CONFIDENCE

When Lisa Lee, a vulnerable young woman, vanishes from a pretty Scottish seaside town, Anna and Fin find themselves at the centre of an internet frenzy to find her.

Her last film on her YouTube channel shows her breaking into an abandoned French chateau with other urban explorers, and stumbling across a priceless Roman silver casket. After Lisa vanishes, the item is listed for auction in Paris, with a description claiming that its contents could have a major impact upon the whole of Christianity.

On a thrilling chase across Europe, Anna and Fin will be caught up in a world of international art smuggling, billionaire con artists, and religious zealotry.

DENISE MINA

---◆---

CONFIDENCE

Complete and Unabridged

CHARNWOOD
Leicester

First published in Great Britain in 2022 by
Harvill Secker
London

First Charnwood Edition
published 2022
by arrangement with
Harvill Secker
Penguin Random House UK
London

*A catalogue record for this book is available
from the British Library.*

ISBN 978–1–4448–4960–8

For our mum, Edith.

When she died
the global Panache Quotient
dropped by ten degrees.

'Art is a mirage.'
Duchamp

1

Lisa Lee had been posting short films on her You-Tube channel for a year before she disappeared. She had still only picked up thirty-odd subscribers. There was no particular reason for that, her films were interesting and well shot, the sound was good, they were just a bit off.

Lisa was a bit off.

She starred in all of her own films but her face was inexpressive, her narration obvious. She'd tour amazing abandoned buildings, point the camera at a table and say *Oh, look, there's a table.* This elusive blandness made her seem medicated, which posed the question of what she was being medicated for and that took you out of the film. This hinted-at back story raised other questions: why was she filming herself breaking into places? Wasn't she worried about getting arrested? Was she trying to resolve something, or escape from something? Why did someone with such a thick working-class accent have such an elaborate, expensive hobby? Was the accent affected? Why would a young, classically good-looking girl have such a severe haircut?

There was too much going on for her to be a one-note internet sensation. Lisa was operating on a lot of different levels.

In the wake of her disappearance her subscribers peaked at just over a million. Her Instagram took off as well, despite the fact that she might never post again, or maybe because of that.

The police asked her dad to take down her films. They thought speculation about them, especially about the chateau, was distracting from the search for her and didn't see how Lisa's disappearance in North Berwick could be related to her exploring an abandoned chateau in France.

They were wrong.

It's worth describing that film for those who didn't get a chance to see it. It's just twenty-two minutes or so. She'd made it six months before but only posted it two weeks before she disappeared.

It begins abruptly — Lisa is walking through an autumn wood of bare silver birches, holding the camera with her left hand and training it on her own face, looking forward as if she doesn't know she's being filmed.

The air around her seems unnaturally still but we can hear the rustle of dead leaves as she walks, the occasional soft sucking squelch from damp soil underfoot. It must be cold because her cheeks are pinked, her breath becomes visible an inch from her lips, but the frost has lifted from the ground so maybe it's lunchtime.

Lisa is twenty, slim, with roughly cropped blonde hair. She's quite intense. When she catches sight of her own face in the viewfinder her nose wrinkles and her shoulder slides up to her ear. She's dressed in combat-casual: black-and-grey camo trousers, jacket over a hoodie. There's a crackle of nervous discomfort about her, appropriate because she's on her way to get into someone's house without permission and creep around, looking at everything.

Hiya. I'm in France! Excitin'. This is an actual shat-oo I'm taking ye into, eh? Is that how you say it? Shat-oo?

2

It's a castle anyway, aye. Kinda.

Her accent is a gentle East Coast brogue, girlish and high pitched.

If you like this gonnae chuck us some stars? And reviews really help other people find me here . . . an' subscribe to my channel, if you like . . . She glances at the camera and micro-cringes, turning away, jerking her chin to point up ahead as she walks on. *That's where we're headed. In there.*

She turns the camera to the edge of the wood and a grey slated turret peeking over the top of the trees. The walls are faded yellow. It looks like a rotting Disney castle.

There. The pointy tower. That's where we're going. See, I heard that a big family was living in there — five kids, mum and dad, granny living with them, you know, like, big for nowadays-families, but one morning years ago they all just walked out and never came back. No one seems to know why. An' they've left everything, furniture and clothes, dolls and all this sort of thing . . .

She walks on, keeping the camera trained forward, scanning the trunks and the ground.

At first glance it looks like an ancient wood but it becomes clear that the history is more complex. Some trees have toppled over. A couple lean drunkenly on their neighbours, one almost perpendicular, its exposed root ball still shaped by the pot it arrived in from a nursery. This is an expensively curated simulacrum of an ancient birch wood, which tells you two things: someone has a lot of money because these things are expensive, and they chose to use that money to create this private world.

Lisa turns the camera back to herself.

I'm completely bricking it, to be honest, I'm always

bricking it at this point, but I'm going in. That's the whole point of doing this, I suppose. In a way. That's the whole point. For me, anyway. Facing your fears and committing to sharing that with other people, sort of . . . She attempts a smile but it warps into a grimace.

A sudden movement draws our eye; fifty feet behind her in the woods. Two men approach, keeping their distance but facing Lisa, following her. One of them looks straight into the camera, a black snood pulled up over his mouth and nose.

Lisa's still smiling awkwardly into the camera when she hears the report of a twig snapping behind her. Fear flares in her eyes.

The film cuts.

Now we're looking at a still: a Catholic altar through a hazy yellow filter. The altar is covered in a simple white cloth embroidered in red-and-gold thread with the Chi Rho symbol: a P with an X through it. A large silver crucifix stands upright in the centre and a set of priestly vestments are hanging on a clothes stand to the side, as if the Invisible Man has been ordained and is waiting for his cue.

I found this cut terrifying when I first saw it. I almost turned it off. I assumed that Lisa had been attacked by the two men in the wood, had been raped and murdered, and this film was a memorial to her. But then the title of the film comes up in a mad, jaunty font:

ABANDONED MANSION IN FRANCE: THEY LEFT EVERYTHING!

This is typical of the edits. They're rough and often meaningless. Lisa isn't a film-maker, she isn't trying to say anything subtle, she just wants to show us

4

things. But it's hard not to read meaning into edits. To watch is to try and make sense of the film. My pattern-recognition instincts were triggered by the cuts but for Lisa editing was just happenstance. Look at this. Now look at that. That's difficult to accept. Our minds resist meaninglessness.

After a few beats the title card is replaced with drone footage of the wood looking down through the naked birch trees to the forest floor. The shot is super high-res, passing overhead in slow motion. Every branch and leaf is picked out in detail, even the drone's own shadow ripples crisply across high branches.

The drone glides out over the lip of the wood, over a gravelled forecourt in front of the chateau, to find Lisa with the two men who were walking behind her in the wood.

They're standing in a tight cluster together on steps up to the front door. A setting autumn sun warms their faces as they grin straight up at us, waving and jumping around, mouthing 'Hello!' It's later in the day, after they've been inside and shed their bags and hoods.

Maybe you only see this because it's slow-mo, if it was faster the subtle shift in mood might not register, but Lisa and the two men glance at each other, realise they're overreacting to the appearance of the drone, laugh at themselves and pantomime their own enthusiasm. They're having a good laugh together.

But there's another man there too, not part of the jolly group, standing at the bottom of the steps, solemn and serious. He's stout and older, dressed in a washed-out metal band T-shirt and joggers. His chin is on his chest. He looks as if he's texting furiously on a phone with two hands. He's actually operating the drone controls and has to concentrate hard.

The drone tilts up to show the chateau's yellow facade and the turrets at all four corners of the building. The roof has caved in towards the back. Beyond the chateau are turned fields and an equine paddock in the distance, outlined by a white picket fence. This is a wealthy area.

The drone swings a turn around the building, slowing as it approaches the group on the stairs. The drone operator looks straight at us, straight into the lens as it approaches, his eyebrows thick and black, his blue eyes delighted, his arm outstretched like a falconer's. The drone alights and a broad, warm smile bursts on his face.

Cut.

We're inside the chateau looking out one of the dirty glass panels on the front door, out to the forecourt and the steps. Lisa narrates in an awed voice:

So, I'm IN. But I tell you what: this floor feels really soft under my feet here. This building is going to collapse soon. I've felt that before in other places I've went, there's a kinda tipping point, sort of thing, where everything feels like wet cardboard and there's not long a building can stand in that state, eh? Like it's gonnae fold in on itself soon. Still, look at all of this: see how fast the family's left here?

Turning slowly into the hallway, she shows us a big set of dark wooden stairs carpeted with grey dust. Next to that is a table laid out for a children's tea party with cups and side plates, a silver coffee pot and even cutlery. Thick dust has settled over the table like a cloth.

They just, like — whoosh — all walked out the front door in a oner and never came back.

6

She sidles past the table to a small door under the stairs, she opens it and shines her phone torch inside. It's a dark corridor leading to stone steps down into a black water that licks lazily at the steps, the movement magnified by an oily rainbow surface.

God . . . Absolutely stinks in there.

She backs out, reaches over to shut the door and her camera accidentally captures the two men from the front steps crossing the hall behind her. They realise they're being filmed and freeze.

Oh, says Lisa and moves so that she's in front of the lens with the men over her shoulder in the background.

Lisa seems taller now that she's made it inside, younger, her eyes bright and wide and her pallor flushed. She points back her shoulder to the men, watching herself in the viewfinder.

This is Florian.

He's tall and skinny, blond with a tentative shoehorn moustache and the perfect skin of a very young man.

This is Gregor.

Gregor is short and brawny with a wry grin. He has cropped dark hair and a chaotic monobrow. His lips are parted expectantly, as if he's on the brink of laughing.

They're the Belgian urbex team I've been chatting to online, you might have seen . . . We all drove down here together. Well — they drove me. Say 'hi', guys?

Florian and Gregor are camera-shy. Florian gives a fast little wave to the camera, squeaks with panic, and they both snicker and scuttle out of view. Lisa waits until they're in the next room and whispers:

We don't always get on in the community, you know

7

that, I've had my battles, but those guys are total diamonds. They've just telt me that I shouldn't say 'shat-oo', it's 'shat-oh'. But they didn't make me feel dead thick or anything. They just, like, they were nice about it, you know?

Unthinkingly, as if she's rehearsing or enjoying the word, she whispers to herself, *shat-oh. Check out their website. I'll put their deets up.*

Through another small door she leads us into a private chapel. This is a new building, an extension made of breeze blocks and concrete.

No way. Look! I tell ye, this family were very religious, there's crucifixes and religious stuff everywhere.

Unfamiliar with Catholicism, she misnames almost everything.

There, that's . . . the wee stage for the priest to do his preaching . . . Benches here, for the people. Tablecloth on the altar — that's still there. The priest's wee dress. Even the silver cross standing up. And I'll tell you what — that is a nice cross too. I know it isn't steel because it'd be rusty as anything by now. Been shut up here for years. It's made of silver, that is. See how it's foxed from the damp and grey, like? That's actual silver. They've just left it. It's a shame.

She turns the camera to the floor; raw concrete covered with a beautiful red Persian rug. Moths have flourished here, dissolving the weave that holds the tufts together so the corner of the carpet crumbles away like a gingernut biscuit left in a saucer of milk.

Sad to see these things just left. This should be saved, all this stuff, because it's, basically, like, antiques.

Cut.

She's in a huge living room papered yellow. Whole strips have slithered off the damp walls revealing

8

smooth wet plaster. The yellow is bright and cheerful, a damask in an oversized pattern. The chateau's decor is full of confident choices like this.

Lisa pans the camera to a patch of deep black velvet mould galloping across the ceiling.

Oh, shit . . . she fumbles her scarf up over her face. *Don't want to get that in your lungs, spores from black mould, it's as bad as asbestos. Have to be careful . . . Sometimes asbestos is why a place got left suddenly but don't think there is any here. The whole building seems redone. The plasterwork under the wallpaper is new. The floor looks pretty new. That little church was new. But they've done all that and then walked out suddenly. Weird. This whole place is weird though. Look . . .*

She turns slowly to a white marble fireplace topped with a massive painting of St Sebastian shot through with arrows. In a better painting by a better artist he'd be looking heavenward in an ecstasy of faith, but it's not very good and he looks like an exasperated supply teacher.

I mean . . .

Cut.

She's in a kitchen, high-ceilinged and bright, painted apple green. Hanging all along the walls are long-handled copper pans, too high to be anything but decoration, higgled-piggledy but somehow a coherent pattern too. Like the rest of the house, the room is cheerful, decorated by someone with a great eye and a feel for the subtlety of colour and textures.

I found this kitchen the creepiest part of the film because some of the things in there were recognisably contemporary: a range cooker in pastel blue from an expensive brand I've coveted online, the same Danish-designed highchair that I had for my girls when

9

they were toddlers. It converts from a highchair into the world's most uncomfortable perch seat. An over-priced toaster and a Bodum coffee press I've seen in a hundred kitchens. But everything was rotting and covered in dust. It made the kitchen feel simultaneously contemporary and ancient, like looking back at the present from the future.

Cut.

Short bit: Lisa's on the big staircase in the hall, staying close to the wall, when a sudden shower of dust falls from the ceiling above her. She shows us it twisting and falling, catching the light like a stairwell chandelier in a Vegas hotel. Lisa's face is sliced in half by the shot and she freezes, mouth ajar, eye bright, looking straight into the camera. As the shower ends a gleeful smile dawns on her face. She survived that.

Cut.

She's in a child's bedroom looking at a windowsill crammed with Furbies, all different colours, fur matted with dust. Their dead eyes are half shut and they look out at the room, tipsy and disdainful.

Whoa! Original Furbies. You could eBay the shit out of these. But you know, you wouldn't though. Obviously. Take nothing. If you're going to rearrange everything you find for better pictures you might as well stay home and do that. There's just no point coming all this way . . . No point.

Cut.

She climbs about in a couple of other bedrooms and a bathroom with a collapsed floor. But the money shot comes in the attic.

She's in a small doorway on the top floor looking into a low-ceilinged room with a run of little dirty windows along one wall. There are steps down into it

10

and it is lined with bookshelves, some of which have fallen and spilled the books onto the floor. By the fireplace is a comfy reading chair with a floor lamp at its shoulder. The mould is rampant in here. Lisa is anxious about that until she sees the carcasses.

Three dead pigeons lie under the window, desiccated, just piles of feathers and bones and beaks. They've been there for a long time. They must have got trapped, she says, got in through the hole in the roof back there and not been able to find their way back out.

Poor things. Poor, poor wee things. Wee trapped things . . .

She is freaked out by the bodies and clings to the wall by the fireplace, scrambling over a pile of books to get past them. This is when she stumbles, almost falls and slaps a hand on the wall next to the fireplace to steady herself.

The wall drops open.

It's a secret door.

Oh! Oh?

She rights herself. She looks at it, touches it, pushes it open a little more. She smiles at us.

Oooh . . .

She looks in through the gap, back out at us, her mouth a smiley little 'o', then she pushes it wider, forgetting to show us what she's looking at.

What the fuck . . . ?

She turns on her phone torch, shines it in and her eyes widen.

Oh my God. Whoah!

She shoulders the door wide and brings the camera up to let us see what she's seeing.

It is a frightening room, windowless, not at all in keeping with the domestic rest of the chateau. Walls, ceiling and floor are painted black. A dead bulb hangs on a bare wire. The floor isn't dusty because this room has been sealed.

In the middle is an old office desk from the 1980s and an orange plastic chair sitting at an odd angle, facing a wall that is blank except for a small, square painting, framed in gold and swathed in cellophane. The image on the canvas can be seen only briefly, winking out at us between flashes of reflected light from Lisa's phone torch on the plastic.

It's a painting of a hand. A hand holding a yellow pen and it is writing something, but the image is cropped so that, if they are writing something, we can't see what it is. The brushwork is soupy and impressionistic, too loose for something so small. It looks like a detail from a larger painting.

Sitting on the desk is a box shaped like a duty-free carton of cigarettes but rounded at the edges. It's silver, foxed and dun like the cross on the altar. There's elaborate raised ornamentation on the side and an inscription on the top.

Whoaw! Lisa grins at it. *Bloody hell, what in the fuck's going on?*

She steps into the room and puts a hand out to the silver box. It's in this moment of forgetting that her sleeve rides up and we see her heavily scarred forearm. We see it very briefly, like the painting of the hand; a mountain range of scar ridges. Lisa has been cutting herself for a long time, slashing deep across the meat on her forearm.

Cut.

She's in a bright place, maybe a garage, filming a dune of broken furniture shored up against a corrugated-iron side wall. One of the guys, Florian or

Gregor, asks her if she's OK. He sounds worried.
Aye! Aye! Yeah, I'm totally fine. Fine.
But her voice is wavering and the camera trembles.
Cut.

2

I watched that film on a nightmarishly ill-conceived holiday before the Year of Sundays, when travel was not only easy but something people moaned about.

I arranged, paid for, and convinced everyone else to come on this holiday for our fractured, blended family, thinking that all those other blended families were just idiots for not getting on really well. As soon as we arrived it was obvious I had made a mistake.

I meant well. We were a tight group and Fin's new partner, Sofia, was having trouble fitting in. He seemed to have given up on us making her comfortable. He didn't want her to come but I intervened and invited her myself.

I'd imagined long walks and big jumpers, reading in bed, movie nights and bonding over big communal dinners.

It wasn't like that.

I didn't just organise it for Sofia, it was for my girls' benefit too. If we could go away together they wouldn't have to choose which family to holiday with. But the scraps and snipes had started as soon as we got here and the girls were skulking around like resistance fighters, dodging tensions, falling quiet when any of us walked into a room.

We were in a lighthouse, trapped indoors by a violent storm, stranded a mile out on a rocky headland in the far south-west of Scotland.

The wind was so loud that it was an effort to hear the telly, we couldn't go outside without the risk of being

14

blown off a cliff into the Irish Sea, and the hot water didn't work. Someone pointed out that they used to pay people to stay in these places. The place was so draughty and cold that we wore most of our clothes and spent all day crammed into the only warm room in the building, the sitting room, reading or staring at individual screens, waiting for it to be over.

Present in the company were my ex, Hamish, and Fin's ex, Estelle — now a couple with a baby of their own — both my girls, Jess and Lizzie, twelve and ten, Fin and his new partner, the nubile Sofia.

Estelle was heating up lasagne that night and the rest of us were sitting around, ignoring each other, waiting. Sofia was talking about lasagne and Italian cooking in general, about ingredients and regional variations. Sofia, that's not her real name, obviously, I'm not a complete bitch, was elfin and very pretty and would not shut up. If she wasn't monologuing about herself she was complaining about the accommodation or her room or the food and tonight Estelle was heating up Tesco's frozen lasagne to serve with plastic garlic bread. We were all bracing ourselves for a scene.

Fin was quite a passive person but since hooking up with Sofia he seemed almost defeated. I'd taken him aside on the first day and asked him to tell Sofia to shut up once in a while, she kept ordering my girls around and telling them they'd get fat if they ate sugar. Fin shrugged and said Estelle asked him the same thing but he didn't know how to broach it, Sofia was very fragile. This was before she gave my ten-year-old a makeover that made her look like a bitter, thrice-divorced Florida golf widow.

We weren't even halfway through the week. The sense of doom was palpable.

15

The girls were watching cartoons on their shared iPad, one earbud each, numb with boredom after a day of enforced board-gaming. To stop myself clucking at them I busied myself on my phone, scrolling through Twitter messages from listeners to our podcast. Doing admin.

I wasn't really reading, just skimming headlines, but I stopped at a name I recognised: Lisa Lee. It was the alliteration that caught my eye. It wasn't from Lisa, it was about her and it was very short. It had been sent five days ago.

Lisa Lee didn't take it. Please tell them.

The sender, called @WBGrates, had included a series of links. I clicked the first one and watched Lisa's film.

I soon forgot that I was in a lighthouse or that Sofia was still jammering on. I was in France on a fine autumn afternoon, walking through a wood. I didn't understand what Lisa was doing in the film, why she was so open about breaking into someone's house. I was scared when Florian and Gregor appeared behind her. I froze along with her on the crumbling staircase, shared her delight when she found the secret room, and I was troubled by how shaken she was at the end. The numbers were clocking up quickly: ninety-five thousand views when I started watching, a hundred and twenty when I'd finished. I was pleased for Lisa, she seemed like someone good numbers would matter to and not just for the revenue.

I went back to @WBGrates's message.

The next link was to an auction catalogue. The silver box was up for sale in Paris this week. There were detailed closeups of it.

It had been cleaned since Lisa found it and the sil-

16

ver was dazzling white, luminescent against a dark background. A close-up of the lid framed a Latin inscription I couldn't understand. Another showed the image on the side, a Roman matron in profile reclining on a daybed. The tresses of her hair echoed the drapery of her toga, these silver details accented with gilding. It was very detailed and quite lovely. The woman looked up at a dove rising from her outstretched hand, wings wide, beak pointing skywards. Beneath these images the catalogue entry read:

Roman casket. Date unknown. Inscription reads: 'Let this, O Pilate of Balaton, follower of the King of the Jews, be a worthy vessel for this proof of his resurrection.'
Provenance and reserve price on application.

I don't know anything about antiques, the auction houses of the world might have been full of boxes like this one, so I went back to YouTube and screenshot the casket in Lisa's film, did the same with the auction image and looked at them side by side. They seemed the same to me. Maybe she did take it. I didn't really see what would be so wrong about that. The chateau had been abandoned, the owners didn't seem to care about all the stuff they'd left.

I googled the story and found a slew of articles from predominantly Christian websites and provincial newspapers, many American: 'Proof of Crucifixion for Sale', 'Christ Box in Auction', 'Hallelujah Gathering in Paris'. It was too much to take in so I opened a long-form article on a news site that I trust.

The box had a shadowy history. Rumoured to have been found in Communist Hungary, it had disappeared for decades and re-emerged in southern Italy in the late nineties only to be lost again. The inscription indicated that it had belonged to the Roman official who condemned Jesus of Nazareth to death by crucifixion. What was special about it was that it suggested that the official, Pontius Pilate, Governor of Judaea, had converted to the new religion, something previously unknown, and it claimed to have proof of the resurrection inside. Many academics thought the casket was a myth until it appeared in the Paris auction, seller unknown. It was still sealed though and had never been studied. There were calls from various churches, religious groups and historians to stop the sale until it could be examined by experts because, one Yale professor said, finds of this significance should be held for the common good. A buyer could store it in a vault and the world would never get to find out what was inside. The sale was due to be held in four days' time and the bidding might reach hundreds of thousands of dollars, or hundreds of millions, no one knew how much it would go for. There was nothing else like it.

Religious people had begun to descend on Paris, eager to be near this precious object. French authorities were telling them not to come. Random groups were pictured, men and women, some with children, gathering outside the auction house, praying in the streets of Paris and camping in parks.

Fin and I are small fish and, although intriguing, this story was far too big for us. The mainstream media were all over it and we'd never get access to interview anyone important.

I tried to remember where I had heard Lisa Lee's name. Had she contacted us a while ago? It could have

18

been one of the emails asking me to pass on messages to Fin — I got an astonishing number of those. I didn't think so though. Her name prompted a bashful glow in me, it felt like it might have been complimentary. I knew it wasn't nasty or threatening, I remember those ones word for word despite myself, but I didn't check because the password for that email account was at home, jotted on a Post-it note on my desk.

Estelle shouted from the kitchen that dinner would be ready in twenty minutes. Everyone shifted in their seats, looking forward to hot food, being a bit closer to bed and sleep and, ultimately, getting out of here. We had another four days of this.

Everyone was being very kind about it. Except Sofia.

Sofia is Milanese and met Fin at a podcasting convention in Leipzig the year before. They had been together ever since but none of us knew her yet, not really.

She'd been unsure of us, I felt, and Fin was a little nervous of introducing her to Estelle and Hamish. I thought if we were warm and welcoming it would have to go well but since we'd arrived here she could not disguise her spiky dislike of all of us. Hamish was too loud. Estelle was too tired and should give up yoga. The girls got too much screen time and their diet was all wrong. I 'sat badly' and snored like a pig.

When we first met I expected us to get on great. She's very cool. She talks as if she's thinking in Italian and translating as she goes, which makes even the most banal comment seem epic and final.

NOW IS THE HOUR WHEN WE SEEK THE CHILDREN.

SWEATERS ARE FINE IF WEATHER IS COLD.

She's small and very proud of her figure. I've heard her tell at least ten people that she has a fifty-five-centimetre waist. She wears tight tops and jackets over flared skirts to emphasise this, platform shoes and her black hair in a high ponytail.

My girls loved her because she looks like a pop star which made me think that she was interesting and fun, that we'd get on well. It wasn't to be. Maybe I'm not interesting and fun. Sofia thought I was a tiresome idiot who had tricked her into coming on this shit holiday, made Fin do boring work things and objected loudly to my daughters dressing like paedo bait.

Sofia and Fin were having a fractious time. She wanted him to come downstairs and do some resistance thing with bands and he wanted to keep reading his paperback.

'Exercise is good for anxiety,' she said, looking around the room for a stray gaze to lock on.

'I'm just reading,' said Fin, keeping his face in his book.

Judging a couple's relationship is easy when you're single. It's fun as well. I like it. I was the only single adult on that holiday and watching them skirmishing made me feel good about that.

Sofia caught my eye. Her face tightened. 'Fin suffers from anorexia,' she announced.

Fin's eating issues are pretty well known. He used to be a pop star, has a big beard and a lot of blond hair, worn as a neat mane. He looks like an uptight Viking. After being outed online when he was really struggling — 'You Won't Believe What Fin Cohen Looks Like Now' — he's open about it, has discussed it on social media. It's always there, the anxiety, the low hum of it, but it isn't the most interesting thing about him and we'd known each other intimately for two years at this point. I didn't really need to be told that by Sofia but I sucked it up.

'Right?'

'Yes,' she said. 'So: it's an anxiety problem. Exercise is good for that.'

'Really?'

'Yes.'

My eyes must have rolled up of their own accord because I was looking at her, then I wasn't and then she was very angry with me.

'What do you know about anorexia, Anna?'

I regretted doing that, it was unkind and she was already feeling unwelcome. I thought I should say something positive. 'Well, a lot less than you, I suspect.'

'Yes,' said Sofia, smiling down as she flattened the skirt on her knees, 'I have had eating issues in my own past, of course —'

I just couldn't listen to her any more and stood up. 'Hey, girls, come and set the table for dinner, please.'

They moaned until I threatened to confiscate the iPad.

'You can have it back as soon as you're finished.'

They scampered off to the kitchen.

'Fin, can I show you something about work?'

Fin nodded eagerly and tried to stand up but Sofia grabbed his thigh and asked, 'What is it?'

'Just a DM.'

'Fin spends too much time at work. It's always taking him away.' She jutted her chin defiantly at me.

Fin looked at the floor.

'Sofia,' said Hamish without looking up, 'let the

21

man go.'

She tipped her head and considered his request.

'Vacations are important for mental health,' she said and looked at Fin as if he was on a weekend pass from a locked ward.

'Let them work.'

She respects Hamish and his booming voice. He's a lawyer and can deliver a line with authority. She relinquished her hostage and Fin leapt up, dropping his book to the floor.

We sat at the corner of the dining table as the girls came from the kitchen with cutlery and a stack of plates and I showed him the WBGrates message. I gave him my airpods, and pressed play.

He was watching Lisa walk through the woods, his mouth open, eyes soft and interested. Sofia's chin landed on his shoulder. She had dragged a chair up behind him and smiled at me, at him, at the screen.

Fin stabbed pause.

'I'll watch too.' She smiled and kissed his cheek. Then she smiled at me, implicating me, somehow.

I shrugged at Fin. Fin half blinked.

'Sofia, can I show you later?'

'No, no, no, no.' Pouting, she flapped her fingers to her palms, asking for an airpod like a toddler demanding a biscuit. 'Lemme watch, lemme watch.'

Fin gave her an earbud and she fitted it, resting her chin on his shoulder again as she wrapped her arms around his torso.

I sighed. Hamish sighed. I think the children may have even sighed. He would not stand up to her in any way, shape or form and so we couldn't either.

It was exhausting.

Fin and Sofia watched the rest of Lisa's film as I

sat holding the phone up for them. She kept flash-
ing triumphant little stabbing smiles at me and I was
counting the hours awake until this holiday was over.

Fin was very into the film. He jumped at one point
and I glanced at the screen. It was the unsafe stairs he
was watching. He smiled back at Lisa when the dust
shower stopped. I watched him be surprised by the
secret door, crane to see what Lisa was seeing. It was
fun, watching him watching, guessing at the scene on
the screen.

The girls finished setting the table and scampered
off. Fin finished the film and sat back smiling.

'Why's she breaking into houses?' I asked.

'It's urbex,' he said. 'Urban exploring. It's a thing
people do.'

I showed him the catalogue entry. 'The WBGrates
message says she didn't take it but why shouldn't she
take it? If it was just left there?'

'It's a basic principle of urban exploring.'

I thought that was a bit naive but didn't want to say,
so I just asked if he remembered a message from Lisa.
Came a year or so ago, I think? He didn't remember
it either.

I went back to the film, to screenshot some links
Lisa had included at the end, but it was gone. The
film had been taken down. All of Lisa's films had been
taken down and her Instagram account had been frozen. I googled her name. She had been missing for a
week. Police were searching for her.

I looked at Fin and muttered, 'You know, I could
pootle up the road to Glasgow and find out what she
said in the email? I could be back by morning.'

'Good idea,' said Sofia, brightening and sitting up.

Fin held my eye, steady, fierce. 'You running away?'

23

'Not 'running away'. I'd be back tomorrow.'

But I was thinking how glorious it would be to be away on my own, in the car, without the tensions and the moods and the Sofia.

Fin was irritated. I knew he thought I was deluded, that I didn't know it yet but I wouldn't come back tomorrow. He was wrong. I did know. I wasn't coming back.

'It's very windy out there,' he said. 'Probably not safe to drive out over the headland in this storm.'

'I think you should go, Anna, I think this is your new mystery!' Sofia's voice was loud and shrill. She really, really wanted me to leave.

'Oi, Sofia,' said Hamish languidly, 'your voice is very loud.'

She spun to him. 'You're rude!' She didn't sound especially offended, just loud and angry.

'Keep it down. You'll either wake the baby or blow the windows out.'

Just then Estelle came out of the kitchen carrying the lasagne and a vegan version and everyone in the house came over to the table.

We ate. The food was very welcome and stodgy and comforting. The wine flowed and a warm smell of garlic bread wafted around us, whipped up by the breezes coming from the rattling windows. Sofia told us all how and why the lasagne wasn't good or authentic and about possibly every other lasagne she had eaten in her life. I wasn't drinking because I was nursing the delicious possibility of leaving. And the mood between Sofia and me was getting worse.

She was keen for me to go and brought it up several times over dinner in the guise of praising my work ethic and my driving, wondering if my roof was surviving in all this wind, talking about other podcasters and how much bigger their listenership was than ours. But the bald antipathy was mutual now. I was annoyed at the morbid amount of attention she paid to what Fin was eating, noticed that she rarely started a sentence with anything but the word 'I' and that one of her eyes was higher than the other. Yes, I was clutching at straws. She wasn't really that bad.

'Look,' I announced to the table, 'I know this isn't much fun. As soon as the storm dies down let's all just go home. What do you say?'

It was a measure of how fraught things were that for a beat pause no one said anything until Lizzie let off a tiny, high-pitched cheer and everyone laughed.

That should have been it. It would be over soon, and there needn't be any hard feelings.

But that wasn't it.

Sofia was even angrier now. She became sulky and sullen. Then she interrupted Estelle talking about a yoga instructor to tell a story at high volume about how her childhood was unhappy because she was always made to sit still. Girls were not encouraged to do sport. The story was met with a distinct lack of sympathy.

'This was sad for me. I was a depressed child.'

Hamish muttered, 'Feel better: bore everyone else.'

Even the girls thought that rude.

'Well, for God's sake.' He waved a hand dismissively. 'If you're complaining about it to a casual dinner table of relative strangers, your childhood probably wasn't that bad. I was sent to boarding school at nine. My parents didn't even like me enough to have me in their house.'

'No, Hamish,' said Sofia, defensive and reddening

about the eyes, 'you know we say, 'Two in distress makes sorrow the less.' My sadness doesn't take away from yours and it's unkind of you to make that point.'

'Well, what *I'm* saying —' Hamish's voice was slightly too loud and I realised then that he'd had quite a lot of wine — 'is: consider your audience before you start bloody moaning. Other people have been through things too.'

Estelle turned towards Hamish, shoulders so square, that it was more than just listening but a wordless way of telling him to calm down. She's good for him. Better than I ever was.

'I mean, ONCE,' bawled Hamish, in a voice so loud we all leaned back a little, 'I was walking with a client who'd got out of Libya and made it across the Mediterranean Sea in an inflatable dinghy and we met this *creature* I know who talked at us for ten minutes about the absolute *hell* he went through commuting on the M25 every day. What I'm saying is *think* about who's listening before you start your stupid sob story.' He picked up his wine glass and kind of gestured in my direction for reasons that were not clear. 'Because, I promise you, you *never* want anyone to feel about you the way I felt about that man that day. Ever. Man was a complete arsehole.'

Lizzie was gleeful at the use of the swear word. Jess tutted. We all ate in silence for a while.

'Ah!' said Sofia, pointing at me as if she had just realised what was going on. 'I see! Because Anna was gang-raped?'

Both of my daughters dropped their cutlery and looked up, first at Sofia, then at me.

Jess was ashen. Lizzie was puzzled. I wondered if she knew what the R-word meant. She tipped her

26

head, I could see her re-hearing it, wondering if it was a swear word, but then looking at Fin and at Jess and she knew this: it was not something you wanted to hear about your mum.

Sofia sort of smirked. 'Sorry, is that . . . ? Sorry. It's public though . . . everyone knows.'

Hamish stared at her, unblinking. 'Shut your fucking mouth.'

Lizzie squeaked.

'Hamish . . .' said Estelle quietly, putting a hand on his arm.

Panicking, I tried to distract them with a story. 'I saw a film today that would take your breath away,' I said cheerfully, and then described Lisa's film, trying to make it so dramatic that they'd forget what Sofia had said. I did a good job but at the end, as the girls were asking what was in the box and wouldn't Lisa get in trouble for going into someone else's house, Sofia spoke loudly over them to ask Fin,

'I said a thing wrong? But everyone knows this already.' She had a spiteful glint in her eye. 'No? The newspapers were full of this story. Everyone knows this.'

Jess made a sound in her throat. Lizzie looked at her dad.

Fin stood up. 'What I know for certain,' he said to the girls, 'is that Lisa Lee did not steal that silver box and put it up for auction. Now: I have never met her or spoken to her. Will I tell you how I absolutely know that for certain?'

Jess blinked and muttered, 'Yes.'

I knew then that she knew I'd been raped. She knew I'd made the allegations and then run away. She knew. She must have heard it from someone, at school, on the internet, maybe one of the vicious snark-blogs about me that said I'd made it up for money or attention, that I deserved it, that I was a lying bitch. But she didn't ask me about it and she was shielding Lizzie. I didn't want them to know these things could happen to girls, to me, to them. They deserved so much better. I wanted to fold in on the stain of me.

'Is it wrong, what I said?' Sofia asked me, a smile twitching at the corner of her mouth.

I was shaken and couldn't speak, but I didn't need to. Fin was suddenly talking, telling the girls how urbex started with storms and Gary Warne.

It was a kindness, the effort he put into telling us that story. He told it to distract us all from our painful present, to make us feel good and forget ourselves for a short while, so we could come back to tend our wounds, refreshed.

It was a story about fear and the big storm that hit San Francisco in 1977.

This became episode one of *Death and the Dana, Season II: The Bloody Casket*. If you didn't listen to it at the time it's worth imagining the narration in Trina Keany's softly growling timbre and lilting south London accent.

3

Hello and welcome to season two of Death and the Dana.

I'm Trina Keany and this is episode one of The Bloody Casket *series.*

The music swells and rises, a couple of adverts play and then —

In this series we will be following a huge international case: the brutal murder of the prominent American evangelical Christian Paul Hammersmith.

None of us thought we would ever get to cover a case this big, much less get unique access to the events that occurred behind the scenes.

We are not that sort of operation. As many of you know, this podcast began as my own small passion project with a limited budget and a tiny audience, until Fin Cohen and Anna McDonald took issue with my conclusions and began commenting on it and contradicting it, bringing a huge audience with them.

We met.

We fought.

And now we're working together with an even smaller budget but a much, much bigger audience.

So, with these few resources, how did we come to be the only people who knew what was really going on? It was because, while the world's media were focused on the fate of the Voyniche Casket, *we began looking for Lisa Lee.*

Lisa Lee disappeared from her family home in North Berwick on a cold March night. The search for her was hampered by suspicions about her father, Bob. Lisa was suspected of having broken into a chateau and stealing the

29

Voyniche Casket to put it up for auction and Bob seemed over-emotional, odd, dislikeable. They were exactly the sort of family where a father might kill his daughter and hide her body.

But Fin Cohen was certain that Lisa hadn't taken it. The reason he was so sure was because of the story of Gary Warne.

Gary was a second-hand bookseller in San Francisco in the 1970s and Gary was a fearful man.

No one was trying to kill Gary or anything, he wasn't in immediate danger, but, like a lot of deep thinkers, he found the possibilities of life paralysing. He was thirty years old, tall and quietly spoken, wore his thinning brown hair in a ponytail and brightly coloured dungarees over rainbow jumpers. This was after punk had peaked in New York City. The Dolls had already split up.

Some of Gary's fears were realistic. He had the normal worries of all small businessmen, owing rent, paying tax, keeping employees insured, robbers and fires and so on, but Gary was also afraid of getting fat, of being thin, of losing his hair, of gaining hair, of dying young and living too long. He was afraid of falling in love and having his heart broken or hurting someone, of looking foolish and never trying, of failing, of being successful.

He knew that his life was being shaped by existential angst, but that was no comfort. It was exhausting being Gary. It came to a head in January, 1977, when the worst storm of the winter hit San Francisco harbour.

Hundred-mile-an-hour winds came in straight from the Pacific. Everyone was warned to stay inside. The TV news showed cars being shoved across streets and walls collapsing. The Golden Gate Bridge was shut to traffic. Foghorns sounded out around the city in a low chorus of maudlin alarm.

Gary invited some friends over to hunker down in his apartment, counting the hours until it was over. But something broke in Gary that night. His heart was racing, he was clammy, he felt such a profound nausea that he knew he would die tonight, that his chest would cave in. He sat with this terror, smoking weed and burning joss sticks, until the fear got so intense that it prompted a flight reaction. He got his friends into a car, there was something he wanted them to see, he said, then he drove them down through the rain-washed city to the harbour, to Fort Point, where Madeleine attempts suicide in Vertigo.

The Golden Gate Bridge was built around the historic Fort, a forty-five-foot-high brick structure at the opening of San Francisco Bay. It's dangerous down there even in good weather, fenced off now, since a number of passers-by were washed out to sea by freak waves. Before that there was nothing but a safety chain made of heavy steel, strung between concrete bollards.

Gary stopped the car and they sat and watched the ocean clawing at the Fort, tearing halfway up the walls, yanking the heavy chain back and forth like a shoelace.

Suddenly, without warning, Gary scrambled out of the car and slammed the door behind him. No one knew what was happening.

He stood by the car, watching with a cold smile as a massive wave slapped the Fort in the face and swept back out to sea.

Then Gary bolted to the edge.

He ran across the flooded car park to the chain and turned his back to the ocean, looking at his friends still sitting in the car, watching like startled day trippers. Smiling, Gary raised his hands out to the side and bent down, wrapping his arms around the chain as a wall of black water rose twenty feet behind him. Then Gary stood up.

31

If Gary was dragged out to sea he would drown, his body wouldn't be found for days, but he stayed. He heard the mournful growl of foghorns and the groan of the wind. He heard the ocean shriek behind him and he held his breath. His heart thundered in his throat.

The icy water hit him hard, washing him off his feet, lifting him inland on a collapsing wave that had come a hundred miles for him. It knocked him to his knees. Then came the heavy backdraught.

Gary Warne died of a heart attack five years later. He was a young man. It was completely unexpected. He didn't live to know that he changed the world that night.

The wave retreated and Gary loosened his arms from the chains. He ran, laughing and skipping, back to the car and jumped in.

He was wet. He was cold. His back was badly bruised from the weight of water but he couldn't stop laughing because, for the first time in years, he felt completely calm.

One by one, all his friends in the car took a turn with the chain, the wave, the near-death experience. They were so invigorated by it that they wanted to do it again, somehow.

Back at Gary's later that night they formed the Suicide Club, named after the Robert Louis Stevenson stories. These are just some of the things they did: they stripped naked in public. They climbed the Golden Gate Bridge and had a dinner party in the girders. They graffitied advertising billboards to radicalise their meaning. And they came up with a simple code, a slogan: take nothing, leave nothing but footprints.

Soon, they expanded their membership and did more crazy things together.

A solstice party on a beach ended with the burning of an effigy of a man made from driftwood. Gradually the

Burning Man Festival changed and grew so big that it had to move. It settled out in the desert.

Guerrilla theatre events, guerrilla gardening, street magic, the Suicide Club did all of these things. And one of those things was urban exploration, later shortened to urbex.

They explored the built environment around them, ignoring the trespass prohibitions. They behaved as if they had every right to be there, reclaiming spaces for public use and held exhibits of films and photo galleries and discussion groups. Schisms arose immediately, disagreements about issues as diverse as staged lighting and whether it's better to declare site locations or keep them secret. Some urbexers make money from their YouTube channels. Burning Man is exclusive and expensive but all of these movements share one core value from the seventies Suicide Club: take nothing and leave nothing but footprints.

This is how Lisa Lee came to have a YouTube channel. She had four urbex films on it when she disappeared, continuing this tradition of documenting a passing moment in the urban environment, framing it for a broader audience, drawing eyes to what she considered extraordinary and beautiful.

Lisa had few subscribers, so few that she replied to almost all the comments. Often her replies were longer than the comments. She was doing this right up until she vanished.

Reading these comments it's easy to see that she was argumentative and a bit rigid in her thinking — she believed absolutely that urbex was an exercise in risk-taking and disapproved of staging and fakery.

She talked a lot about whether it was OK to reveal the address of a site: if videographers kept them secret they could turn into a puzzle for other people to solve and lots of other sites got flooded with urbexers, she said. At the same time, telling everyone where a place was could attract more casual visitors and even people who wanted to steal things and strip lead or copper. She could see both sides tbh.

So Fin was certain that Lisa Lee would not pilfer from the chateau but others weren't sure.

Who could say how they would behave if they stumbled across a solid silver Roman casket, one potentially worth millions. Lisa might not know what it was but she'd know it was a big lump of silver, and that the house was deteriorating so quickly that it would soon be impassable. No one else seemed to want the precious thing. There would be lots of ways to justify taking it away.

Maybe Florian and Gregor took it. How much did we know about them? Maybe the drone operator took it. It wasn't necessarily Lisa.

So Fin and Anna decided to ask her.

They went to her YouTube channel and found that the chateau film had been taken down just a couple of hours before.

Then they found that her Insta account was frozen.

It was weird, so they googled her and that was when they found out that Lisa had gone missing a week before and the police suspected her father of killing her.

4

Hippies doing naked street theatre didn't exactly captivate Jess and Lizzie, but they really did care about Lisa Lee. She wasn't miles older than them and North Berwick was only seventy miles from Glasgow, not far, they might know someone who knew her, they might one day be her.

She had been missing for a week. Her father said she answered the door to someone and seemed to evaporate. When he came down to the hall he found the front door open into the night and he hadn't seen or heard from Lisa since.

Hamish used the iPad and came across a police appeal for information. It was a press conference with her father. He held up the screen to show us and turned the volume up full. Even then it was barely audible over the wind so he Bluetoothed to a speaker under the wall-mounted telly and we all watched the tiny screen as the disembodied sound blared at the far end of the room. It didn't really matter. The sound wasn't important.

On a small stage three seats were set at a trestle table in front of a blue backdrop with a recurrent white 'Police Scotland' logo on it.

Lisa's dad, Bob Lee, sat between two uniformed police officers, a man and a woman. He was reading a statement from a handwritten A4 sheet that had been folded in quarters and kept wilting shut.

Bob was a big man, broad-shouldered, wide in the middle, hands like hams, with electric-blue eyes rimmed in red. He introduced himself, his Yorkshire accent softened by the Scottish East Coast. 'I am Lisa's father, Robert Joseph Lee.'

I wondered who'd advised him to call himself that. It made him sound sinister. Serial killers are often referred to with their middle names to differentiate them from other people with the same bland first and surnames. To make it worse he was wearing a bad, cheap white T-shirt that was fresh out of the packet. The material was thin, the neck was gathered and tight. It didn't fit him and made Bob look as if the police had confiscated his clothes for forensic examination. The officers flanking him didn't like him, it was obvious. They looked down at the tabletop, frowning. It all felt as if they suspected Bob and were trying to provoke a confession by making him repeat his stupid excuse in front of the entire class.

As Bob spoke and confirmed that Lisa had gone missing, the time and place, a lot of dull statements about how nice she was and how everyone liked her, no one would want to hurt her, the woman officer's face twitched a sceptical commentary. Bob's eyes flicked towards her, nervous half-glances, and he struggled to stop his chin convulsing. Halfway through a sentence he broke off, his mouth yawning wide, his face frozen. The sheet of notes he was holding folded closed in his hands.

Neither officer attempted to comfort him with a touch or a kind word. The male officer glanced sombrely at the camera a couple of times.

Bob caught a ragged breath and finished his statement in a strangled voice:

'— Please. We're very worried. Lisa has struggled with her mental health since her mother died. She

36

has been in hospital and needs her medication. We are very worried. Please come home. But if someone has taken her: we beg of you, please return our Lisa. Please . . .'

He lost the struggle with his chin and dropped the statement, covered his face with his big hands and his back heaved with silent sobs. The officers looked uncomfortable.

It ended.

'It's usually the dad,' said Hamish sadly. 'He's the first person they'll be looking at.'

'The internet thinks it's him,' said Fin. 'Armchair vigilantes are posting his address.' I felt alarm tickle the back of my neck. They did that to me once. I felt for Bob.

'They've released a photo of her,' said Estelle and held up her phone to show us.

It was taken a few years ago. Blue and silver water glinted behind Lisa, on a summer's day by the sea. The white sunshine glare seemed exotic and unreal in our grey and draughty lighthouse.

She wore her hair longer then, pulled over one shoulder, and her sun-kissed skin was as flawless as felt. She was smiling dutifully, lips closed, eyes narrowed, trapped forever halfway between a child and a woman. It didn't really look like the determined nervy girl in the film. She looked like the sister of that girl, the untroubled sister, alike but not alike. Her scarred-up arms, the very thing that made me kind of love her, were not in frame.

This was how Bob saw her, how he wanted other people to see her, how he wanted her to be. Untroubled, scar-free, a child bathed in sunshine.

'Why is Hamish picking on me?' Sofia asked Fin.

Fin raised his face to answer her and then sagged.

I stood up. 'Look, Lisa wrote to us at the podcast. We can't remember what she said but it was before she went to France. I can't find it here, the password's at home. I can't just stay here if it would help. I have to tell the police. Would it be OK with everyone if I go?'

'YES!' said Sofia, almost before I had finished the sentence.

'Girls? D'you want to come with me?'

'No, no, no,' said Hamish. 'It's too late and too stormy.'

'Would you like to stay with us, girls?' asked Estelle, holding my eye with a fierce look that suggested Sofia would be scraping the wall for bits of her face if she brought my rape up again.

Jess, the more appeasing of my two girls said thanks, Este, she'd stay, but neither of them wanted to. Lizzie said she'd just come with me because it was very boring here and she wanted to see her friends.

Hamish wasn't happy about me leaving and he certainly wasn't letting the girls go. The drive out onto the headland had been frightening enough and the storm had worsened since then, it was late, the wind was strong, but he'd take them both home tomorrow if Lizzie felt the same way. One more night wouldn't do anyone any harm. Maybe I should stay too.

But I was determined to leave. I made it sound urgent — Lisa might have said something important, a vital clue in it for the cops. I should go.

Downstairs, I scooped all my stuff into a couple of bags, left them by the door and came back up to hug the girls. I found Jess alone in the kitchen and picked her up, even though she's too big for that really.

'I'll see you at home.'

She whispered in my ear, 'Mum? Can I ask . . . ?'

I knew what she wanted to ask about.

I sat her down and held her hand and explained that, one night, when I wasn't much older than her, just after my own mother died, I got a bit drunk at a nightclub. Four famous footballers took me to their hotel room and raped me until I was ripped and bleeding. I crept out the next morning as if I was the one who had done something wrong. I went to the police and then everyone called me a liar. They said I wanted attention, that I was a bitch; unlikeable, vindictive and jealous of these men. The press and public turned on me, hassled me, doxxed me. Someone broke into my house and tried to murder me in my kitchen. Another girl who spoke out was killed. I ran, changed my name, shut up and have been hiding under a fake name ever since, because people only give a fuck when it suits them. There is justice but only for rich people. No one cares about crimes of sexual violence against people like me, unmoneyed, parents both dead, unless it fits their own agenda. And I told her that the footballers who raped me went on to have successful careers, that two of them have a nationwide radio show together now, you can hear them chortling away every Saturday afternoon. I told her that no one cared because people really like football, there's a lot of money in football, and evidence isn't really all that important. Facts don't matter. We all choose to believe whatever we want to and that usually means whatever we don't have to think about too much or change. And then I ruffled her hair and winked and said, 'Good luck out there, kid.'

Well, no, I didn't say that at all. In a jolly-hock-

39

ey-sticks voice so piercing that even I found it alarming, I trilled, 'Let's talk tomorrow, maybe? It's a long drive.'

'You *are* Sophie Bukaran, then?'

I wanted to slap my name from her mouth. Jess knew. She'd heard it in school or from one of those princessy little shits at that snooty fucking ballet school her father takes her to.

'Oooo, what a big topic! Let's talk tomorrow.' I carried her out to the living room, squeezing her so tight that she lost her breath, realised what I was doing and let go, dropping her so abruptly that she almost fell over. I grabbed Lizzie and lifted her up, holding her as a barrier between me and that conversation.

When I put Lizzie down Jess was looking at me, hurt and angry.

I said I'd see them all in a couple of days, punched Hamish on the head — I meant to hit his arm but he moved — waved a manic goodbye to everyone else and ran downstairs.

I was pulling my coat on when Fin came down after me. 'Sure you're safe to drive, Anna? You don't seem OK.'

'I didn't drink.' I pulled a hat on and did my coat up.

'I didn't mean that . . .' He picked up my two bags by the door.

'I'll just go straight home,' I said. 'I'll just go straight home and see if anything's happening. Might be nothing anyway. They might find her by the time I get there! Then I'll be home and see what's in her email.'

'Anna, will you be OK . . . ?' He didn't seem to be referring to the drive. Fin knows me well, knows I come from a family with a history of suicide and I've

40

had heavy ideation in the past. The one thing that isn't reassuring is spontaneously blurting that you're not going to commit suicide. I just wanted to get the fuck out of here.

'So, yeah, I'll call you.' I turned my collar up and took my bags off him.

'Well, if you don't mind —' he was pulling his coat on too '— forward me the email when you find it, will you?'

'Yeah, yeah.'

He dropped his chin to his chest, huffed a sigh and whispered, 'I'm so sorry, Anna, it's not fair to you or the girls . . . '

But behind him, at the top of the stairs, I could see Sofia's shadow fall across the landing. She was loitering and listening, Mrs Danversishly.

Fin bristled as if he sensed her presence.

'Let me carry the bags to the car.'

He opened the front door and we stepped out into the storm.

The front door slammed tight behind us. A bitter rain needled our cheeks.

I looked at Fin to see if he was as pleased by the sight of chaos as I was and he proper grinned for the first time in ages.

I opened my mouth to the rain and he laughed, deep-throated, and, still smiling, nodded me sideways to the car.

Our first step onto the path was a reckless drop. One hundred feet below us the Irish Sea growled and shrieked. Vicious wind buffeted us back. It felt very unsafe out there.

A low wall ran all the way round the lighthouse. I'd thought it an odd, affected detail when we first

41

arrived, but I saw now that it was there to stop light-house keepers being blown over the cliff in weather like this. We hung close to the building until we got to the corner, heads down, feeling our way to the sheltered side of the building.

There was a small windbreak round the corner, inches deep. We both gasped deep breaths before we stepped towards the car and I opened the back door to throw the bags in. I turned to tell Fin I was sorry, look, Sofia's OK, I'm sure everything will get better when I'm gone, but he couldn't hear me. He kept shouting 'WHAT?' and staring at my mouth.

I tried again but my clothes were soaking wet, rain was running through my hair and dripping down into my collar and I still had a long drive ahead. I gave up, squeezed his arm and just got into the car, slamming the door behind me.

I waved and then sat panting, dabbing my face with my sleeve until his shadow moved from the rain-warped window. I started the engine.

The lights on the dashboard lit softly, the rain murmured against the roof and windows, and my heart swelled at the prospect of being alone, of thinking my way through this, of strategising what lies to tell the girls, but the passenger door opened and Fin slid into the car.

I turned, expecting him to say, oh, remember — whatever — or please call me if x happens or take care of yourself. But he didn't. He didn't even look at me. He shut the door and looked forwards. Then he locked the door and pulled his seat belt on.

'Drive.'

'Oh no, Fin, fuck, no.'

'Drive.'

'That's not fair. She hates me. I'm leaving so she'll stop saying vicious stuff in front of the girls. You're making this worse.'

A flash of light at the side of the house signalled the front door opening. A long shadow fell to the corner. It began to move towards us.

'GET OUT, FIN.'

'DRIVE, ANNA.'

'NO.'

Sofia caught up with her shadow, rounded the corner and looked straight at me, her face melting through the sheet rain on the glass.

For reasons I don't understand, excitement maybe, raw reflex or just badness, I threw the car into reverse and sped backwards, careening out of the windbreak of the house and into a sideswiping gale. A deafening thump hit the side of the car. It was the eighty-mile-an-hour gale ramming the doors. The car tipped very slightly and Fin grabbed the side of his seat.

The white headlights washed over Sofia, bleaching her features to an old, tough-as-nails Italian nonna. Her ponytail reared up behind her like a cobra rearing to strike a pose. She wasn't even wearing a coat. Her eyes were wide. She took a step towards us.

I gunned the engine, yanked it right, and Fin and I sped off into the night, at fifteen miles an hour.

5

The wipers fought a losing battle against the heavy rain. It was coming in sideways from the north and I was driving blind over the road off the headland, a thin tarmac strip that meandered for a mile, weaving between giant boulders, dipping down, twisting on the upswing.

It took us ten minutes, an engine stall and a lot of swearing to get to the shelter of a thick hedge on the road. I stopped, pulled the handbrake on and loosened my fingers on the steering wheel. I've never had exhausted elbows before.

Fin looked back into the veil of rain, back to where the lighthouse probably was. The radio DJ warbled calmly, as if nothing at all was happening.

'Fin, you can't just leave like this.'

He looked out of the side window.

'You've got to stand up to her!'

He didn't say anything.

'Estelle'll blame me for this.'

He shook his head softly.

I tried again. 'You've got to go back. You brought her here.'

He muttered *fuck off* at the window.

'Fucking off is exactly what I was trying to do.'

He chewed his cheek. 'It's not that big a deal. We're coming back tomorrow anyway.' Then he turned to me and gave a sickly smile. 'Aren't we?'

He'd known I was lying about coming back. I mentally Rolodexed through all the reasons it was OK for me to lie and run away but not him. It was different because I had problems. Because my background was tragic. Because I was special. Because feminism. None of it worked.

'You're so passive, Fin, you've got to stand up for yourself. You can't always leave it to me, for fucksake. At least text and tell her that it was your idea to get into the car.'

Reluctantly, he took out his phone and unlocked it.

'Tell her I didn't force you to leave. You need to learn to stand up for yourself. Defy her. Make a decision.'

'OK, OK,' he said. 'Just drive.'

I drove on into the dark. The road was bordered with hedges and trees and that tempered the wind but the storm clouds were low and black and the night was velvet. Fin's face was reflected in the windscreen, uplit by the phone he was writing the text message on. I saw him compose the awkward text, frown and cringe and finally press send.

He dropped his phone to his lap. 'How long d'you think it'll take to get —' but his phone lit up and interrupted him, text following text, buzzing loud, light pulsing bright as each one came in.

It seemed like quite the rant. I hoped it wasn't all about what a shit I was.

It was a difficult drive. I had to concentrate hard to swerve around the fallen branches and debris scuttling across back roads, anticipating the wind breaking through the maze of hedges and sideswiping the car so hard that it broke our tyres' grip on the tarmac.

Forty minutes later we passed an actual street light and it felt like a triumph of sorts. Fin still had his face in his phone but he was scrolling now, so I knew he

45

wasn't answering texts from Sofia.

'What are you reading?'

'Background. This story is huge.'

'It's too big for us, isn't it? We're too small to fight our way through teams of professional journalists.'

'And too lazy.' He smiled.

'Well, let's dignify that by calling it 'considered'.'

'Languid.'

'Reflective.'

We were smiling together. It had been a while.

He looked back at his phone, 'Still, no one else is especially concerned about Lisa Lee. It's the contents of the casket everyone's interested in. And the monetary value. The focus is on the auction in Paris. Her disappearance is just a footnote part of the Curse of the Casket. Everyone thinks her dad killed her.'

'Curse of the Casket?'

'Yeah. People have been dying around that thing since it was found in Hungary in 1978.'

'Very expensive, portable things do tend to be cursed, I've noticed.'

'We could go to North Berwick and talk to the dad. I think we'd be the only people who bother to. I'll call Trina, see if she thinks there's anything in it.'

'Where are you reading this stuff?'

He'd started a Reddit thread but, as was so often the case for us now, it was being added to so quickly it was almost confusing and contradictory. Fin had given up and gone to long-form articles by journalists, waiting for the thread to settle down.

'Jess knows my real name.'

'Sophie Bukaran?'

'Yeah. She asked me about it. And if she hasn't looked it up before she will now.' I flinched. 'She'll read all that graphic stuff.'

He didn't know what to say to me. In the watery windscreen reflection, I watched his hand rise to touch my shoulder. It fell back to his thigh when he knew I'd seen it. He shook his head. 'Fuck.'

I nodded. 'Fuck, indeed.'

'She was going to find out one day,' he said, wondering if that was any consolation.

'She's twelve.'

He nodded heavily at the storm. 'Fuck.'

We drove on. I think we were both feeling sad about the girls knowing. I find it hard to sit with sadness. I'd much rather have a fight. I asked him if he'd replied to Sofia's texts but he knew I was changing the topic, that it was a prelude to a nagging session about his unassertiveness.

'You've got to start standing up for yourself more, Fin.'

'OK then,' he said. 'Anyway, do you want to hear the history of the Casket and the story of the Curse? It's got history and mystery and drama and murders.'

Losing ourselves in other people's stories was what Fin and I did together. It was our connection.

Our rough-and-ready podcast had made us very famous within a very small, strange world that we hadn't known existed. We were listening to a podcast called *Death and the Dana* when an old friend of mine was mentioned and, I felt, maligned. We'd recorded what were really just soundbite comments as we tramped around Europe trying to find out what really happened but a lot of people listened because Fin was already a name. Then the whole multi-media mess of the thing was collated without our permission — we hadn't copyrighted it. Our listening numbers were astronomical.

We changed the form, apparently.

The thing was awarded prizes by people we'd never heard of and we were guests of honour at conferences on podcasting, crimes of sexual violence, on corruption.

My new identity was blown and the history of my rape and persecution was rehashed all over the public sphere. I'd been living in silent dread of my children finding out ever since. How could I possibly explain it to them, excuse myself, talk them through the traumatising details? Which details would they home in on, identify with, form their own identities around? I tried not to think about it. I got so busy that I didn't have to think about it.

We got a publishing deal and I wrote a book. It was hard, so hard that I never thought I would do it again. Yet here we are. But this book you're in the middle of, my writing yet another bloody book and everything that happened afterwards, it was all because of Bram van Wyk and Marcos.

I'll get to them.

And because of Lisa's letter.

When we set up a podcast site we asked for other stories. Then the emails started coming.

Some were compliments, some were snark, but a lot came from people asking us to investigate: please find my missing son, my mum, my friend, please convict the men who raped me, my mother's killer, prove I'm innocent, no one cares. A lot of those people had never had the chance to tell their story to anyone before.

The deficit of justice was terrible to witness.

Awful things happen to people sometimes, no one

really cares and some things are unsurvivable. They just are.

If you wrote to us I want you to know that we read those letters, every single one, but it wasn't good for us.

Fin found it so hard that we asked people to stop writing. Thank you for trusting us but please just stop.

But we were stuck.

We'd sit up staring at the full email inbox, willing ourselves to read just five more tales of devastation, just three more, just one more and then we could stop. It was impossible not to think of the courage it took to write those things.

For me the worst ones were about sexual assault. It wasn't the details that bothered me so much as the people who did what they were supposed to do after they were attacked. They reported, spoke out, let a stranger swab the sore bits and cuts, let them test and touch them and then nothing happened. Or their rapist got a sentence that was little more than a sabbatical because of drink or drugs, benefit of the doubt, unreliable witness. No one cared. It was hopeless. It was pointless. It got to be too much for me, to be honest. I got a bit down.

For Fin the worst were the eating ones. It was all so samey, he said, the way people felt. So similar. He'd always believed it was different from person to person but at base they all hated themselves enough to do this. Now he wasn't just struggling but he felt responsible for all these others, for the harm and hurt and the refusal to believe they mattered.

It was a day's work to open my eyes some days.

When I did Estelle was always there. She was pregnant by Hamish but still stayed with me, making me toast and tea, getting me to do a little bit of yoga, go for a walk. Hamish painted my new home and assembled all of the furniture. He'd lost a lot because of me. He'd never make it onto the bench because the papers knew I'd lied about my identity for the ten years we were together and he hadn't noticed. Generations of his family had been judges but he'd never make it. He said he didn't care any more, but I knew he did.

We all spent a lot of time together. I know this interdependence wasn't healthy but it was the best any of us could manage at the time. We should have moved on really.

So, another deep dive into the impossibility of justice was not what we wanted. We were looking for escapism, for a story to take us out of ourselves, for a mental holiday.

I was thinking about all of this, about whether Lisa's scarred arms were any business of mine when she hadn't mentioned them in the film, when Fin's phone pinged a text notification.

'Sofia?'

It wasn't from her but an unknown number.

Someone had seen our request for information and wanted to help us find Lisa Lee. They had a lot of resources, a lot of contacts, a private plane, and wondered, if we found her first, could we ask her the name of the person selling the casket? It was signed 'Bram van Wyk'.

'Is that a name or an anagram?'

Fin wasn't sure but they knew that we were in Glasgow (we weren't) and were '*podcasters made famous by the* Death and the Fana *podcast series*'.

This was a typo on the first line of the Wikipedia entry about us.

'Well,' I said, 'he's clearly done a lot of research.'

'How did he find my number though?'

It wasn't impossible but it was an effort.

'What does he want with Lisa?'

'Yeah, that's what I'm worried about.'

We got to Stranraer, the nearest big town, and it was a balm to the eyes to see lights on in houses and well-lit streets. It had taken us forty-five minutes to do what was usually a twenty-minute drive. I pulled up in a narrow street where the wind felt less insistent for a rest.

Fin had texted Sofia and said she was OK about it. She was going to come home tomorrow and they'd have 'a talk'. I didn't really know if that meant they were splitting up but didn't like to pry. She knew he'd left with me, but not for me. That was all I cared about.

We were at a fork in the road and briefly considered taking the turn for the East Coast and North Berwick. We'd have to go at some point to get audio and maybe an interview but the weather was awful and we wouldn't get there until one in the morning so we decided to take the left turn and follow the motorway up the west coast to Glasgow. We'd get a look at Lisa's email and some sleep before we went.

I braced myself, took off the handbrake and headed for the main road along the blustery coast road.

Traffic was sparse and slow, crawling along at thirty miles an hour. Lorries and cars were staying as close to the centre line as they dared, cowering from huge waves washing over the road from our left.

It was alternately terrifying and very dull so Fin read bits of the rapidly expanding Reddit threads to keep me awake.

Lisa had been an outpatient in a psychiatric unit in

Edinburgh. Someone met her in there and refused to say what Lisa was being treated for but wanted to say that she was very nice and quiet and wouldn't steal things. Anyway her dad was rich.

An old classmate said Lisa was a school refuser. She'd stopped coming in when her mum was ill with breast cancer. They nursed her mum at home for a long time but when she died her dad had a bit of a breakdown and Lisa had to nurse him. Then Lisa stopped going out at all. Only her little sister left the house. Social workers got involved. That went on for a while until —

Fin's text tone pinged and he broke off to read it.

We'd reached a part of the road that was flooded. The surface felt oily and uncertain. I was squinting as hard as I was hoping, driving blind, but was aware of a hiss from Fin's phone. He was watching something. I could see the flickering light from the screen reflected on the inside of the windscreen and a shallow image of his face. He was smiling.

'What's funny?'

'Private plane guy isn't a hoax. He's a publicity hound. There's a news interview with him about the casket.'

'Turn it up,' I said, very much wanting something else to focus on.

He did.

This was the first time we heard Bram van Wyk's smoke-ruined voice. His accent was South African, all burred 'r's and razor-sharp 't's, but he drawled, elongating vowels as if he was terribly tired or his teeth hurt or both.

'I tell you this now: this casket is the most significant find in archaeology since Tutankhamen. And now it's going to

be sold on the open market — to who? Should these things be sold like that, to whoever has the most money? These people don't care about history, they don't care about truth. I'm not a religious man myself but even I can see that it means more to the faithful than a capitalist pig like me.'

The clip finished. Obviously, I couldn't see Bram van Wyk but Fin was captivated.

'He sounds like a giant red flag snapping in a high wind,' I said.

Fin snorted. 'Yeah. Touching, all that stuff about caring about the faithful. He's the Don King of the antiques market, apparently. He didn't mention Lisa Lee in the interview. I don't think he really gives a toss about her.'

'Tell him to fuck off.'

Fin composed a text and I heard the little swoosh as he sent it.

'I know you didn't tell him to fuck off.'

'I answered more in terms of: thank you for thinking of us, and we'd love to meet you but it's just that we're terribly busy looking for Lisa.'

'You need to be more forthright, Fin.'

'I'm forthright.'

'Confrontational, then. You can't let people push you around all the time.'

'People don't push me around.'

'Sofia does.'

'No, she doesn't. Can I smoke?'

He rolled us both cigarettes as thin as matches and we smoked them. Smoking together was a ritual for us, a bonding signal, but not a very positive one. It meant one or both of us were feeling reckless, as if something bad was going to happen and we were both excited about it.

Writing this now I can smell the thin smoke rolling around the inside of that warm car, I can hear the rain battering on the roof, feel the tension in my shoulders from clutching the steering wheel. I can feel nicotine pumping through my blood, my blood pressure rising and tiny hairs on my face lifting gently. It feels like a premonition of the madness to come.

The traffic in front of us came to a standstill and I could see vehicles in front taking turns to ford a deep puddle. We were going so slowly that, at this speed, it would take about another three or four hours to get home.

Fin smoked and asked if I wanted to hear what he had pieced together about the history of the Voyniche Casket.

I said yes, please.

This became the second episode.

6

When Maria K.'s father got a promotion his family knew they would never be able to trust him again.

He was a man of no real importance in Communist Hungary, yet, quite suddenly, he was lifted several civil service grades and transferred to one of the most coveted placements in the service.

He was being moved to Lake Balaton.

Lake Balaton was a glamorous and exclusive holiday resort for senior Communist Party members, a Hungarian Côte d'Azur. The weather is glorious there, good sailing, great swimming, with wonderful local produce and wines. It was a favoured resort of the Romans too, who called the Balaton region 'Pelso'. High-ranking officials would retire there at the end of their glittering careers running the Empire. They built huge villas on the shore, staffing them with slaves from all over the known world. Much of the present-day infrastructure around the lake, ferry ports, the layout of the roads and bridges, dates back to the Romans.

When Maria's family moved there in 1977 the region was rundown. Buildings were still pockmarked from the last great battle of World War II. Bombs and chunks of shrapnel were often found in the woods and ditches and hilltops.

Still, the Lake Balaton civil service placement was highly coveted. This was why the family were suddenly afraid of their mild-mannered father, because Communist Hungary was not a meritocracy. It was a police state. Success in the civil service was not about ability but how much someone contributed to the perpetuation of the regime. People were rewarded for spying on each other, betraying fellow workers, neighbours, family members.

When the Nazis withdrew in 1945 the Hungarian Secret Police walked straight into SS headquarters in Budapest. Form determines function. The building had a torture chamber in the basement, an execution chamber, a great many small, windowless, sound-proofed cells and a furnace big enough to burn several bodies at the same time.

But while the SS only had a few brief years to establish control of the population, the Hungarian Secret Police had thirty-five. One third of the entire Hungarian population were registered as informants at the force's height. Suspected infractions were treated brutally. A cabinet minister, tipped off that he was about to be investigated, put on his coat, went home, murdered his entire family and then killed himself. He was Minister of the Interior. He knew what they would do to them.

During the '56 Uprising known informants were lynched from lamp posts by angry mobs. Their bodies were left hanging for days, their mouths stuffed with money. They were hated and feared by everyone, and more so by people with something to hide.

Maria's mother had a terrible secret: she was Catholic. Religion wasn't banned in Hungary as it was in Czechoslovakia, but its leaders were harried, persecuted for petty infractions and held under house arrest. Maria's mother was an active Catholic. She knew underground priests, hiding places and the names of her fellow congregants. She had every reason to be afraid of the Secret Police.

The family said nothing about the unexpected promotion except that they were pleased. Lake Balaton! How nice! Lucky us! And they moved with their father into a modest house in a small town two kilometres south of the *lake shore. But they were afraid of him now. The trust was gone. They didn't know what he had done to get this or who he really was.*

I should say that the sources for this episode are variously: an unpublished interview with an anonymous man in Beirut, Hungarian secret service files that were found and released after the fall of the regime, and rumour. Pre internet, all of these sources were available but they were never linked together. Simple keyword searches by citizen detectives have uncovered this story but that doesn't mean the danger facing those involved is no longer real. We will only use the name 'Maria K.' in this episode. This is to minimise identifiers of those involved. We don't believe in curses or hexes. We believe that the cause of the deaths in this story is more prosaic.

Maybe Maria's father didn't know why he had been promoted either. Maybe the man who actually deserved the cushy transfer had died or been arrested for something and they picked Maria's dad at random, as a replacement, but if this was the case he couldn't tell his family that. It would make them even more suspicious. That's exactly what a spy would say.

He knew they didn't trust him, were afraid of him and, soon enough, that they no longer loved him. It broke his heart. He turned to drink.

One day on his bus journey home he was particularly unsteady on his feet. The bus turned a corner and he stepped on an old woman's shopping bags. They argued and he said a bad word, right in her face. She slapped him. Just then the bus came to a stop and he shoved her as the doors opened. She fell out through the open doors, hit the pavement with the back of her head and died on the spot.

Maria's father was arrested for murder.

During his trial the father's co-workers gave evidence

that he always smelled of vodka, kept his briefcase with him at all times and was often weepy or sleepy. The witnesses on the bus said that, as the old woman lay dying in the street, he tried to cheer everyone up by starting a singsong.

It was all very out of character. It didn't sound like him at all. The family didn't believe the bus story. It was a fiction. His arrest was political. He'd got involved with matters he shouldn't have and then the authorities had to get rid of him.

They didn't attend his trial. They didn't visit him in prison. They never mentioned him again. From then on they kept their eyes down, kept to themselves and studiously avoided the attention of anyone in authority. If no one ever did anything interesting again they might just survive.

Maria was the eldest child and she did well in school but, striving not to stand out, left as soon as she could for a menial job in a bakery on the 4 a.m. shift. It was hard work in a hot kitchen for very little money, but she finished at three in the afternoon and met very few people.

Without their father's wage the family were poor and they often went hungry. A lot of people grew their own food but that invited accusations of involvement in the black market. Maria needed a private patch of well-hidden land. She began to watch out for obscure plots that no one knew about.

One day, on her way home from work, she found it. It was on the banks of a small stream below a dairy farm, an awkward quarter-acre running downhill to the water, about a quarter of the size of a tennis court. No one seemed to know it was there and no one had ever cultivated it so the soil could be very rich. Before she planted anything, though, she needed to pick out the stones.

Every day she walked past on her way to and from work, and every day she filled her pockets with rocks. She took them away, dropping them at the side of the road. On fine days she gave herself twenty minutes, ten minutes if it was raining. After two weeks she stood back and looked at it. She was ready to turn the topsoil.

The next day she brought a big serving spoon and did a little digging. She did this for a few days, never going too deep, until one morning her serving spoon hit something hard. Thinking it was a rock she tried to dig it out but it was too big. She wiped the soil away to see what it was and there, in the dark, she saw a patch of pale green. She tapped it, feeling for the resonances in her teeth. It wasn't stone, it was metal. It was an unexploded bomb.

Maria ran.

At work she asked about bombs and her co-workers told her that minesweepers came after the war but, yes, there were still some bombs out there, especially in uncultivated land. You had to be careful. One boy lost his legs playing in a wood. A farmer was blown up at the edge of a field. She asked if anyone had ever seen a bomb and a lot of them had. They described them, the glinting brass shells and steel casings. Were any of them made of copper? They laughed at that. Copper was a soft metal. You might as well make a bomb out of cake.

She told her mother that she might have found something old, made of copper on a riverbank. She didn't know if she should leave it there or bring it home. Maria's mother was troubled enough to ask her priest, Father Lamberg, for advice and he said Maria should dig it up if she wanted a bit of old copper, but if not she should plant onions. He was from Vienna. He didn't know the Hungarian law governing archaeological finds.

Most countries offer a reward if people find historical

treasure, sometimes fairly substantial amounts of money, a cut of the market value, an insurance guestimate or just a flat rate. Not Hungary. In Hungary archaeological finds must be surrendered to the state as a civic obligation. A finder might not even get their expenses back. This was well known around Lake Balaton, where Roman finds were not unusual.

Maria knew that if she had found something valuable it would draw the eye of the authorities so she didn't tell anyone. But she went back.

It was a fine autumn afternoon. She sat down, lit a cigarette and smoked for a while with the sun on her face. If anyone saw her they'd just think she was sitting, smoking. Gradually she let her hand drop to the warm soil and felt the cold copper brush her fingertips. She picked at the edge of the hole for a while. Then she started digging out the metal. It took longer than she expected.

It was getting dark but she kept going, determined not to leave until she got it out. Now she was digging by moonlight.

Her mother would almost certainly think Maria had been arrested, she always thought that, but what Maria had uncovered was so valuable that she didn't dare leave it.

It was a copper cooking cauldron, dented and damaged, bright green with oxidation, deep and full of silver objects. She dug them out and washed them in the stream until everything was sitting in a neat row on the moonlit bank.

This is what she had found:

The big green copper cauldron, battered, still with a tidemark trace of the last meal cooked in it two thousand years ago.

A massive Roman serving plate of solid silver, expertly decorated with gilded exotic animals.

Twin silver wine jugs with bacchanal scenes and handles shaped like rearing panthers.

Two wine goblets, matching.

And the casket. This was the least impressive item. It looked like an outsized silver pencil case with rounded edges, one of them crumped by the weight of the soil.

To Maria the hoard looked valuable enough to draw the attention of every secret policeman for fifty miles. Panicked, she put it all in the cauldron and humphed it home. There she found her mother sitting at the kitchen table, reciting a novena for her safe return with Father Eugene Lamberg.

Eugene Lamberg was ordained in January 1976. He was twenty-four, a Lutheran convert who had given up his studies at the University of Vienna, and an aristocratic life of freedom and privilege to be smuggled into Czechoslovakia. Converts often have a rigidity and commitment that far surpasses those raised in a faith, and so it was with Father Lamberg.

He knew he had a vocation but normal seminaries weren't hard core enough for him. He wanted to study under Bishop Davídek, the head of the Czechoslovak Underground Church.

Father Felix Maria Davídek was ordained three years before the Communist coup in Czechoslovakia. In 1950 he was sentenced to twenty-four years in prison for owning a radio and for 'spiritual activities'. After fourteen years, under a general amnesty, he was released. When they came for him Davídek refused to leave his cell in protest at the persecution of religion. They had to physically drag him out of the prison.

The Vatican made him a bishop.

For the rest of his life Davídek expected all Czech priests to be deported to Siberia at any moment. If that hap-

pened the faithful would have no access to the sacraments or spiritual guidance of any kind. The official Church had to retain a public face so that people still knew they were there but they were policed without mercy or compassion and their activities were very constrained. Davídek established a religious community in the woods, in secret, out of sight of the authorities, and set about recruiting an army of the religious to offer the word of God to those who sought it.

Part of the community was a seminary with a syllabus that included film criticism and computer studies. He was preparing a reserve team of contingency priests in case of mass arrests.

Davídek ordained almost anyone who asked him to. This included several married men and three women. He wasn't authorised by the Vatican to do this. When the Vatican ordered him, Davídek thought the message was a trick by the Secret Police. Anyway, no one could understand the pressure and conditions they were under, he reasoned, unless they too lived in a police state. He ignored the order and carried on.

John Paul II became Pope in 1978. He had lived under the Nazis and the Communists, had studied in an underground seminary. He fully understood the pressures on Davídek and his congregation. He issued an order demoting Davídek, disbanding his seminaries and rescinding all of the contingency ordinations.

Father Eugene Lamberg's priesthood was revoked.

Lamberg ignored that. He travelled the Soviet bloc under fake papers. He lived on little. He ministered to many and every day he risked arrest and imprisonment or worse. By all accounts he was a wonderful priest but he did not go unnoticed. He was too elegant, too tall, he spoke with a distinct Viennese accent and he had very nice teeth which *made him stand out. Everywhere Lamberg went people asked the same questions: who's the guy with the nice teeth and why would anyone leave Vienna to come here?*

The Secret Police had extensive files on him. After a while he befriended some of the agents who were following him and, when the Wall came down in '89, two of them converted. Eugene Lamberg came back from his new home in Boston to attend both confirmations. Lamberg was one of the few people to survive the discovery of the casket but he didn't escape unscathed by what people assume is a curse.

In 2014 the assisted suicide of a cancer patient led to the arrest of her priest, Father Des O'Brian. He gave himself up willingly. It was only when he was fingerprinted that his real identity was revealed: Fr Des O'Brian was really Eugene Lamberg.

But this was long in the future. Before this, in 1977, he was the priest Maria found praying with her mother for her safe return. Maria showed them what she had found and Lamberg offered to put them in touch with a junk dealer he knew called Ludovic Voyniche.

Lamberg never spoke about this. Our account of what happened then came from an interview with one of Maria's younger brothers, given many years later in Beirut. This version is corroborated by Secret Police records that were released when the regime fell. These records tell us what Maria was doing day by day, minute by minute, and they tell us who killed her.

12 November 1977: Maria's mother bought a flódni cake from a shop. Buying shop-made cakes was not something ordinary people did. It certainly wasn't something Maria's cash-strapped mother had ever done before. The cake shop was there to serve the big houses, not ordinary people. Everyone else made their own, if they had any need of a cake at all. Someone working in the cake shop informed the police. It was noted that Maria's mother, perpetually beset by money worries, had recently paid off all of her debts and had new shoes.

The Secret Police began to watch Maria's mother. All of their reports were meticulously typed up and filed. This led them to identify Maria as the source of the money.

This is the start of the Maria K. files.

Saturday 19 November 1977: 08.47 a.m., Maria gets off a bus at Budapest Airport, approaches Agent 71213 (Ludovic Voyniche) at a stall and sells two matching Roman goblets (silver) for US$80. Agents had been warned about her. 71213 was interviewed later and said he had also bought a steel serving plate. Scrap value only. Had asked Maria if she could get more and she said she would come back next week.

24 November 1977 8.20 a.m. Maria was seen on the bus to the flea market. Sold Agent 71213 an old copper pan and two reproduction Roman wine jugs for US$98. Showed him a metal box but could not agree on a price.

8.46 a.m. On the bus back to Budapest. Observed disembarking at Moscow Square and walking to the train station. Boarded the train for Lake Balaton with a return ticket to Budapest. Observed by five separate agents (!) disembarking and greeting her mother.

They smoked cigarettes and chatted. Maria gave her mother an envelope, walked her to the bus and waved her off.

Secret Police sightings of Maria stop abruptly there.

The case was stamped closed on 24 November 1977. It's a mark of how assured the Secret Police were that they didn't bother faking a report of Maria getting the train back to Budapest or make up an excuse.

They just closed her file.

Maria hadn't even been reported missing when her mother was notified that a parcel was waiting for her the local post office. She didn't know what it was. Expecting, perhaps, a present from Budapest, she walked into the village and found that it was a large parcel, wrapped in brown paper and tied with string. Several villagers gathered around to watch her open it. They were excited.

She untied the string and was careful not to rip the good paper. It was brand new. She could reuse that. She folded it back carefully and found Maria's clothes, her shoes, her washbag, her two books, her pencil case, her nightdress, her hairbrush, and, at the bottom of the parcel, her identification papers. Maria's mother dropped the parcel and ran home. Thankfully the other children were at school, because the door had been kicked in and their modest house had been ransacked. The casket was gone.

Eventually Maria was found hanging in a chicken shed a hundred kilometres north-east of Budapest, her knees almost touching the shit-encrusted floor. The farmer called the police. He and his wife had been woken up by a noise, looked out and saw footsteps through the snow leading round the back of the house to the shed, three sets of footsteps in, two sets out. He knew not to look until he had called the authorities because the prints coming back out matched each other and were distinct: they were from military boots.

The casket had disappeared. But there were always rumours.

Maria's brother, who we'll call Michael, fled Hungary. By 1992 he was married with three children, living quietly in Beirut which was a surprisingly easy thing to do.

There was nothing notable about Michael. He lived in a modest apartment, ate and dressed in an unremarkable manner, wore a tie to work. He agreed to be interviewed

by a journalist who had heard the rumours of the Voyniche Casket's existence as long as they could guarantee his
anonymity. He was afraid of the Hungarian Secret Police.
They were still operating, he insisted, serving different
masters now but still out there. But maybe no one cared
any more and he wanted his sister to be remembered. There
was a casket and it was silver, he said, his sister found it
in a field. He drew the Chi Rho symbol from the lid for the
journalist, described the inscriptions, the words Pelso and
Pilate and Judaea.

The interview wasn't even slated for publication yet.
The story needed confirmation, it was a long time before
the corroborating Secret Police records were scanned or
even filed, and none of it seemed terribly likely. Christian
groups were flooding into formerly Communist countries
and stories were flying around, many of them nonsense.

One evening Michael and his family were eating dinner. The doorbell rang. Maria's brother went to answer it,
carrying his napkin with him to the door as a signal to
the caller that their dinner was being interrupted and they
should keep it short. He opened the front door and the
family, still sitting back at the table, heard him give a surprised 'Hello?' then 'Oh!' and then quiet.

They waited for him to come back to the table but he
never did. They went out to the hall. The front door was
open, the napkin on the floor, but he was gone.

An hour later a pipe bomb blast went off two streets
away. One casualty. Michael was blown apart.

None of the usual factions claimed responsibility. No
one mentioned the explosive unpublished interview and
rumours of the Voyniche Casket faded until it appeared
again in 1998, in the southern Italian city of Bari, in the
hands of a disreputable South African named Bram van
Wyk.

7

It took us four hours and change to get back to Glasgow. While we limped home on the wet motorway Fin stayed on his phone, skimming articles and tips, relaying the story to me in chunks and lumps.

We both saw the parallels between Lisa's disappearance from her hallway in North Berwick and Michael K.'s abduction and subsequent murder in Beirut, but we couldn't fathom who would be taking people from their houses or why. And the two incidents were more than twenty years apart, a long time for an individual to hold the same grudge. Even maniacs get bored and move on to other projects. That made us think that maybe it wasn't an individual. Maybe it was the vestiges of the Hungarian Secret Police that Michael K. was still afraid of.

And then there was the why, of that we had no idea. It wasn't to steal the casket: Maria K. didn't have it with her or her mother's house wouldn't have been ransacked, neither did Michael K. or Lisa.

No one else in the world seemed to have made the connection but maybe no one else had a Reddit army. We thought we should at least visit her dad and tell him.

I stopped at a red light on an empty street at Charing Cross. My arms and back were aching from hours of careful driving and my gums throbbed from all the cigarettes. I was looking forward to getting home and being alone and, mostly, brushing my teeth. I wasn't thinking about Lisa as we made our way through the town, just about Jess and Lizzie sleeping and not thinking about what Sofia had said. She was vicious. I hoped she hadn't said anything else after we left.

The city was quiet and still. Far off in the distance emergency vehicles sang to each other and the roads seemed molten with rippling run-off hurrying down to the river. The rain had been very heavy here. I was worried about my roof caving in. I was always worried about my stupid roof.

Fin said could he come to mine because he didn't have his house keys or even a change of socks. I was not pleased.

'You have great faith in the universe turning up to look after you,' I said.

'I just need somewhere to crash,' he said, pretty indignant for a man with no house keys or money on him.

I took the turn and snaked up the steep hill to my home, a mews cottage in Park Gardens Lane. I bought it when I moved out of Hamish's house.

It was on the far side of the girls' school from the old house, close enough to keep me in their daily lives but far enough away from Hamish and Estelle that we wouldn't run across each other all the time. It had been a coach house and stables with a living space upstairs for staff. It was down a cobbled lane and faced onto the backside of enormous Victorian town houses. Both it and the rest of the coach houses on the terrace were nuzzled into the side of a small cliff and above us loomed a grand crescent of even bigger houses.

In the 1920s, when a carriage and horses stopped being an aristo necessity, it was redesigned as a cottage by a famous architect. The facade was tiled in art

68

deco stripes of silver and brown and a fine balcony was added to the first floor, the wrought iron curly and handsome. The rooms were tiny but the top floor was a big, open living space with a wooden staircase that led straight onto the roof garden and the street above.

The cottage had a lot of flaws: the windows were small, the walls were damp, the roof garden was in perpetual danger of getting waterlogged and caving in and, because it was listed as a building of historic importance, I couldn't change much about it. But I loved it.

Towards the top of the hill the shimmering tiles came out of the blue rain, glinting a welcome at me. The sight calmed me so much that I became aware that my phone had been vibrating in my bag on the back seat. Frenetic. Multiple messages. Shit. The kids. Hamish and Sofia. Something had happened. Shit.

The pilot light of my shame flickered and flared in my belly, the boiler came on and dread flooded my body.

I parked, pulled on the handbrake and steeled myself before reaching around to grab my bag, but a sudden, stark-white light flooded the cabin, so bright it was painful. Fin and I covered our eyes and keened as our pupils twanged.

The light was coming from the parallel lane across the road. Fin shouted at me to move. Squinting so hard I was barely using one eye, I let the brake off and rolled back, out of the harsh beam, and stopped. We peered over at the cause of it.

If Death had a car, this would have been it. The big black chassis was a foot off the ground, windows blacked out and the engine rumbled, rolling exhaust fumes up the side of the buildings on either side. It was unusually flash for such a shady back lane. I assumed something skeezy was going on in there, an adulterous couple or a spontaneous hook-up, but that was none of my business. I had other worries.

I reached in and took the phone out of the bag, glancing at the face of it nervously. The messages were not from Jess or Lizzie, or Hamish. They were all from Sofia and even a cursory glance told me this: she was going berserk, in a house with my kids in it.

I held it up to Fin. 'You didn't text her, did you?'

He cleared his throat. 'Look —'

'How have I become the focus of this? All I did was invite her on a free fucking holiday.'

But Fin didn't want to talk about it. There were things going on I didn't know about, he said, sorry but forget it, then he opened his door and turned away, swinging his legs out into a curtain of grey rain.

'My kids are there with her, Fin, I've left them there.'

He got out and slammed the door behind him. I got out and shouted over the roof that he was an arsehole. A total arsehole. But he wouldn't look at me. Furious, I slammed the car door too and looked up to shout yet another forensic insight about his character but I stopped. What I saw made my heart break.

He stood in the heavy rain, wretched as a lost dog, underweight, beleaguered, defeated. All around him fat raindrops exploded on the pavement, tiny spiked crowns, the street lights illuminating the tips.

'Stand up for your fucking self,' I hollered. 'Stop letting yourself be pushed around all the time.'

Behind me, a fast-moving shadow cut the beam of the stark-white headlights and shouted, 'Howzit!' I

70

spun around to look as it stepped sideways out of the beam.

It was a tall and beefy man in an expensive tan suit and pink shirt, pressing a red velvet hat trimmed with gold to his head.

'Hey, hey, I'm Bram van Wyk.'

'Bram Van what?' I asked.

'*Wyk*. Wyk. Van Wyk. It's an Afrikaans name.'

The origin of his surname seemed like something of an irrelevant detail, standing as we were in shitting rain in the street in the middle of the night.

I shrugged, baffled. 'And?'

'So you guys are Anna and Fin, yah?'

I nodded warily.

'OK, good. Looking for this Lisa Lee girl, yah? Can I come in?' He waved his velvet hat at my house. I was worried. I didn't like him knowing where I lived.

Fin said, 'I told you not to come, Mr van Wyk.'

'But I came anyway, to help you. If you say no — absolutely fine, I'll go away, but I really think I can help.'

'How?'

That stumped him, but only momentarily. 'Can I come in? Out of the rain?'

I hesitated but it was wet and we were cold and I was worried about Fin's health.

'Just for a minute.'

Bram van Wyk grinned. His front teeth had a big gap in the middle. It was cute. As I turned away to lead them to the house, feeling in my bag for my keys, I found myself running my tongue across my own front teeth, wondering why I didn't have a gap and wishing I did. Behind me Fin pointed out that the blinding car lights were on. Yeah, don't worry, said

71

Bram, it was automatic. Neither of us questioned this, but we should have.

I fitted the key, felt the ratchet purr of the lock and was so glad to be home that I could have kissed the door.

As we piled into the narrow white-tiled hall, a hang-over from the stables, and the familiar smell of damp and faint vanilla hit my nose, the tension melted in my shoulders. Home.

I peeled off my wet coat and hung it up to dry over the radiator. Fin looked at me nervously.

'Get your coat off, idiot.'

I swear he told me to piss off under his breath but he did what I told him and then we pulled on ripped old sweaters from a basket. It's a cold house. I offered one to Bram but he demurred, I suspect because he thought it would make him look silly.

'It's very cold in here,' I said. 'What about a blanket?'

He dropped the mad red hat, took the wool blanket, pulled it over his shoulders and smiled a shy thank you.

He was in his late fifties, tall, with skin so sun-damaged it looked almost bleached, and his pallor was tinged with grey, like a man in the early stages of a heart condition. He was still handsome though, wore three gold rings and sported a careful trompe l'oeil stubble-beard to suggest a chiselled jaw he didn't have any more. His clothes were expensive but casual. He wore his shirt untucked and kept pulling at the hem, irritated. It made me think that he'd been buff for a long time but his physique had gotten away from him and it bothered him. The line of his suit was ruined by the cross strap of a heavy green canvas satchel any-

72

way.

I led the way up the stairs to the big living room, with its arched brick ceiling and French windows onto the balcony. I put the lights on and heard Bram give a gratifying hum.

'Nice.'

I invited him to sit down. He squelched over to a sofa and lowered himself gracefully, and took off sodden blue suede loafers to reveal bare feet. He looked at the ruined shoes sadly.

'Damn,' he said, 'I was just getting them *perfect* on my feet.' He looked at me and shimmied his shoulders like a cat settling down in a warm corner.

If you saw Bram on TV his charisma wouldn't really come over. He was of a generation unused to beaming that towards a lens, but in real life he was warm and likeable.

Fin made some tea in the kitchen at the back of the room while I lit the stove and gave Bram some kitchen roll to dry his shoes with.

'So,' said Fin, putting the tray on the table, 'I saw an interview with you in Paris from this morning, Mr van Wyk.'

'Oh, please, just Bram.'

'How did you get to Glasgow?'

'I flew. I have a plane.' Bram took the cup Fin offered him and cradled it between his big hands. 'It's a lot of weather you have here.'

We agreed that it was a lot of weather. Fin said Glasgow is Gaelic for 'dear green place',that it was a poetic way of pointing out that it rained incessantly here.

I was looking at Bram's bare feet. Nicely manicured toenails, I noticed, but not recently. The cuticles were eased back but the nails were roughly cut and uneven. He had fresh pads of hard skin on his heels. Something had changed for him.

'Would you permit me to smoke?'

I said yeah, fine, and he took out a box of Sobranie Cocktail cigarettes. It was an unexpectedly fey choice for such a butch man. He flipped the pastel pink lid open with his thumb, lifted the gold lining paper and offered them round. The cigarettes were all different colours, from pastel green to hot pink, all with gold filters. They looked like sweeties.

I took a yellow one and Fin chose green. Bram took a pink, to match his shirt, he said, and lit us all up with a slim gold Dunhill lighter he kept in the packet. The cigarette was much too strong for me but I persevered to make the other damaged, middle-aged kids think I was cool.

Fin poured him a cup of tea. 'So, you said you could help us find Lisa Lee?'

'Yah, I really want to help find this girl.'

'Why?'

Bram smiled and sipped his tea. He swallowed. 'Why what?'

'Why would you come all this way to help us?'

'Well,' he shrugged, 'she's a missing girl. She's vulnerable.'

It seemed like a thin lie but neither of us really knew what to say.

'Ah,' said Fin. 'So, are you like Batman? Flying around the world saving random people?'

Bram laughed. 'No. Her mother died, didn't she? Less than a year ago, I think? I lost my own mother when I was young.'

'But why does Lisa matter so much to *you*?'

74

'Why does she matter so much to *you*?' He had a point. He sighed. 'Listen, I was in Paris because of this casket — you've heard of this?'

'The silver box thingy that Lisa found?'

'Yeah, the Voyniche Casket. People are gathering there for the coming auction, a lot of religious people, people with money, everyone is coming. It's Holy Week this week, you know that? It marks the week running up to the crucifixion of Christ on Good Friday and the resurrection from the tomb three days later, on Easter Monday. They went to look for his body in the tomb but found nothing except the linens he was wrapped in. Now, this Friday, Good Friday, is the day of the auction. So, I'm in Paris, at the build-up, it's crazy, all religious people there, praying and crying and hoping for the Rapture on Friday, maybe, and I'm wondering: what are we all *doing* here, trying to see this *thing*? To buy this thing? We should be helping each other. Then I see the father give his appeal. It felt like a cry for help. That poor kid, all alone. I just had to come.'

He looked up to see if we'd bought it. Again, it wasn't a very good lie: Bram looked more Monte Carlo than Medjugorje. But he had flown all the way here in a terrible storm, and was desperate enough to find Fin's mobile number and my address, probably from a source that wasn't entirely legal. We couldn't work out what we really wanted.

I guessed, 'Are you Catholic, Bram?'

'No. No.' He put his cup down. 'Honestly, I'm a godless fuck.' He flashed me a smile. 'But even godless fucks have a moral code. Are you Catholic?'

'No,' I said. 'My background is Muslim but we're secular.'

75

Fin said, 'We were Jewish enough for Hitler.' I didn't know what that meant so he clarified. 'Genetically Jewish, but not religious.'

Bram dabbed at his shoes with kitchen roll. 'Well, I don't come from a faith tradition but I do want to help save this kid. What can I do?'

Fin caught my eye. He didn't believe him either.

'We make podcasts,' he said. 'Is it OK if we record you?'

'Sure!' Bram said. In fact he'd record it too if we didn't mind. We didn't. He took an actual cassette recorder out of his battered satchel. 'I record everything instead of making notes. This way I can instantly check what people say: police, gangsters, Scotland Yard, dealers, everyone. Then it's not just down to my memory, yah?'

He opened the deck, checked that the blank tape still had space on it, slapped it shut, pressed record and sat it on the middle of the table.

Fin was interested because blank cassette tapes are difficult to source. Bram said he 'had a guy in Antwerp' and he could put Fin in touch with him if he wanted. As he talked it occurred to me that he might not be recording us as much as himself, to remember which lies he'd told and to whom.

Fin asked him why he would be having conversations with the police at all.

'Oh, I work with the Met finding stolen antiques. Arts and Antiques task force. I've helped them with many cases. You can call them if you like. They'll vouch for me.' But it was the middle of the night and he didn't offer us any contact details.

It was supposed to reassure us but his knowledge of the police made me think he'd been in trouble.

Fin said, oh, OK, thanks for that, maybe later. He fitted a directional mic on the DAT machine, switched it on and pointed it at Bram.

'Can you start by telling us what's going on in Paris?'

'Sure —' Bram drew a breath but a loud, aggravating ringtone interrupted him, a tinny rendition of 'Auld Lang Syne'. He took out his phone and answered the call.

'Yah. Very soon, my treasure.'

He hung up and refreshed his smile at us. It was twenty to three in the morning, a very odd time to take a call.

'Right now Paris is crazy. They're selling off this silver box of Roman origin that claims to prove, as a fact, the resurrection of Christ, in Holy Week, which I find interesting. They are selling it to the highest bidder, again, a very interesting notion, that history should be in the hands of the richest person. This box has not been opened before, can't be X-rayed, we can't see inside yet so no one knows what's in there. All the religious groups are coming and so on. Crazy. At this same time a girl called Lisa Lee hits my feeds. She found the box, we think, but she is not the seller of the box, we think —'

'Who's *we?*' asked Fin.

Bram shrugged. 'Everyone? She's missing, yah?'

'Yeah.'

'So, I'm in Paris in all this, it's a crazy case I've been following for a long time. I've seen many casualties from this casket, over the years, poor people, people with no power, killed or ruined or losing family members and no one cared. No one gave a damn about those people. I saw this and I swore I wouldn't

77

stand by and watch again. Lisa Lee is a person like this. I want to help.' He took a drag on his cigarette. 'So tell me — what can I do to help?'

On the recording you can hear us all smoking in silence, the wind groaning outside and the metallic ping of raindrops falling down the wood-burner flume, hissing on the hot metal lining.

Bram was charming but obviously up to something. I didn't trust him, not really, but I said we were going to visit Bob Lee in North Berwick in the morning to tell him about the parallels we'd seen with other people connected with the casket, that Lisa disappeared from her hallway and it sounded like a 1992 incident in Beruit —

'His napkin was on the floor. A pipe bomb. He had three kids. OK, I can help. Let me drive you to North Berwick now, you can sleep in the car while I drive, we get there by morning, super early, and then I'll bring you home.'

I wasn't keen on getting in this duplicitous stranger's car but could tell that Fin was intrigued by Bram.

Bram could tell that there was tension between us. 'You guys need to talk to each other. I'll use the washroom,' he said and rose gracefully from the low sofa.

I directed him downstairs.

We listened for the snib on the toilet door and, when we heard it snap shut, scrambled over to the desk. I turned on my old laptop and found the Post-it with the password on it while it fired up. Fin told me that, listen, he did text Sofia to tell her it was his choice to leave but reception was bad, she didn't get it until after she'd sent those texts to me. Anyway, he said, if he hadn't jumped into the car I'd have arrived here and been rushed by Bram when I was on my own and it would have scared me, so, not all bad, was it? If you think about it.

We locked eyes. 'Fin, when I hear you talk about me or imagine how I'm feeling I always sound like a fucking hapless victim and I wonder if you've even met me.'

The screen burst to life, lighting the walls and ceiling blue. We were suddenly underwater. Fin looked shame-faced. 'We should just —'

I opened the file of *Dana* podcast emails and searched for 'Lisa Lee'.

The subject line read 'Hi?'

This is what it said.

I hope you don't mind me writing, I know you get a lot of messages. I heard Fin Cohen talking about ethics and responsibility in new media and I don't know what to do.

I made a film in an abandoned house, it was still full of a family's stuff, they left everything, all personal things, all just left there. I think something happened in there. Here's some photos.
[She enclosed a file of PDFs.]

The guys I went with want to post images but we argued, I don't think it's right to do that. People'll find the place and steal things. It seems like stuff that's really important to someone.

It was too much. I feel like something happened in there. I'm stuck here. I just want to get away. I don't know what to do.

Any advice would be great. I'm drowning.

Lisa Lee
North Berwick

It was confusing. It could have been a hint that she'd kill herself or just mean that she wanted to run away. We forwarded it on to the address the police gave in their public appeal for information. Then we watched the screen expectantly, as if they'd write back immediately to thank us. Nothing happened.

I imagined a sleepy police officer scrolling past without reading it, a firewall bouncing it back, someone reading it and rolling their eyes, failing to see the connection.

We didn't know what else to do, though doing something felt urgent. She'd asked us to help her and we didn't. I think I'd read it and rolled my eyes, I'd failed to help her when I could. For some reason it made me think of my daughters trapped in the lighthouse with Sofia. She needed to get out and I knew that feeling all too well, to just turn and bolt and never look back. I get out in different ways now, escaping into chores and exercise or stepping out of my own life into other people's stories, but that urge to run was so familiar.

'We could talk to the guys she went with,' said Fin. 'Find out what happened.'

I posted a question on all our socials: if Florian and Gregor were out there could they contact us, please? We didn't get their contact details before Lisa's film got taken down and we really wanted to talk to them.

Then we stood and watched the screen again. It was the middle of the night. We got some irrelevant comments, a 'hi' or two and a frankly eye-watering dick pic that was deleted immediately.

Wrong address, evidently.

Fin downloaded the photos Lisa had sent us.

There was something delicious about us being together, tired with hot eyes, nerves nicotine-jangling. It took me back to our first adventure and the intimacy of these moments, the waiting for answers and queasy-fear, taking mutual joy in a hunger-busting bag of crisps or a clean public bathroom. It was intense. It was immediate. All that mattered was the next place, the next clue, the next task and it took us away from the long-term irresolvable complications of home.

We heard Bram flush the toilet downstairs.

Lisa Lee had sent us eight photos of the chateau, all taken with a bird's-eye lens, clear and focused and copyrighted to 'FlrGr'.

These were beautifully composed panoramic scenes of the front room and of the kitchen, of the entrance hall seen from the staircase. Some were of eye-catching details: a doll half eaten by a black mould that had worked its way across the hillocks and valleys of a rose-print duvet cover. The hem of the priest's cassock in the chapel, silver threads, loosed by moths, hanging heavy as a drowned woman's hair.

But we didn't get the chance to examine them closely because Bram snapped open the lock on the toilet door and opened it. He was coming back up the creaky stairs.

Fin slapped the laptop shut.

Bram arrived at the top of the stairs and smiled at us. 'What were you looking at?'

We didn't have time to lie though because his 'Auld Lang Syne' ringtone sounded again.

'Yeah? NO. OK. Marcos — *Marcos* — OK, Marcos. Just wait. Stop. *Stop* now. I WILL. I'll be out in a minute.' He hung up without saying goodbye and bent down, took the damp kitchen roll out of his loafers and put his shoes back on. He held up the kitchen roll. 'Recycle bin?'

I couldn't quite believe it. 'Did you leave someone in the car?'

'It's been five minutes.'

We'd been talking for over an hour.

'Who's Marcos?'

'My son.' He pulled his satchel over his head and gathered his cigarettes.

'How old is Marcos?'

Bram stopped and thought about it. 'I don't know. Eleven or something? I'll take you to North Berwick. Come on.'

Fin looked at me. His eyes were red and excited. I shook my head: this was not a man who cared about missing kids, but Fin was pulling his jumper off. He was going with or without me.

As he packed up the DAT machine I looked around my living room. If I waited here I'd be moping around all night, trying and failing to sleep, blinking in the dark as I listened to the rain, sleepless and miserable, worried about Fin, waiting for Jess and Lizzie to wake up and call me and ask me about that thing.

8

The headlights were still on full and the engine was running, spewing smoke out of the exhaust. It was big and black and the windows were tinted, the wheels chrome. It looked like a hearse for a millionaire.

Bram fell into the driver's seat and Fin took the passenger side without even asking me. Their seats were shaped like expensive, massively comfy gaming chairs. I opened the back door and found it was just a normal bench seat. Annoyed, I threw my bag on the floor and got in. It was roomy enough that I didn't see the kid before I got in.

Marcos was playing a game on an iPad furiously and didn't look up. He was still a child, with a kid's softness in the contours of his face but he looked like his father, same eyes and sandy hair. His hair looked chewed-into and uneven, as if he'd cut it himself. They were dressed alike too, Marcos in a pink cotton shirt and three-quarter shorts. His face looked puffy, suggestive of chaotic hormones and bad diet.

He didn't acknowledge us. 'HAT.'

'Oh shit, I left it.' Van Wyk glanced up at the rear-view mirror and pulled on his seat belt. 'I get you another one, my treasure.'

He started the windscreen wipers. Marcos dropped his iPad.

'Go and get it.'

Bram's shoulders came up to his ears.

'GO BACK AND GET MY HAT,' screamed

Marcos at a pitch that would have made a dog beg for mercy.

Bram flicked on the handbrake but hesitated, biting his lip and waiting. Marcos opened his mouth wide to shout again but Bram opened his door to stop him and held out a hand to me for the door key.

Afraid Marcos would scream again, I gave it to him, only then realising that he'd be alone in my house, that it might be a ploy, that Marcos might have been primed to do this. My hand was on the door but Fin was already out, having had the same thought, and ran after Bram. I was alone with the kid. The iPad game played a jaunty tune as explosions went off in the background.

'Is Bram your dad?' I asked.

'Probably.'

'You live together?'

He shrugged.

'I'm Anna.' I wasn't even awarded a look. 'Didn't you want to come inside with your dad?'

He half glanced this time, his eyes gliding across the back seat before retracting.

'How old are you?'

'Thirteen.'

His accent wasn't South African. It sounded like a neutral English accent, possibly posh, possibly not, depending on the context.

'Live with your mum?'

'In holidays.'

'Boarding school?'

'Yeah,' he said, gruff but pleased at being spoken to. 'Switzerland. Children need stability.' He said it as if he was repeating something a therapist had said to him. 'Mum lives in Malaga.'

'She there now?'

'Boston. Coming home tomorrow.' Eyes on his iPad still, Marcos made a strange noise with his lips, a kind of farting noise. 'He's sending me back, flight leaves from Paris tomorrow night.'

I nodded. 'Parents are a lot sometimes.'

He liked that. 'Phh — yeah.'

I liked him and thought perhaps it was mutual. 'What are you playing?'

'Fuck off,' he said and raised his face to meet mine. It was so rude that I laughed with surprise.

'You're a cheeky little bisum.'

He smiled at that. 'What's a bisum?'

I didn't actually know. It was just something I'd heard Scottish people say. 'A type of ferret, maybe.'

Bram and Fin were back out of the house, locking the front door, their forms shadowy in the dark and the rain. They turned towards the car.

'Did your dad tell you that we're looking for a missing girl?'

'No,' he said, but then whispered, 'Lisa Lee.'

'Did he tell you about the Voyniche Casket?'

Outside Bram and Fin struggled towards us through the storm. Just as Bram's hand landed on the driver's door handle, Marcos spoke quietly. 'He's tricking you. He's had a copy made.'

'Of — ?' I began but Marcos slapped me a backhanded wallop on the upper arm to shut me up.

The doors opened and the storm tried to muscle its way in as Bram and Fin fell back in and slammed the doors shut.

Bram was clutching the velvet hat. He dried the rain from his face with it, holding Marcos's eye in the mirror. Then he threw it over his shoulder, hitting

85

Marcos in the face.

'Fat fuck,' said Marcos gratefully.

'It's a piece of shit tourist hat,' Bram told the mirror bitterly. 'You need to throw it away before we leave Glasgow.'

'Fuck off,' said Marcos. 'Bastard.'

Bram smiled at that and took his cigarettes out. 'This kid doesn't believe I love him. How can I prove it?'

'Be a father,' said Marcos.

Bram turned to Fin. 'We just met. His mother is . . . secretive.' He looked at the boy. 'Why do you like that hat so much? Because it's a present from your old man?'

'You ruined it, getting it wet.'

'It's a cheap piece of shit. I can buy you ten more in any tourist shop.'

'Fuck off.'

Bram snorted a laugh and pulled out, taking the the flooded streets at motorway speed. The atmosphere in the car was weird. I didn't think they knew each other very well.

'What a big car,' I observed calmly.

'Yeah,' said Bram. 'A hire car.'

'Don't think I've ever seen a hire car this size.'

'Yah, it's the biggest one they had.'

'Easy to spend money,' Marcos told his iPad screen, sounding like a jaded fifty-year-old.

Bram shrugged a shoulder carelessly. 'I got it, I spend it.'

He lit a purple cigarette and held out his open packet to offer them round. I looked at Marcos. 'Do you mind us smoking?'

'Don't give a fuck what you do,' he said.

Bram was driving fast, swerving between cars, over-taking. The rain was coming towards the car like a hail of arrows.

Even if we had been aware of being followed at that point there was no way we could have seen the car.

I shut my eyes and turned my face to the window, taking in deep second-hand-smoke breaths so that no one would see how scared I was by his erratic driving. Next to me, as reassuring as an air steward's voice, Marcos played his game and the iPad sang little tunes.

'OK,' said Bram, 'you guys have heard of Bari? It's a city in Italy.'

'Not until we read about the Voyniche Casket.'

'I was there, when the casket reappeared briefly. I handled it.'

'No, wait, wait, Fin, record this —'

Fin wasn't pleased at being ordered around by me but got the DAT machine out anyway. Bram asked him to get his tape recorder out and press record so he would have it too and he did.

Bram tapped the ash from his cigarette, took a deep draw and then he told us the most amazing story I've ever heard.

9

It was unusable. The wind and the air conditioning made it sound like someone whispering next to a washing machine on a spin cycle. Much later we listened carefully and managed to transcribe most of what he said. Parts of this are an approximation though. Real speech is all ums and ahs and asides that go nowhere. Real speech is virtually unreadable.

It's a hard life but I made a lot of money and retired by my early thirties. In 1998 I was living in the South of France, Antibes, enjoying a quiet life. Nice place, you been there?

No one had, not even Marcos.

I'm rich. I have a nice lady in my life, a sailboat, life is good. Until I get a call from a priest I know. He needs a favour. He has a chance to buy this casket, a piece of history, but no money. Can I bring cash and meet him in Bari?

Well, it was nothing compared to the reserve price now, but still, it was more than I had. I found it for him though. I knew the priest from Boston, when I met Marcos's mother, eh, Marcos? We knew each other for a long time before Marcos. We were friends. I know her family . . .

So this priest, he's from back then in Boston and he asks me for this favour, it's a big favour. He'll make it worth my while. He has something I need destroyed. He's sort of blackmailing me but I still trust him. I like him. He was treated badly. Eugene Lamberg is Viennese, clever man, very religious. But a sad man. He has a lot of sadness in him, maybe that's why he's such a good priest, well, he was a priest for a while but one of those popes took the title away for a technical reason, I don't understand why. They keep these paedophiles and get rid of men like Eugene. I don't know. Anyway, Eugene is a good man. A better man than me.

I was a very bad man, a drug smuggler. Back in Durban, where I'm from, all us yacht club people, we started importing, moving things around, making big, big money. The eighties were a blur: money, crazy profit, everyone having a good time. A lot of coke and girls and parties. I travelled the world, this little guy from Durban, I met interesting people, tried not to get killed by those interesting people. It was fun. Until it wasn't.

That was sudden.

I got arrested in Mozambique. Prison there was . . . well, I thought I'd die in there. Then I got out and my girlfriend at the time overdosed. I came home after a trip and found her. She had been there for a week, in our apartment. She was beautiful . . .

He paused here. On the tape it lasts a minute and eight seconds. That is a long conversational pause. I don't know what was true in all of the things Bram told us but I do believe that he found someone dead at some point and it affected him deeply. Breaking out of that memory was effortful.

Yeah, so . . . it stopped being fun, got super scary very fast. The drugs business was suddenly full of crazies and bad, bad people. I got out of there and ran out of money in Boston. You been to Boston, Marcos? No? Your mum didn't take you to meet her family there? Never? Oh. OK. Wants to move on, maybe. Sure. They were rough and ready. Not for everyone. She's protective of you, maybe? Her precious treasure.

Marcos was very tense as Bram asked these ques-

89

tions. I didn't think he felt so valued that his mother couldn't share him with the rest of her family. He thought she was ashamed of him or bored by him.

Anyway, I ran out of money and road there. But look: I'm a smuggler. It's a transferable skill. Things were happening. It was there that I found the antiques business.

Art smuggling is a great business, same big money, same smuggling routes, and if I get caught all I get is a fine. That's it. Drugs, I get thirty years, but for antiques — nothing. And you're not selling to hundreds of fucked-up, desperate people, just secretive people, rich people who have the police and customs officials in their pockets. This is a good business for me. This is a clean business.

I made a lot of money in Boston and met Lamberg there. It was a good time. Then the Soviet Union collapsed. I had to go. Too many opportunities for me not to go. Money to be made. Art has no value in a collapsing economy. People want oil and bread, not paintings. I learned a lot about it. I became an expert in religious artefacts. You know what icons are? Paintings that don't just depict God, they embody God. Seriously. You look at these paintings, ancient, hundreds of years old, and, you know, even a godless man like me, I can see it. When I lay my hand on them I can feel the presence of God in these things. I am reaching all the way through history back to God.

Anyway, anyway — I'm all off-track. So Eugene knows me, he has a contact, but the seller doesn't trust anyone. Doesn't even trust a priest to be discreet. He's afraid of the authorities finding out about him. It is very illegal what he's doing. He's selling all of the treasures mixed up in this Yugoslav war, from the museums and government, he's selling them to raise money for certain groups who are doing . . . things illegal. You don't want to know. Balkan shit.

90

But I'm a good cover, yeah? I'm a rich, bad man, yah? Got the SA accent, everyone thinks, sure, this guy is a bastard. I'm a good front.

I go to meet Eugene in Bari and he tells me about this casket. He saw it before, he'll know if it is the real one. What's inside? I ask him. He doesn't know. No one knows. But he says that Roman documents are cylindrical, this casket is shaped to hold a long thin thing, so maybe it's the crucifixion order? Or maybe it holds some of the linens found in the empty tomb of Jesus on Easter Sunday, we don't know. No one's opened it yet. Only the market is involved, not archaeologists, and it's more valuable if it's not broken open. So, we're going to get it off the market with me as a front, buy it from a junk dealer: a man called Ludovic Voyniche.

Bari is not a beautiful place. I think it was bombed flat in the Second World War, but it's straight across the Adriatic from Durrës in Albania and this was at the end of the Yugoslav Wars. A lot of stuff was moving through Bari at this time. A lot of bad men there. I was worried, carrying all my money in a suitcase, but my old friend needs it, so . . .

That war was profitable but a fucking mess. I hate that war. Too many sides, what the fuck is going on? Balkans. I trust capitalism. Everyone is a bastard. I get it. That war was about beliefs. Identity and religion — same thing. Fucking nightmare.

You know, I'm a white man from South Africa. I was born in '68, we knew we were rich, nasty, white bastards. White South Africans my age look back now and wring their hands and say oh, we didn't know how bad it was, we believed it was a good system, I mean that's total bullshit.

We knew we were bad. We all knew. We had big cars and servants and swimming pools. Until I was fifteen, I didn't know how to hold a broom to sweep. Can you imagine? The first time I held a broom I held it at the top, like a gearstick. I'd never used a broom and I was never even in a room when anyone else was using a broom.

We grew up rich. We had steak every night and new shoes every month. I grew up on our family estate near Durban. Yeah, hey, Marcos, this is who your old man is: we had a lot of land out there, yah? My parents adored me, only child, see, like Marcos, my only child. I was their treasure. My mother was a beauty, Elizabeth Taylor-standard. In the newspapers, at horse races and regattas all the time. My father was born to money. Everything I did was wonderful. They spoiled me, I admit it. I won't let that ... yah, Marcos and I just met. I didn't even know I had a son but that won't happen to you, Marcos, eh?

Marcos looked up and told him to fuck off and that he hated him.

We edited that out before we sent the recording to Marcos, in case he ever listened back to it. It's hard enough to lose a parent without you telling them to fuck off being the only documented moment in your fleeting relationship.

But in the Balkans no one is the bad guy. They really believe that. In South Africa, we knew where our privilege came from. We drove by the shanty towns.

So, anyway, I'm in Bari with Eugene and all this money in a big bag while this is all going on across the Adriatic. There's another priest with Eugene. Father Desmond O'Brian. I never forget that name. He explains that the Vatican needs a front man because Voyniche won't sell to them. He asked Eugene to find funds and a rogue to act for them. That's why Eugene asked me.

I think, honestly, that Eugene hoped Des O'Brian would see him doing good work for the church and get him back his ordination and work as a legitimate priest, church sanctioned, if he gets this casket for them. Because otherwise why is O'Brian even there? I'm bringing the money, Eugene is the contact. Why even bring O'Brian? I've seen Eugene working as a priest in Boston. He's a good man, he deserves it, but this O'Brian watches him like a hawk. Terrible tension between them. They don't trust each other, these men.

People will kill to get this thing. Is it for resale value or because it proves Christ lived? Do they want to stop someone else having it? Why though? And who? If it's the Christians we would have heard, they can prove they've been right all along. Why not tell everyone?

Or is it for cash value? Because in this business, my business, there are things so valuable that they are never seen by the public, they're used to pay debts, to guarantee payments for shipments of guns or drugs or information. Is this it?

Anyway, so the three of us are hanging around in a shit hotel for three days, keeping low, waiting for a call. Then Lamberg comes in to breakfast: it's today.

A boat is waiting for us in the harbour. Just me and Eugene. Des O'Brian will stay in Bari. If they see him they'll run. We're going out alone.

Eugene and I get to the docks. It's a nice boat for tourist fishing, thirty-footer, luxury, you know this kind? Well, it's a nice boat. So we get on, crew of seven maybe. We cast off, get cocktails, we're served lunch. Three hours out we're very cold, the sea is rough, black clouds coming from the north. This is when a small fishing boat appears on the horizon. It comes straight towards us and ties up.

Two men board our boat. One tall, one medium height, a bit older. The smaller man has a supermarket shopping bag but no muscle with them. That might seem strange but that was art smuggling back then: no guns, no shouting, no threats. It was a gentleman's business.

Back then.

I start talking to the tall man. I think he's the guy, you know, because he's not carrying the bag. I'm talking to him and he keeps smiling and nodding. Turns out he doesn't even speak English. We laugh about that.

The little man, he shuffles forward, shakes my hand and introduces himself as Ludovic Voyniche.

Voyniche is ordinary, keep this in mind, he's not small or tall, he's not old or young, he says nothing much but he's not unfriendly. He's the most ordinary-looking man I've ever seen. No one knows who he is or what he does. The police don't know who is supposed to police him. Governments don't know if they can tax him. He calls himself a middleman because 'dealer' makes you think he might have a warehouse somewhere full of things to steal.

So Voyniche opens the plastic bag and shows us the casket. It's beautiful. We look at it. We touch it. Eugene has seen it before. He says yes, this is it.

That part is important because, I tell you, I know that casket. It is burned on my brain. I give them the money. I'm relieved because now Eugene will have to give me what he promised in return.

Voyniche and the tall man get on their boat with the bags of cash and they go off, back to wherever. No one knows.

Voyniche doesn't like that the casket is called after him, you know? Doesn't want to be remembered. Remembered is investigated. He doesn't want that. He lives on Terra Nova *now, you know what this is?*

We didn't.

Terra Nova *is a luxury ship, ocean-going, residential. They sell apartments on this ship. One small bedroom for ten million American. The rooms are OK, nothing special, you can decorate, it's not the Hotel Cap Estel, but this ship is full of rich people and it travels the world all year. The whole place is a safe. Residents on this ship don't pay tax, are never searched, don't have to see anyone they don't want to. See? Total security. Total discretion.*

Anyway, Lamberg and I, we turn our boat around and we go, fast, back to Bari, back to the hotel. We go fast because they might come after us, take it back to sell again, you know? We go full speed back to Bari, so fast I was sick on the way.

But we get there. We act calm, we have a box of frozen fish that supposedly we'd caught, we didn't attract any attention. We thought of everything. Well, no. Not everything.

At this point the only people who know we have this casket are Lamberg and me and Voyniche and the tall guy. Only us.

In the hotel room Des O'Brian examines the casket. He slumps onto his knees and starts crying, right there, in this shitty hotel. Lamberg too. Overwhelmed. O'Brian asks do I mind if they pray? I don't care.

They kneel together like little boys. They're weeping. They're so moved, it's touching to see. They're very happy, these two men.

So we part, Lamberg and I. He is with Des O'Brian and the casket, I have nothing but I'm free of my past. Eugene has promised me that he will go straight home to Rome and destroy an object that could be very bad for me if it is found. Ties me to . . . things. So I'm done with all of that and I head back to my girlfriend in Antibes. Now I'm broke but I'm free.

When I get there I buy the paper. A murder in Bari. A priest has been thrown from the roof of his hotel with his throat cut. It's Eugene Lamberg. Poor bastard.

95

I waited to hear about the casket. Nothing. I waited twenty years. Silence. I don't know if it's in the Vatican vaults or some cupboard somewhere but Eugene would not have had the time to destroy this thing he promised to and I'm out a lot, a lot, a lot of money. I had to go back to work. Soviet art is all gone. This is before the Chinese market opened up. I was reduced to smuggling artefacts out of Egypt. I sunk them into plaster of Paris models of the Sphinx to get through customs. Every three weeks the customs officers see me and I know they think 'here's this dumb guy again with his tourist crap'. When inside is a statuette of Amun. It worked out but, going back and forth, it was rough for a few years.

But then the casket reappears in this auction. Where was it all this time? Who put it in this chateau? My friend Eugene Lamberg lost his life, I lost my life savings. Who did that to us?

There was a slightly awkward pause in the recording. Fin clears his throat a couple of times before he tells Bram that Eugene Lamberg is alive, was arrested for murder in 2014 and had been living under the name Father Des O'Brian.

Bram refused to believe that. Fin was wrong, Des O'Brian was a common name, someone used Lamberg's name, no, no, no. Fin didn't fight him, he just said OK. I noticed that his driving was getting faster and more erratic. Then Bram asked for details: age, height, hair colour. Fin found it all in the article and, finally, Bram asked us which prison Eugene was in now?

Fin checked the article we'd been sent about the curse of the Voyniche Casket: Lamberg had been released, Fin told him, into the care of the Pontifical North American College in Rome.

Bram fell silent and sped up even more, driving so fast that when we hit water on the road surface the car skied sideways and made us all hold on to the seats. The atmosphere was so intense that even Marcos was sitting up straight.

You guys want a podcast? You want a fucking story? Come with me to Paris. Or maybe we'll go and see Lamberg. Let's go see how he's getting on.

We agreed vaguely and, in hindsight, I don't know why. We were trying to appease him, maybe, or we were tired or scared by his driving, because finding Lisa alive seemed unlikely and we didn't have much of a story yet.

We were just trying to help find a missing girl but, when I listen back to this recording, I can see that we should have asked Bram van Wyk to stop the car and got out at the side of the motorway.

10

I must have crashed out because I woke up, startled to find myself crumpled on the seat, my head resting on the cold window. Outside either the terrible storm had passed or we were in the eye of it because the air was still.

We were driving into the dawn on a broad road across a flat coastal plain. Marcos was asleep, slumped next me. Fin said he had dozed off briefly too. His eyes were pink and swollen. Bram was smoking a yellow cigarette and seemed resigned to the fact that Eugene Lamberg wasn't dead after all, had lied to rip off Bram's retirement fund and possibly committed two murders. He was back on board. Fuck Lamberg. We were going to find Lisa.

We opened a window to let the smoke out and the gentle sea breeze woke Marcos.We started to talk about breakfast.

It may have been the straightness of the road or the hour but I kept noticing a car behind us. It was the only other car on the road so it was easy to spot. It was grey, small, and it hung back noticeably. I didn't say anything to anyone because I was sleep-deprived and they could just have been going where we were going. I forgot about it until Glasgow Airport.

A heavy fog hung low so that the North Sea was just a grey notion where the land ran out but slowly, a high hill rose in the distance, and, at its foot, by the sea, there sat North Berwick.

The GPS directed Bram along the back of the town,

down a walled road until, quite suddenly, we caught our first sight of the sea.

I felt a familiar burst of excitement at the sight, Fin felt the same, but Bram didn't understand. We told him about the tradition of children being driven to the seaside and told to scream when they first see the sea. Bram said that wasn't a thing where he was from. He grew up in Durban. They'd be screaming all day.

Because it was still too early to visit anyone without a warrant or a warning that their house was on fire, we decided to find Bob Lee's house but go and get something to eat and wait for a couple of hours before we knocked.

We passed along streets of nice council houses and into the town proper. The architecture was Victorian or low-key modern. The visitors' centre and new library deferred to the dimensions of the other squat sandstone civic buildings. There was money here. Cars were big and plentiful, villas were freshly painted and gardens clean and pretty. Even the bus stops were graffiti-free. Down at the shorefront terraced houses were traditional and uniform, whitewashed and trimmed in pastel colours, each a complement to its handsome neighbour. A wide putting green separated the seashore from the road. It was a tasteful seaside cliché until we came to Bob Lee's house.

'Oh God,' said Fin. 'Who would do that?'

The house was as shocking as a shit on a trifle. It was an outsized concrete box in the middle of a paved-over garden, taller than its neighbours and sitting proud of the line of the houses. The front door was a huge black-matt rectangle. White blinds were pulled down on all of the windows but all of the lights were on. The whole building glowed like a paper lantern.

'Statement, isn't it?' said Fin.

I had to agree. 'But what's it saying?'

'Um, 'our planning committee accepts bribes'?'

'Whoever built this doesn't care what people think,' said Bram with respect. Marcos tutted at his dad.

It was early but whoever was in there was wide awake. Waiting to knock seemed redundant.

Fin fixed the mic as we all got out, stiff from the drive, tremulous with tiredness, and walked up to the door.

The path was a steep concrete ramp. I arrived at the front door a little out of breath, my lungs tight from a night of unaccustomed smoking, and stepped into the black yawn of the porch. I pressed the button, heard it give out an electronic two-tone call inside. Footsteps. Someone was coming.

The door was opened by a uniformed police officer, bulky in his stab vest and utility belt. It felt ominous.

'Hi,' I said. 'Is Bob Lee in?'

He didn't speak for a moment but looked us over and thought about it for a moment, running his tongue across the front of his lower teeth, but then took our names and addresses, writing them down, looked us over again, and then opened the door wide, nodding to a room on the right. He told us to go in there and wait.

The hall was warm and cavernous. White walls and orange wood flooring with a matching big staircase. A slim lift was fitted into the back of the hall. The lay-out was so similar to the chateau it seemed as if this geometrical combination of stairs and halls and walls was an incantation fated to follow Lisa Lee.

We shuffled into the room on the right, watched by

the cop, and he shut the door behind us. Marcos fell into a seat. Bram looked around as if he was thinking of buying the place, knocking walls with his knuckles and peering around the blinds at the sea view.

The room was very masculine. The walls were wood-lined to match the floor. Two large brown leather sofas faced each other, scattered with Union Jack cushions. Flag cushions are a choice and this was a very pointed choice in Scotland, where fans of flags tend to favour Saltires.

The walls were bare apart from one big inspo poster framed in silver. It was a chunk of a poem, not even a stanza, written out in silver script with leaves in blue and grey tumbling in the foreground:

> *Earth in beauty dressed*
> *Awaits returning spring.*
> *All true love must die,*
> *Alter at the best*
> *Into some lesser thing.*

I had forgotten that Lisa's mother had died, that this was a family already struggling with loss.

The door opened carefully and a man on the brink of a breakdown stood in the doorway. Bob Lee wore a grey T-shirt and joggers which may or may not have been pyjamas. He was stooped, simultaneously wired and withered, as if he had lost weight suddenly. He looked as spent as a match.

'Who are you?' he said. 'Are you here to accuse me too?'

I've never felt less confident about what we were doing. I said no, I explained that we were looking for Lisa and how we operated and Bob was cautiously

101

interested. 'Lisa wrote to us before she disappeared and we wanted to tell you about it.'

Bram swung round to face Bob and me. We hadn't mentioned that to him yet.

'You got an email from Lisa?' asked Bob. His at-home accent was untempered Yorkshire, which made sense of the belligerent cushions.

'Yes. A few months ago, about her trip to the chateau. She sounded as if she was thinking about running away.'

Bram lurched over between us. 'Where is the chateau?'

He wasn't talking to Bob but to me. He seemed desperate. It was weird.

'She didn't say in the email —'

'Do you know?' he demanded of Bob. 'Did she tell you?'

Bob's eyes slid to me, as if he was asking for a referee. 'Lisa didn't run away. She didn't take her passport or clothes. She evaporated.'

I slid between Bob and Bram. 'Lisa just said that she and the boys she was there with had argued. But, Bob, we asked online for information about Lisa going missing and someone sent us a clipping about a disappearance in Beirut that was similar. A man disappeared after answering his front door too and that person had contact with the silver casket Lisa found.'

I gave him the article on my phone and he sat down to read it. Bram, chastened by the snub, moved off across the room and sat down next to Marcos.

I couldn't tell if Bob had slept last night, if he was just up or about to go down, but he was moving slowly. He looked up. 'Can you send me this?'

'Of course.'

'Could you tell the police as well? They're not listening to me.'

'We already have and we sent them the email from her.'

Bob gestured to us to be cautious. The shadow of a police officer lingered in the hall. I saw Bob look us all over, trying to work out the connection. We were a dictionary definition of motley.

I pointed at the framed poster on the wall. 'That's a lovely quote.'

Bob smiled wanly. 'You like poems?'

I nodded. I do like poems. 'Yeats?'

'Yeah,' he breathed, 'W.B. Yeats, yeah. Got that on a card when Lisa's mum died. Really spoke to me, you know?'

'There's a line missing though,' I told him. 'And it changes the meaning. The last line is 'Prove that I lie'.'

He looked at the quote, lips quivering as he reread it with the additional line. I saw him warm at the defiant challenge to love.

'Prove that I *lie*. *Prove* that I lie.' He nodded. 'I like that. It's nice. Nicer. Thanks for that.'

He got a bit tearful then but breathed in deeply. The tears switched off as soon as they had started.

He was grateful for a crumb of hope. I had the feeling that Bob had been very depressed for a very long time. It would be hard for Lisa to live with that.

He wasn't sure about being recorded so Fin turned it off, showed Bob as he deleted what we had already, and apologised that we had all piled in here, but the police officer told us to.

'Aye,' said Bob, 'they don't want a complaint coming in that they've kept us prisoner. They're turning no one away. Sent in next door's Deliveroo last night, and two justice warriors from Sheffield who were sure I'd killed Lisa. They were surprised to get in, I think they wanted to stay outside and shout at the house. We ended up having tea and biscuits. It was awkward . . .' He lost the thread of what he was saying and looked at the floor. 'What was her letter about?'

'Lisa wrote it after she went to the chateau. She said she'd argued with Florian and Gregor. Do you know them?'

'No.'

'Did she talk about an argument she had with them?'

'No.'

Bram leaned over to Bob and gave him his warmest smile, 'Say, Bob, where is the chateau, did she say?'

Bob smiled back as if he was going to be sick.

'She must have said where she was going? Told you? In passing even?'

The smile died on Bob's lips. He stood up.

'You,' he said, his voice low, 'you're just like everyone else. You want the furniture and all the stuff in there. Ever since she posted that film my phone has been tapped, her computer hacked, it's a bloody scavenger hunt.' His voice cracked and he turned to me. 'And now my Lisa's missing . . .'

I thought he was going to fall. I jumped up and took his arm, and helped him onto the sofa. He sat on one buttock, slumped, eyes unfocused. The policeman outside the door shifted his weight.

'Why are you here at this time in the morning?' Bob whispered to Bram. 'I think you're all well dodge.'

We had no defence. Maybe we were dodge.

'No, forget that, we don't need to know where it is,'

I said, 'Look, I think he's asking because it might help find her. We're clutching at straws and we all saw the film of her there.'

'She spent ages on that, waste of bloody time. I wanted her to join the army. I gave her a choice, army or navy. I said to her she couldn't spend all day on that YouTube rubbish. It's not real life.'

The floor creaked outside in the hall. We all waited. I saw the shadow shift and withdraw. We heard a padding and a hand brush a wall. The cop had gone down to the back of the house.

'They'll be listening. There's cops all over,' said Bob. His voice was raw. 'They think she stole that box and ran away, or that I killed her. Lisa wouldn't steal. She's well brought up. She'd never take anything that didn't belong to her.'

But the police were just doing their job, he said. They had procedures they had to go through and the box was worth a lot of money. She didn't know that though, did she? They only know that now. She wouldn't steal it. And he understood why they suspected him, he understood where they were coming from. Totally. And they hadn't scrimped. They had helicopters out the first night, searching the sea, and two days ago they had fifty or sixty officers combing through the woods on the hill over there. He knew that's why they were being like that with him but he couldn't take it right now.

They'd searched the house and dug up his garden looking for Lisa's body. They'd confiscated his clothes and had taken photos of everything in the house. They'd brought in cadaver dogs.

They'd taken his computers away and then come back and asked him about the porn he'd been looking at because there were women in them, not girls or anything like that but just normal women, and they'd said the women were about Lisa's age, weren't they? Those women? About your daughter's age . . . He looked plaintively at Fin.

'I'm as white bread as the next man.'

I don't know if Fin uses porn, I don't want to know, but he nodded kindly and Bob appreciated it and both of them looked sad about Bob being asked about the porn he watched by a policeman at a time like this.

Fin explained that if he gave us a recorded interview, told us how he felt, it might help engage people, help us find Lisa. We'd need more than a twenty-year-old coincidence and we only knew about that because someone told us.

Bob thought about it and said, yeah, go on then. These are bits of what he said.

Lisa was downstairs. We'd ordered pizza that night so it was no surprise when the doorbell rang. Lisa shouted up that she would get it. She'd left a fiver by the door to tip the delivery man. It's a small town. Everyone knows everyone. Lisa thought she'd know the delivery driver so she liked to tip big.

I was in the shower and Amy was in her room. I got out the shower, dried myself, put my softies on, my trackies, and then I realised something was wrong. Not wrong exactly, but not right. There was a cold draught coming under the bedroom door and Lisa hadn't called up to say, you know, the pizza was here, come and get it.

The house was very quiet.

I opened my door and felt the wind pouring up the stairs, sea wind, from the front door being open. I called out to Lisa. She didn't answer. I went down and found the front door hanging open and the fiver on the wooden floor. It's one of those rubbery notes. It was surfing the breeze, down the hall, towards the kitchen.

She's gone. Looked out. Gone. Nothing. Not even a sound of a car. Just gone.

We've looked later: her passport's here. Her phone's here. She's just gone.

A physical sensation. I'm walking down the stairs in the dark, just feeling for the edge of the next step with my toes, you know? Tapping, tip of my toes, just tapping to see if I'm going to fall, feeling my way down. If you've ever lost your kids in the supermarket you know that shaking, fingers tingling, heart racing? Then you find them and it's over . . . but this is never over. It just gets worse and worse.

She's alive, out there somewhere, and if only I can find her. I can fix this. I still feel I can fix it. When her mum died I lost it. Lost my mind. That's been hard on her. Lisa had problems before . . . I didn't notice early enough.

Alison, her mum, was dying and that's all I thought about. Built this house for her. For Alison. Fuck the neighbours. We didn't go out anyway. Alison liked it. I'll never leave here. Never.

When she died I sat by her bed for days. Wouldn't let them take her away. It hit the girls hard. The little one, Amy, she's more resilient, she's got lots of friends. Never in the house now, unless she's asleep. Lisa. Found blood on her tops, on the arms, that how I found out about the cutting.

But even the TA won't take you, not with those scars on her arms. Won't take you if you're nuts.

Amy's applied to boarding schools, can you believe

that? Twelve and she got a teacher to help her. Clever. Lisa thought it was funny that Amy was trying for boarding school, said good for her, like.

Christmas was rough. First Christmas since Alison. Not good. Lisa went back to Paris after, just for a couple of days. She'd money to do that because she got a sponsor for her YouTube channel. Big money. She was going to go to Miami next. She's got all this to look forward to, you know?

They've heard about the casket on sale there, in France. It's all over the papers, isn't it? They've read about the film and how she's found the box in it and now it's on sale. They think she's lifted it. Or I've killed her, that's what they think.

'Dad?' A small girl stood in the doorway. She was about Jess's age and peered through sleep-swollen eyes. 'I think the policeman's in her room.'

Bob nodded. 'Just let him, Amy.'

'He shouldn't be in there,' she said. 'He's sitting on her bed, Dad.'

Bob went over and hugged her, weeping and whispering lies: it'll be all right, there's nothing to worry about, she'll be home soon.

Amy's face was squashed against her father's belly but she watched us impassively, taking in every detail as if she might have to pick us out of a line-up, until Bob let go and sent her back to bed for an hour before. We could hear Amy walk back upstairs heavy-footed. When Bob sat down his face was puffy.

'You want anything else from me?'

We didn't. We got up to leave.

'Bob —' I pointed at the condolence poster and asked —'did Lisa like that quote?'

'Hated it. Made me move it out of the kitchen. Said it did her head in.'

He saw us out and shut the door behind us.

A wary sun rose through the fog over the sea.

We stepped down into the concrete garden and let Bram and Marcos go ahead. We both knew now that Bram was here to find the chateau, not Lisa, but I was excited about something else.

'I didn't want to get Bob's hopes up,' I whispered, 'but I think Lisa is WBGrates. That DM was sent two days after she disappeared. I think Lisa's alive.'

Fin nodded. 'And no way does a channel with thirty subscriptions get sponsorship. Someone gave her money for something.'

'Oh shit,' I said.

'I know.' Fin dropped down the step to the path. 'She stole the casket, didn't she?'

11

Bram was going to drop us in Paris with Marcos and go on to Rome himself. He was going to see Father Eugene Lamberg, to doorstep him and demand answers. I was glad we wouldn't be there.

We were keen to get to Paris. It might not help us find Lisa but staying here wouldn't do any good either. She had come into money, lied to her father about the source and, we were both sure, was alive somewhere, hiding.

We thought the better plan would be to tell a compelling story and try to shake the tree that way. Fin said Paris would be a great starting point, a good soundscape to the story of Lisa's disappearance. Plus it was a free trip, which is our favourite price.

The storm rose again as we hit Harthill and the drive back was wild and taken too fast. Bram was angry and sullen. He was scary when he was like that. I could see him as a glowering international drug smuggler and yet here he was, in the world of podcasting with us, like Pablo Escobar volunteering at a local preschool.

Fin was in the front seat asking questions, passing casual comments on the traffic, doing a good job of maintaining the fiction that Bram was trying to help us find Lisa when it was clear that he had another, darker agenda.

I was in the back seat, trawling through messages about Lisa. They were flooding in but I stumbled across a few screenshots of Florian's and Gregor's contact details from the end of Lisa's film. (If you sent that to us, several people did, thank you very much.)

I sent a message asking Florian or Gregor to contact us and would they speak to us? And then I messaged @WBGrates: hey, I said, we'd seen a poem they might like to discuss if they called this number? It wouldn't send. WBGrates had deleted their account.

I looked up and found that we were on a back road running along the side of the Glasgow Airport runway. I'd never been this way before and I would soon find out why.

We were slowing down to pull off the road when I glanced out of the back window and saw the car, a Peugeot, I think, drive past us at the speed limit. It was the careful driving that caught my attention, and that it looked the same car as the one on the road behind us in North Berwick.

'Anyone else see that?'

'What?' said Bram.

'A car. A grey car just passed behind us.'

But no one else had.

Bram drew left, into a car park in front of a small, square office building of black glass. He parked at the doors.

'Marcos, get the bags from the boot,' ordered Bram.

'Fuck off.'

Fin and I froze. Marcos smirked at his iPad. When Bram spoke again his voice was a strangled whisper. 'Get. The bags. Out of the boot, you little shit.'

We both held our breath. Even Marcos sensed the danger. He closed his iPad and opened the door, got out, clutching his velvet hat, slammed the door shut and barrelled over to the building entrance, turning away to hide his face. We could see him smiling though. His face was reflected in the black glass. Then the doors slid open, Marcos stepped in and they shut behind him.

Bram slapped the headlights off, yanked the key from the ignition and, muttering curses to himself in Afrikaans, got out and walked round to the boot. As he passed my window I could see his fists were balled tight.

'Fin, he's going to batter that kid.'

'Yeah, we shouldn't leave them alone,' said Fin.

We jumped out, hurried over to the automated entrance and ran in. The doors shut behind us and we looked back out through the smoked glass.

Bram had left the boot open and was carrying a heavy bag, coming at the doors through rain like stair rods, eyes narrowed, lips curled into his teeth.

'Shit, he's scary,' said Fin.

We hurried through a second set of doors and found ourselves in front of a reception desk manned by a pretty woman wearing a blue uniform and a lot of make-up.

'Good morning.' She tipped her head and smiled mechanically. 'Are you with the van Wyk party?'

'YES WE FUCKING ARE.' Bram stormed past us and threw his bag at the foot of the desk, making it judder.

He clattered his car keys on the top. 'Two more bags in the boot. Hire car. Get them out and take the car back.'

Her smile faltered. 'Oh, I'm afraid —'

Bram slapped the desk. She jumped and then looked down at his hand. 'I can take care of that for you, sir.'

He had slapped notes down in front of her, a couple of hundred pounds. The money was wet because

112

his hand was wet and it looked crumpled and grubby. He took his empty hand away and walked round the desk to Marcos.

The kid was slumped in an armchair, playing his game again, still smirking but less confidently this time, the hat on the seat next to him. I didn't think he had seen his father angry before.

The woman slid the notes down to her side and smiled with genuine warmth, told Fin and me that she'd be right back, perhaps we would like to take a seat in the lounge area? She almost skipped off out into the rain.

Bram loomed over his son.

Marcos glanced over to the food bar, a black countertop with baskets of biscuits, a mini fridge and a coffee machine. 'Get me some Haribo, fat man.'

'What did you say to me?'

'Get me some Haribo. Get me the sour ones. Tangfastics.'

'What would you do if something happened to me, Marcos?'

The kid dropped his iPad and looked at his dad. 'What?'

'If I died, if I was killed, if I wasn't here any more.'

Marcos put his iPad down carefully and stood up. 'You've never been here! I DON'T KNOW YOU!'

'BECAUSE OF YOUR CUNT OF A MOTHER —'

'Leave her out of it.'

'She is IT. She's the reason we never met before. I DIDN'T KNOW YOU FUCKING EXISTED UNTIL LAST WEEK.'

I'm not going to tell you that fight word for word. I'll leave it there. The point is that Bram didn't know he had a kid and Marcos wasn't invested enough in having a father to give a shit if he died.

That was the essence of it. And something about the hat as well, Bram wanted to get rid of the hat and Marcos wanted to keep it.

The mother seemed to be called Janine, was rich and mean and didn't want them to know each other. Until now. Marcos was surprised that she let them meet, obviously he knew that he had a father but she only told him Bram's name a week ago. Bram didn't know he had a son but somehow was not surprised that they were spending time together, or that it was a full week instead of a tentative, supervised lunch.

'TIME IS SHORT,' yelled Bram. 'SHE KNOWS ANYTHING COULD HAPPEN.'

It made me think Bram was ill and dying. He did look pale, kind of sweaty sometimes. He looked like a man who shouldn't be smoking or running far.

Anyway, the things they said to each other were too much, they were intended to hurt.

Bram said things about the mother that he wouldn't be able to take back as he stood over Marcos, hands fisted, arms rigid, shouting into his face so loud that he ruffled Marcos's hair and sprayed him with spittle.

Finally it reached a pitch. Bram's head rolled on his neck and he fell back a step. I thought he was going to hit the boy. I stepped towards them. Fin backed up to the wall, which tells you a lot about the difference between us.

There is a simple arithmetic to interpersonal violence: the person willing to absorb the most physical injury usually wins. You bet a broken finger, I'll see you a skull fracture. This is not usually me. I'm not giving up my face or a femur or any fingers but Marcos was a kid and I was thinking a lot about protecting kids at that time. I picked up a chair and aimed for Bram's chest.

Marcos turned to look. Bram turned at the waist. They were staring at me.

'What the hell are you doing?' asked Bram.

I stood there guiltily, holding the chair in mid-air. 'I thought you were going to hit him.'

'Hit who?' said Bram.

Marcos giggled.

At that moment the doors opened and the woman came back in carrying two enormous Louis Vuitton weekend holdalls with the energy that comes from an unexpected two hundred quid.

She froze when she saw us. I lowered the chair. She blinked and looked away, looked back and managed a smile.

'I'll just check you in, ladies and gentlemen.'

She took our ID to register us for the flight. Fin didn't have his passport with him, he hadn't been home, but she said all she needed was photo ID. He gave her a card.

'Is that because it's a private plane or can anyone travel on photo ID?'

'Oh, depends where you're going,' she said. 'Within the EU you don't need a passport. Not yet anyway.'

I mumbled to Fin, 'Lisa could be in Paris,' and he nodded.

She moved on to Bram's and Marcos's ID then and when she was finished with us we broke up the band, all sitting quite far away from each other. Marcos took the long glass window overlooking a hangar. Bram had to deal with the woman and Fin and I perused the mini fridge and baskets of biscuits.

Fin chose a packet of vegan crisps that were almost

all air. I hated myself for registering the low calorie count. I tried not to get sucked into his eating problem. It was hard though.

Bram was smoking. I could smell it before I saw it. It had been so long since I smelled smoke in a public space that I turned to look. A green cigarette was hanging from his lips as he handed the woman another fifty-quid note. She smiled warmly over at us, her wet hair brushed back from her face, and announced to the room that we wouldn't be able to take off for another two hours because of the storm. Bram shouted at her for a hot moment but then, quite abruptly, accepted it and sat down.

We waited, scattered around the lounge, listening to the whistle of the rain and the low clacking of the woman's keyboard. I checked our messages. Florian and Gregor had contacted us. It was a caps-lock reply addressed to FIN AND ANNA OF DEATH AND THE DANA. They were SUPER MAJOR FANS! They were GETTING TOGETHER! Please FACE-TIME! They wanted us to call them but not for two hours so that Florian could get dressed and cycle over to Gregor's house.

I showed Fin the manic message but he nodded over to Bram, telling me to listen.

Van Wyk was on the phone talking quietly and respectfully to someone. I think we both hoped it was Janine but it wasn't. It was someone called Philippe and Bram was begging him for a name.

'I can't, Philippe, I don't have that kind of money . . . I understand. Mh-hm . . . But I would never do something as underhand as that. I wouldn't do that, Philippe, you know me. Only on the contract? No way you can give me the name unless . . . ?

But I don't have —'

The loud angry sound of a gull shrieking filled the lounge and Bram hung up abruptly. It was a call coming through on Marcos's iPad. Marcos panicked and fumbled the iPad so that it slid onto the floor. He left it there, struggling to get his earbuds in and answer the call.

'Hello?' He sounded breathy. 'Oh. Oh? OK, Mom . . . No. It's fine. No.' He looked at Bram, his face panicky. 'No. Bye.'

She hung up first.

Marcos picked up his iPad. He turned away to face the window but we could see his reflection and hear his ragged, angry breathing. He was crying.

No one spoke for a while.

Marcos, young, furious, alone, looked out of the window, kneading the edge of the seat with one hand. Fin looked at me, asking if he should speak to him. I shook my head.

He had expected to get away from this strange man he didn't know and didn't like. I was sure he'd told me about Bram having a copy of the casket made because he thought he would be leaving him soon. Now he sat crying and we all just listened, to his misery ebbing and the incessant hiss of the rain.

'Marcos, my treasure,' said Bram carefully, 'was this your mother on the phone?'

'I'M STUCK WITH YOU. SHE SAID NOT TO COME.'

'Well, it's not so bad —'

'FUCK OFF AND DIE, YOU FAT BASTARD.'

12

We were still waiting to board the private plane of a retired South African drug lord: not a phrase I ever thought I would type.

It was a quarter to twelve and we had been waiting for almost two hours. I had slept for a bit and woke up puffy and sweating. Fin was working on his laptop, trying and failing to clean up the unusable recording of Bram in the car.

We had gotten to know the space quite well. It was comfortable, warm, with deep recliners, a big TV mounted on the wall showing the news, muted and subtitled. We were looking out through a wall of angled glass to a bare concrete forecourt and an aircraft hangar. A buffet had been set out: baskets of pastries and fruit and crisps, a selection of wine, whisky and individual bottles of champagne in the fridge, and a machine that made a decent approximation of an espresso.

The weather was so fierce outside the windows that the deep puddles on the tarmac were tidal.

Marcos dozed on a couch while Bram was making and taking calls in between arguing with the woman and her manager about whether it was too windy to take off. His phone calls seemed to cheer him up a lot. When a final one tipped him over the edge into a good mood he bribed the woman on the desk to get us all bacon rolls and opened himself a mini bottle of champagne.

Fin had to explain veganism when the rolls arrived.

'What, *nothing*?'

'Yeah, no animal products.'

'Eggs though?'

'No, no animal products.'

'Cheese though?'

'No.'

Bram shook his head. 'That's crazy.' Then he raised his glass. 'To good fortune.'

'Something happen?' I took a bite of my bacon roll.

'I'm in the auction. I'm bidding.'

'I thought you didn't have enough money.'

'Well, I'm acting for someone else.'

'Who?' asked Fin.

He was reluctant to say. 'Ahhh, private. I didn't really want to do that but —'

'But you want to know the seller's name?'

He looked at Fin, wary. 'How do you know that?'

Fin looked around the room, 'It's quiet in here.'

Bram was surprised. 'Oh. Yeah. So it is.'

'Who are you an agent for?'

'Yeah, who is it?'

He wasn't going to tell us until we stopped prying. Then he blurted, 'Paul Hammersmith. A Christian billionaire. Very rich but if he bids it changes the whole dynamic so he needs someone else to be him in the room. You can't say his name to anyone.'

'We won't,' I said.

Fin was intrigued. 'Change it, how?'

'Rivalries, you know, factions don't want him to have it. Don't tell anyone that. And he's very, very rich and, if they know Hammersmith's in the bidding, the price will go higher and higher and higher. Anyone who wins the bidding knows they can sell it on to him afterwards with a big mark-up. So he wants to work with an agent, maybe two. They can't know who it is otherwise there are no limits. They'll be watching the room for his agent, but no one will suspect me, a rogue. But you two can't tell anyone about that before Friday and if you do I'll deny it.'

'We've got no one to tell,' said Fin. 'But if we keep quiet will you let us come with you to see the casket, maybe even record the auction?'

Bram shrugged with the easy-going manner of a man who didn't keep his promises. 'Sure.' Then he sloped off to sit by himself and enjoy his roll.

It was time to phone Florian and Gregor.

We found them sitting on a bed, Florian in front, Gregor behind him, in a small room with dark purple walls and white shelves crammed with electronic junk and graphic novels. On one wall hung flyers and posters for movies and bands I'd never heard of.

Gregor's white fleece was zipped up to his chin and they were both smiling wide, Florian showing off his big white teeth as Gregor chewed the neck of his top with delight. They seemed much younger than they did on Lisa's film, just two teenagers in a bedroom.

We introduced ourselves.

Fin asked if they would mind if he recorded our conversation and they said sure, that was OK, but it wasn't that interesting and we found we could summarise it in a couple of lines at the start of an episode. A lot of what we talked about wasn't Lisa Lee at all.

It started with me asking how they met, just to get the levels.

They met at *kleuterskool*, which seemed to be kindergarten, and had been friends all their lives. Everyone else went off to college but they didn't, they said, and sort of fluffed why they hadn't. If I had to guess I would have assumed they'd both failed their exams. Then Florian went off on a rant: *Oh my God! Anna McD! It's actually you!*

I'm a legend, apparently. I won't lie: I loved this. They were nice guys and they'd heard of me, knew my backstory and didn't think I was tainted by it. It's nice to be admired and quite rare in my case.

'Hey,' grinned Florian, 'my stepsister was raped at college. She listened to your podcast. She quotes you all the time.'

'Me?'

'Yeah: 'We are everywhere . . .' oh, I can't remember what you said but it got her through this.'

Gregor did remember though, and mumbled the quote through his roll-neck to the back of Florian's head. I'm not going to quote myself because that's unstylish.

'Yeah! That's it,' said Florian.

'How is she, Florian?' I asked.

Florian grinned at me, the perspective fish-eyed. 'She's surviving, Anna McD. She's going back to college next year. The rapist left.'

'Didn't go to the police?'

'No. She was drugged. She only realised when the film was posted online and the drugs had left her body. She couldn't go to the police because she'd done a spell in rehab and been a bit, you know, things they don't like in a witness. The other students on the campus made his life hell though.'

I didn't know if that was right but Fin said things get messy in the absence of justice.

'Well, tell her I said hello.'

'I will.'

'Tell her I said —' I ran out of steam. I wanted to

say something inspirational but I'm not terribly good at that sort of thing and had forgotten that because I was so tired. 'Um, all the best.'

'Oh my God, she'll love that,' he said, and then we all laughed because it was so banal.

Fin did some intros and showed them we were in a lounge waiting to get on a private plane. They were as surprised as us, and then we got on with it.

Florian and Gregor didn't know Lisa Lee until they all went to the chateau together. They met online, in a community of urbexers. They'd been liking each other's stuff, commenting on locations and images by more established people for a long time. Lisa was pretty old school in her principles, they liked that about her. She got in touch with them about a year ago to say she was thinking of coming to France to visit a couple of locations. They decided to team up. Florian and Gregor live in Belgium, in Kortrijk, just over the French border, and she took the Eurostar to Lille where they picked her up.

'She emailed us about your trip,' I said, 'and mentioned you guys were angry with her.'

'Yeah,' said Florian. 'Still are angry.'

Gregor mumbled something into his fleece, looking at the back of Florian's head and Florian cringed.

'But we're sorry she's missing. That's why we're calling you.'

I asked about the ethics of posting a film that burglars might use to empty the house.

'Yeah, well, is that our responsibility?' Gregor raised a reluctant shoulder. 'We don't all agree.'

Florian turned to him. 'They'll find the site soon, if they haven't already. Someone will post the coordinates.' He turned back to us. 'Then the site will be flooded by explorers and the more people in there, the more likely that things will go missing.'

'Diffusion of responsibility?' I said.

'Yeah.' Florian nodded. 'It's difficult.' He explained that the ethical dispute had been going on for years and, like many debates in small communities, it was bitter and nasty and hard to stay out of.

When urbexers posted images of a great new location there were consequences to keeping it a secret. If they didn't share the address it tended to send other urbexers into treasure-hunt mode to see who could find it and declare it publicly. This competition could get vicious. There had even been criminal cases when accounts or sites were hacked to find locations that were being kept secret.

I'm afraid I stopped listening very closely because my phone was ringing. When I saw that it was Jess I declined the call. Then I sat, listening to Florian and Gregor, wondering what kind of mother would decline a call from her twelve-year-old daughter. I was a coward. I looked up and found Florian still talking.

There was a big rush to be first and get to sites before everyone else but that's not what urbex was supposed to be about. It's not a competition, that's the opposite of what it was. When it's a secret people forget what they're supposed to be doing and the site becomes a notch on their belt. But the urbexers before them, the previous generation, found that if you give the location in the film or documentation there is no rush. People go if they're interested. Or people don't go and just enjoy your films, they find their own places. Exclusivity makes it something it isn't. Lisa and Florian and Gregor agreed about this. It was one of the things they had in common. But then they got there and saw that it was full of stuff, some of it quite valuable, they knew they couldn't post and pretend there wouldn't be a stampede. It's kind of what the fight was about. That and other things.

'What did you decide?'

Well, said Florian, they didn't want to use images of valuable things. Their pictures were mostly of the hall, the living room and the ceiling. They did a lot of nice images of the black mould.

'Which was exceptional,' said Gregor, grinning.

'Yeah.' Florian nodded and smiled, nostalgic for a moment. 'Normally the sun doesn't hit the mould or it would dry it out but at the end of that day we got this image of sunlight catching a burst of spores and they were . . . well, it was just magical.'

'We were lucky to see that,' said Gregor.

'We were.'

They drifted for a minute, lost in the memory of the day, until I drew them back by asking how Lisa felt about that. She didn't agree with them posting interior images but then she used the drone shot. She said it was too good not to use, but Florian and Gregor thought using the drone was far worse. It made it too easy to find the place.

They talked to each other for a bit about how great Alan was and it took a minute for me to work out that he was the drone operator.

'Yeah, Alan Johansson. We all paid a share of his costs but we weren't even going to use it because it made the location so obvious. She wanted to use it. She said it would be all right, she'd make it safe before she posted and we should wait for her to tell us.'

'But she came with *us*.'

'She didn't know Alan. Why should we wait for her

to give us permission to post our images?'

'What did she mean by 'make it safe'?'

They didn't know for sure. Better locks or security, tip off the owners or something.

But the location had leaked online now. Mobs of people were heading there right now.

'In the email she seemed to think you were still angry with her.'

They snorted at that. They were still angry. It was rude. She was their guest at that location. They'd found it and invited her to come with them. They were nice to her. They knew she'd gone missing but they also knew she wasn't going to contact them because she didn't like them at all any more.

'She was real hard work,' said Florian. 'Different in real life, you know? She had phobias. She was nervous.'

'Hm,' said Gregor. 'Hm. She was on meds for phobias.'

'She slept most of the way there. Four hours in the car.'

'Five,' said Gregor.

'Yeah, more like five hours because we stopped for food and switched over driving, remember?'

'She wasn't really asleep.' Gregor seemed uncomfortable. 'She was pretending . . .'

'Why?'

'Uhh.' Gregor looked sideways, 'Yeah. Kind of, stopped getting on . . .When we got there she wasn't really talking . . .'

They were sweet guys, socially awkward young men who, I suspected, didn't know many girls.

'I *liked* her.' Gregor flushed red and his head kind of shivered on his neck. 'In an internet-girlfriend way.

But she didn't like me back. I was embarrassed . . .'

Florian laughed hard. 'Yeah, he liked her a *lot*.'

Gregor blushed and laughed into his roll-neck. 'I was very embarrassed . . . But Lisa didn't even like Flor and all the girls like him.'

'Because I'm a weakling, an unthreatening boy. They know they can beat me up.'

Gregor punched his back. 'You're not weak.'

'But I look weak, like I'm not a threat. Ladies love that.'

It was so raw, all that young person honesty, how unaffected and open Gregor was about the pain of rejection and Florian was about being weedy (he was very weedy). Lisa Lee was pretty, probably seemed exotic to them, and she came a long way to team up with them. She was probably oblivious to Gregor's romantic hopes until she was in their car.

'And she got really freaked out in the chateau,' said Gregor.

'Yeah,' said Florian. 'She came out and she was crying and a mess. She wouldn't tell us why.'

'But she's nice,' interrupted Gregor, tipping his chin up to talk over his roll-neck. 'She's a nice person, a shy person.' Then he slipped back behind Florian again and they both stilled so completely that I thought the connection had frozen until I saw Florian's eyes continued to drift to the right.

Fin left a pause. 'Did she steal that silver casket?'

'No, I don't think so. But we left before her.'

'You didn't drive her back to Lille?'

'No, Alan Johansson took her to England on the ferry. She didn't want to travel with us.'

'Can we talk to Alan?'

'Sure,' said Florian and sent us Alan's contact

126

details. 'I'll tell him who you are. You'd have to visit him in London though, don't try to text him. He doesn't answer emails either. He's an odd man.'

Fin thanked them and asked if they'd spoken to Lisa after that.

They hadn't. Gregor had texted her a couple of times but she didn't reply. He said she was brave though, coming on her own. And leaving with Alan because he didn't like her. Alan didn't like them either, though they really liked him. But Alan didn't like anyone. He was moody person.

'Where is the chateau?'

Bram had slipped in behind us to ask the question. The atmosphere changed as suddenly as opening the door in a sauna.

'It's in France, yeah? What's the address?'

Florian blinked nervously. 'Who is that?'

I told Bram to fuck off but he didn't.

Florian and Gregor looked scared. 'Who is he?' Florian's finger came towards the screen. He was going to hang up.

Fin asked for a second and took his wireless earbuds out of the charging case so it would be a private conversation. He gave me the left one, kept the right with the mic for himself and then walked away with the now-silent phone.

I heard him say, 'Forget him, he's the man with the plane. Are you being hassled?'

'Yeah,' said Florian from the other side of the room. 'Fin, man, it's real scary, getting crazy.'

Gregor said, 'Jesus freaks. They're fucking crazy people. Real scary people.'

'He's not religious, that man, he's just our ride.'

'Yeah. Well, they're storming our social media

127

accounts and physically turning up at the school where my sister works, putting letters through my door and so on. We're going dark until this is over.'

I looked up and saw the woman coming across the room to talk to Bram, a happy smile on her face.

'Boarding for the van Wyk party,' she told him, 'I'm afraid you'll have to hurry or you'll miss your slot.'

Bram went to wake Marcos but I saw him throw the velvet hat under the seat first, into the shadows. Then he woke him.

Fin came back over and, together, we said hurried goodbyes to Florian and Gregor. They looked disappointed and a little hurt by what had happened.

I missed the frank admiration from the start of the call as they said goodbye and waved dutifully at us, as if we were elderly relatives leaving after an acrimonious Christmas Day.

We just had long enough to text Alan Johansson, tell him we'd spoken to Florian and Gregor and ask if we could visit this week.

He texted by return: Florian just said, yeah, come the day after tomorrow. He sent us his address.

I remember feeling pretty smug at this point, as if we were getting somewhere now. We were going to Paris, the centre of everything, we were going to visit Alan, and we'd pieced together a couple of things: Lisa had money from somewhere, she was alive and had probably taken the casket and sold it.

We didn't yet know that a body had just been found in woodland, less than a mile from North Berwick. Or that we weren't flying to Paris.

13

If you've never been on a private plane, it's like some-one with a passion for beige bought a minibus and went buck-wild. When I used the loo I was surprised at the white toilet paper, that's how beige everything was.

The storm had eased and take off was surprisingly smooth. We were buffeted a little on the way up but soon rose above the low clouds to a bright summer's day in another world.

Then the pilot announced that we were flying to Rome.

'Rome?'

Bram shrugged. 'Marcos doesn't have a flight to catch any more and Lamberg's there.'

'Where's my hat?'

'We didn't agree to go to Rome.'

'Where's my hat, Bram?'

Bram grinned at Marcos and reached into his pocket, took out a fistful of mini bags of Haribo gummy bears and dropped them in his lap.

'I don't even fucking like these ones. I like the sour ones.'

'I'm getting closer, kid. Give me a chance.'

'I want my hat.'

'Well, I'll get you another hat, kid. I'll fill it with sour Haribo.'

'Fuck off,' said Marcos, but he tore a packet open and started eating them.

We explained that we couldn't go to Rome: we had

to get to London the day after tomorrow for a meeting. Bram waved our concerns away. We would be in Paris then, he said. It was a two-hour train journey to London from the Gare du Nord. We could be there and back in an afternoon. The flight plan was in. We couldn't change it now.

I pointed out that Eugene Lamberg had murdered someone and Bram said he found that hard to believe, you shouldn't believe everything you read in court reports, but he smiled as he said it.

'You have to meet Eugene. He's . . . different.'

When I suggested that he might have told us we were going to Rome before we got on the fucking plane Bram rolled his eyes, undid his seat belt and stalked off to another seat.

I called after him, 'We didn't agree to this.'

He waved at me to shut up. Marcos got up and moved too, sitting as far away from his father as possible. When the flight levelled off Bram sparked up a cornflower-blue cigarette and came back and sat next to us.

'I'm sorry. I need to see Eugene. You can record this, yeah? I mean, Lisa finds this casket, Eugene had the casket, maybe he did kill Des O'Brian, and took the casket with him. Where has it been all this time? That's interesting, no? We'll stay in Rome tonight, I get you a nice hotel, then we'll go to Paris tomorrow.'

I suggested a moment of honesty, an amnesty; we were looking for Lisa and he was looking for something else, clearly. What was it?

Bram looked out of the window. We waited.

'OK. I need to get something else she showed in her film. Something in the chateau. If no one will tell us where that is, perhaps Eugene will help.'

'What is it?' asked Fin.

'That's not important,' he said, as if that made it true.

I was about to say that the location had been leaked online, Florian and Gregor had told us that, but Fin gave me a warning look and I didn't.

Fin asked what had happened with Marcos's mum and Bram went off to investigate. Marcos was sitting at the front of the plane with earbuds in and Bram stood in the aisle and made him take one out and talk about the call from his mum. Marcos was mumbling. I heard Bram say, 'It's OK. I'm glad, though.'

But Marcos wasn't glad to be stuck with Bram. He was very not glad. 'I DON'T KNOW YOU. Why am I here?'

'She wants us to know each other.'

'Why? I never met you in my whole life. Why is it for a whole week?'

'Well, I might not be here all the time, you know . . .'

'Who the fuck are you? You could be a fucking paedo for all I know.'

'I'm *not* . . .'

'YOU JUST LIE ALL THE TIME. YOU'RE NOT EVEN SOMEONE I KNOW.'

'I'm not sure we should be listening to this,' I said to Fin. 'I think this is private.'

Fin agreed but it was hard not to hear in this small space.

'GET AWAY FROM ME. YOU'RE A LIAR.'

'Shut up, kid, your voice is so fucking annoying.'

Bram and Marcos didn't seem terribly concerned about privacy. We tried to stay out of it. Fin put on headphones and listened back to what we had planned out so far, leaving me at a loose end.

'YOU'RE A FUCKING PAEDO.'

You can use your mobile phone on private planes. I couldn't put it off any longer.

Jess answered immediately. They were still at the lighthouse but Sofia had left first thing after an argument with Daddy and Este last night. Jess didn't hear anything they said, which seemed unlikely but very Jess-like and diplomatic. Was I OK? Oh, look, here's Lizzie. Lizzie, speak to Mum.

Lizzie asked me what that noise was and I told her I was on a plane. She told me I'd get into trouble for using my phone and then asked me what rape meant.

I said I'd tell her when she was older. Jess was hissing at her to shut up in the background.

'Oh, OK,' she said and rambled about Hop sleeping all night so everyone was in a better mood. Then Daddy got up and announced that no one was to call Hop 'Hop' any more. His name was Hamish. But they were still going to call him Hop.

It stands for 'Hamish, his own person'. The girls gave him that name because their dad had planned out his whole life, from which Oxford College he'd attend, to his sporting passions (rugby) and they were angry on his behalf. It wasn't fair and he hadn't been as ambitious for them. They could have resented the baby for that but they didn't. They were busy petitioning for their little brother. Small girls are amazing. Most of them get the moxie kicked out of them by puberty but there's always hope. Jess came back on.

'Did your name used to be Sophie?' asked Jess.

'Um, yes, Sophie Bukaran. That was my name at one time.'

'I like that name —'

'Anyway,' I said, quickly changing the subject, 'I

132

can't talk long. I'll call later.'

I hung up and sat for a moment with my eyes shut, trying to breathe in, and not think about my slippery avoidance, Jess's silencing, all of us.

'I like this story.'

I opened my eyes and found Fin smiling. 'Did you call Sofia?'

His face twitched. 'She's keeping me well abreast of developments without prompting.'

I couldn't talk about it any more. I looked over at Bram. 'Is he terminally ill? Or is someone planning to kill him?'

Fin followed my gaze. It did seem plausible. Bram was the kind of man people would want to kill.

'I don't trust him.'

Fin patted my hand fondly. 'Do you trust anyone, Anna?'

I sat back. 'Why would you ask me that? That's a very suspicious thing to say.'

He laughed, but only a little. He knew I meant it.

We were over the English Channel and I was scrolling on my phone. There was an Instagram story from the first people to locate the chateau from Lisa's film. It was two hundred kilometres south-west of Paris and they'd gone there and posted images of what they found.

All of the familiar rooms were completely empty. Great drag marks through layers of dust scarred the floors. It was picked clean when they got there, they said, every stick of furniture gone. Someone very greedy got there first. They must have brought moving vans and everything.

Just then the steward came out of the cockpit to offer us a meal. I shut my phone off and put it away.

Bram would not like that news. I didn't want to be the one to break it.

We gathered around the table, which was a bit of a crush, and he gave us single-sheet menus printed on fine paper. Fin and I chose a packet of crisps each. They were served with plates, napkins and cutlery. Bram and Marcos had rice and chicken that smelled like plastic, served face-melting hot straight from the microwave.

Fin asked Bram about the man he was an agent for. Bram was less guarded this time. I think he was trying to impress Marcos.

He wiped his mouth with his napkin and waited until his tape recorder and our machine and mic were running. He cleared his throat.

'Paul Hammersmith,' he said, 'is a rich man. You have no idea how much money is a lot of money. Actually rich. Really rich. Hammersmith is a good — a holy man. He's doing what he thinks is right by his own beliefs. I respect that. I don't share his faith, I envy it a little maybe, but I respect it. The Christian artefact market is on fire right now. You've heard of the Good News Museum?'

We hadn't.

'I'll tell you.'

Bram van Wyk leaned over the table so that Marcos could hear him clearly and then he told us the second most amazing story I have ever heard.

14

The sound quality was even worse on this recording. The engine drone made it sound like a twenty-three-minute gargle. But anyway, Bram told us a lot of lies about Paul Hammersmith. When we fact-checked what he told us we found that he'd made a lot of it up. This is the version Trina Keany gave in the third episode.

Paul Hammersmith was an apostle. He believed passionately in his mission to bring people to Jesus. How the Dollar Store King of Kansas arrived at that conclusion was complicated.

Hammersmith came from nothing but made a fortune through retail with hard work and a ton of good luck.

He grew up in rural Kansas and stayed there. He was witness to the social deprivation and needs of his neighbours. He wanted to help. He was a good man and a Christian but he and his wife ascribed to prosperity theology, the idea that riches were a reward from God for a life well lived. If he just gave his money away to help people he would be denying them a chance to develop their own relationship with the Almighty and experience the beneficent rewards that Paul had.

So, from a small town ravaged by poverty and poor schooling and opioid addiction, a place with little infrastructure and limited access to clean water, internet and electricity, Paul decided the responsible thing to do would be to build a museum celebrating the Bible. Plus anything he gave to the museum was tax-deductible. Paul didn't like paying tax. He didn't like a lot of the things the government were spending his money on.

He established a trust and a board and bestowed vast funds on them. Four years later they had built an enormous campus with a museum, research facilities, exhibition spaces and climate-controlled storage areas.

The spending spree that followed changed the world of biblical artefacts forever. With an almost infinite budget and a very tight brief the trustees filled the museum with Bibles, bits of Bibles and anything related to the Bible. They hired theological academics at exorbitant wages. They commissioned researchers to seek out objects related to the Bible and buy them at any cost. They spent money with wild abandon.

They bought manuscripts of the New Testament from the third century, Torah scrolls, ancient coins used around the time of Jesus, untranslated cuneiform tablets, scraps of the Dead Sea Scrolls, material, bowls, stools, a number of odd shoes, illuminated medieval manuscripts and archaeological finds from the Holy Land. The collection was vast and priceless.

The market was not accustomed to the prices they were paying. The spending spree overheated demand to such an extent that churches all over the world were being robbed of religious artefacts. Even very minor collections were being pilfered. This did not go unnoticed. The sale of items of historic significance is heavily regulated, especially since the sacking of the Iraq Museum in Baghdad during the American Invasion of 2003. The trustees claimed that all due diligence would be done on all of the purchases and opened their doors to the regulators.

The international panel came in and began their examination with the papyri collection. They found clean and credible provenance for one in every two hundred and fifty fragments they had. The museum's acquisition practice had caused a feeding frenzy for international smugglers, shady dealers and fraudsters. Further complicating the mission, the market had attracted new players.

Tom Hansen, a Norwegian billionaire and opportunist, began buying pieces indiscriminately, knowing that Hammersmith's team would buy anything from him at any price.

Elena Callis of the American Cypriot Callis family got involved. She was a patriot and extremely religious and determined to keep as much as she could out of the hands of non-Orthodox Christians. The Callis family were infinitely rich and, though American for three generations, proudly traced their lineage back to the establishment of the Cypriot Eastern Orthodox Church in 431 CE. Outraged at the thoughtless hoarding of resold icons by Hammersmith and his sect, they made it their mission to block any and every purchase Hammersmith attempted. They outspent him, employed buyers to actively seek relics related to the history of the Orthodox Church and basically messed with him at every turn.

Following in the wake of these three big fish were a lot of bottom-feeders, buyers and thieves and zealots. It was turning bitter.

Then the Voyniche Casket came on to the market. It was unopened and Paul was worried about what was inside. Some suspected a document, possibly some last comment made by Christ. It might support Hammersmith's beliefs or it might be more in the 'give unto Caesar that which is Caesar's' manner of thought. Paul very much wanted to be the first to see the contents so that he could control what, and how, that information was released and, if the museum could acquire it fairly, in an open auction, it would make them front-page news all over the world and bolster their reputation. Once opened, regardless of what was made

137

public about the contents, the casket could attract more visitors than the Pyramids.

But Hammersmith couldn't bid openly because it would treble the price. Callis and Hansen would work together to block him, and the Vatican would be bidding too. The Hungarian government had issued a statement asserting their ownership and promising to sue whoever bought it. So Hammersmith needed an unlikely frontman, someone the other buyers would never suspect of working with him.

This is how Bram van Wyk came to be involved. No one would expect Hammersmith to be reckless enough to trust him and Bram was out of the game, everyone knew that.

Bram lit a cigarette, sunshine yellow this time, and finished off with a comment to Marcos: 'So, you can see who I move with. I know these people. This is your father.'

'You're not my fucking father. And you're a five-time loser. Mum said so.'

Bram glared at the boy through hooded eyes. Smoke seeped from his lips, a physical expression of his loathing. Marcos dropped his eyes to the table. Bram's breathing was very shallow.

'Bram . . .' Fin reached for him across the table but Bram drew his hand slowly away and kept staring at Marcos.

As if he was stopping himself from doing something terrible, Bram got up carefully and slunk off to the back of the plane, sat down, facing away from us but a soft cloud of his cigarette smoke drifted over our heads, drawn forward by the air conditioning.

Marcos looked frightened.

I whispered, 'We won't leave you alone with him.'

He nodded, blinking, grateful.

'What happened with your mum?' asked Fin.

Marcos didn't really know. 'She says I've got to spend time with him while I can but she's quite . . . emotional. She says things like that.'

I wondered at a mother sending any child off to spend unsupervised time with a father that volatile. My indignation burned off when I remembered that I'd run away and left my girls with Sofia, the rape-blurter.

Marcos kept his eyes on the back of Bram's head and whispered, 'You don't think he killed that girl in North Berwick, do you?'

I was quite shocked at that. It hadn't occurred to me. But Marcos was frightened of Bram, ashamed at the sordid state of his family life and his mother's carelessness, so I told him that we'd just run away from a family holiday, Fin and I, even though I'd booked it and paid for it, and they were glad to be rid of me because I was a bit much sometimes.

He liked that. 'Are you two related?'

'No, not really. Fin's ex is my kids' new stepmum.'

He enjoyed the messiness of that, I think, and understood that I was trying to empathise with him.

Then he asked me, 'Are you a nightmare?'

'No,' said Fin, too quick and defensive for it not to be a little bit true, 'she's not.'

But Marcos had me pegged as a fellow troublemaker. 'It just seems to happen . . . ' I said. 'I'm not trying to be.'

'No,' he said sadly, 'me neither.'

After a while the steward came and cleaned up and asked us to take forward-facing seats and do our seat belts up.

We were beginning our descent into Roma Urbe Airport.

15

It was a glorious spring day in Rome, warm and bright outside, but not in this small, noiseless room on the first floor of the North American Pontifical College. The white stone walls stole the warmth we could see outside the long window to the balcony. Hard wooden chairs were pushed up against the wall and the window was shaded with grey net curtains.

It smelled of dust.

A young priest with thinning blond hair, a Connecticut accent and a snippy attitude picked lint off his sleeve and set out the rules: we must not call Lamberg 'Father'. We must not ask for or accept a blessing from him. Regardless of our history with him we must remember that Eugene was a visitor to this seminary, he was not a member of the college. He was here as a pilgrim, staying in the quarters reserved for lay members who came to visit Rome. Eugene could visit with us for one hour, no more, and then we would have to go. He trusted that we would support Eugene's return to society and pray for him at this difficult time. Everything he said was pitying and distancing. It laid out Eugene's position as crudely as a tourist map.

Did we understand?

He had mistaken us for members of a congregation that Eugene had served at some point, people who knew him and his history and sympathised with him. Explaining who we really were would get us chucked out so we all nodded dumbly.

He left, shutting the door quietly, as if he was

trapping us in there but didn't want us to know.

We looked around at the blank walls and stern seating. Fin caught my eye and touched his breast pocket. Recorder still running. Reminded by this gesture, Bram took out his tape recorder and sat it on the table, pressed record and then left it there. Over at the window he pulled back the curtains and stepped out onto the balcony.

We followed him into the fresh air and sunshine.

We were looking down into a courtyard of potted trees arranged around a modern water feature. A low jet fell over rough rocks, encircled with a brass crown of thorns. Far away, beyond the opposite wall of rooms just like ours, peeked the pink dome and spire of St Peter's Basilica. We were in the centre of Rome yet all we could hear was a gentle whisper of falling water amplified by the enclosed courtyard.

'Bram van Wyk.'

Bram stiffened at the voice and turned back to the figure in the room.

They looked at each other through the open doorway as a net curtain drifted lazily between them.

Eugene Lamberg looked like an actor in his breakthrough role as a sexy priest. Fit for a man in his early sixties, he moved like a dancer, had thick salt-and-pepper hair and as good a jaw as any man could ask for. His pale blue eyes were framed with dark lashes. He wasn't wearing a collar or cassock, just black jeans, a black cashmere sweater and brogues, but everything looked expensive and freshly laundered.

They looked at each other and I thought they might come to blows until Eugene's face burst into a sudden warm smile and his hands rose at his sides. 'Hello, my darling.'

141

Bram flew into the room and they hugged, happy but confused at the intensity of their mutual delight, Bram lifting Eugene off his feet, then Eugene lifting Bram, slapping each other's back and laughing at the other's tears.

Finally they sat down next to each other, neither really able to speak, so I introduced myself and Fin and Marcos, quite formally because of the strange setting, and told him why we were here.

They sat knee to knee, Eugene holding on to Bram's hand tenderly, unembarrassed. He listened, jerking around to look at Bram a few times, as though he couldn't believe his friend was there. Then I saw him steel himself and make a commitment to listen to me.

'This girl is missing in Scotland? Did she leave and come here?'

'We don't know where she is. We've no idea where she went.'

He stroked his chin. 'Then why are you here?'

I told him that the police were doing what they could but we had noticed that Lisa had gone missing after answering her front door. It was like the disappearance of a Hungarian man, Michael K., — but I used his real name — in Beirut many years ago, and he was from Balaton.

Eugene nodded — he knew the K. family very well. He was close to their poor mother and knew that Maria had been murdered by the Secret Police. 'And now the casket is being auctioned.' He squeezed Bram's hand. 'Is this why you're here?'

Suddenly exasperated, Bram stood up, told Eugene that he'd just heard that he was fucking alive, that he'd believed he was dead all these fucking years, that he'd been murdered by Des O'fucking Brian in Bari and

142

that he had grieved Eugene, the loss of Eugene, and how dare he not get in touch? How dare he? And did he murder Des O'Brian and steal the casket? Is that what happened, you fucking fucker? You sack of fucks! How did the fucking thing end up on sale again? Was he fucking selling it? Who the fuck did he sell it to?

Eugene stood up slowly, holding Bram's eye and paused. 'Yes, I murdered my friend and stole the casket to sell it and —' Lamberg gestured around the bare borrowed room — 'as you can see, I am now a millionaire.'

Bram laughed despite himself.

'I thought they'd killed you in Bari too, Bram. This is before the internet, pre-Facebook, you couldn't just look people up —'

'I'm not on fucking Facebook,' said Bram, angry, as if that was the issue.

Eugene laughed at that, trying not to, biting his lips between his teeth.

They liked each other. They couldn't hide it. And it was nice for Marcos to see his father with a friend, sparring and giggling and being loved. It seemed to warm him to Bram, if just a little.

Eugene explained to Bram that it was Bari, it was all Bari. The hotel was full of Mafia. 'We were followed, I think. Maybe they didn't even know what we had, just that we'd gone to a lot of trouble to get it so it must be valuable.'

'Could Voyniche have killed him?'

Eugene shrugged. 'It's so long ago. And Bari is . . . well, you know Bari. We'd have been safer in the Siege of Dubrovnik.'

'And my picture . . . ?' said Bram, looking broken.

Eugene lifted his face by the chin and read him. 'I

143

didn't have it. I'm sorry. I lied, to make you help me.'

'Who did have it?'

Eugene didn't know. Bram said he saw it in a You-Tube film. It was in the room where the casket was found but Eugene couldn't help him. He didn't know anything about YouTube. He was sorry.

Bram looked at Marcos, playing a game on his phone, and dropped his voice so he couldn't hear him. 'I'm done if I don't find it.'

Eugene empathised and hugged him and said he was sorry, so sorry, if it was within his power to help he would. Sometimes we're just done and we have to accept it.

They hugged again and Bram cried a little and whispered that he was done. Done. And Eugene stroked his back and listened and wiped the tears from his cheeks.

And yes, Eugene was flirtatious, not just for a priest but for anyone. It was as if his avowed celibacy gave him a freedom to interact in this kind way with anyone, make them feel special and seen, without the threat of anything going any further or turning uncomfortable. At one point he asked Bram for a cigarette and Bram asked him acidly how he knew he hadn't given up.

'Because you smell so very delicious.'

They giggled at that and we all went outside to smoke on the balcony. He liked Sobranie Cocktail cigarettes, he said, they reminded him of the seventies. He picked a green one because it was his favourite colour.

We all leaned over the ledge, enjoying the sun and the nicotine buzz. Eugene told Marcos stories about the old days in Boston when he and Bram were young and foolish and full of hope. Most of the stories were about getting things wrong because they didn't understand American culture, how strange and awful the food was — 'overcooked meat covered in sugar' — and how polite the people were to each other, because they all had guns. Bram almost got shot every other day, Eugene said.

Marcos said his mother — Janine — was from Boston, and Eugene's left eyebrow rose as far as it would go and then stayed there, half an inch from his hairline.

'I didn't know I had a son,' said Bram. 'She just told me about him. Wants us to spend time together before, you know . . .'

'She was very young, Bram,' said Eugene reproachfully.

'She was thirty-four!'

'Oh, this was later?'

'2006 not 1990. Eugene, look at him.' They both looked at Marcos. 'Does he look twenty-eight?'

And then they laughed together so boyishly that we all laughed with them. Eugene told Marcos that he'd served as priest to his mother's family and Marcos asked shyly how that could be? The man who led us up to this room said Eugene wasn't a real priest.

'Well, you know how, sometimes, if people are shot or sick they can't go to a regular hospital in case they get reported to the police?'

Marcos nodded lightly that yes, he did know that scenario, which seemed quite a lot for a boy of his age to know.

'Well,' said Lamberg, 'just the same way: sometimes people can't go to a regular priest. And sometimes these are the same people most in need of spiritual guidance. They can revoke my priesthood but not my

145

vocation. I operate in the grey areas where the Church doesn't care to go. Lucky for me Americans are not an obedient people. That's why the paedophile priest scandal broke there, I think. In Europe we are more deferential to authority. Land of the free, yes?'

A sudden shrill voice cut across the courtyard. A mono browed nun in a grey habit shouted up to us from the courtyard: smoking was forbidden here and we should put our cigarettes out at once.

'I'M TERRIBLY SORRY, SISTER,' Eugene called back, 'WE DON'T SPEAK ENGLISH.'

After the hilarity had died down he said we should get out of here: the retreating nun was quite a powerful character in the seminary and he didn't want to get into trouble. He was a guest and relied on their charity.

We decided to go for a walk, along the banks of the Tiber to the Via della Conziliazione.

'What could be more appropriate?' said Eugene, slipping his arm through Bram's.

As we made our way downstairs I realised that Bram had abandoned the tape recorder he had been lugging around. He must have noticed his satchel was lighter. I didn't know if it was deliberate, maybe he was going to try and come back without us, but it didn't feel like that. If felt as though he had left it because he might not need it any more, as if something was coming to an end.

As we crossed the grounds to the exit gate I wondered if it was OK for Eugene to leave. Fin was still recording and caught his reply:

'It's a conditional discharge. I can do as I like so long as I don't break the law, it's fine.'

Fin said, 'Can I ask about the murder you were

convicted of?'

Eugene looked a little uncomfortable for the first time. He stopped before the gate and crossed his hands and dropped his gaze. He spoke quietly, in a flat voice, as if he had said this many times and it still pained him.

'She was a very dear friend, very ill, had been ill for a long time. A painful cancer. She had young children but was wealthy and had very good care. She would have lived a long time with terrible pain, increasingly confused, disabled, erratic. She didn't want her children to remember that. We prayed together for an answer. We both came to the same conclusion. Suicide is a mortal sin and so is murder but I can repent a murder. An old theological conundrum. I helped her die and assisted suicide is a crime, technically, but it's treated leniently. The judge said he would have let me walk out of court if it was within his power, but it wasn't and I respect that.'

Marcos said, 'That was brave.'

Eugene squeezed his arm. 'What are we for, Marcos, if not for each other?' he said quietly. 'Let's go for a walk.'

We left the grounds and walked slowly downhill to the electric-green Tiber. The water level was low, revealing banks of sticky brown mud. Native Romans who knew that the weather would soon get better, were waiting this day out in big jackets and gloves, but we were walking, heads erect, enjoying the low spring sun and the strangeness of a weather system that meant us no harm.

This is when I first saw the blue Nissan. It was parked in a side street. I spotted it several times over the next few hours but put it down to tiredness. I'd

147

thought we were being followed back in Scotland too. I was jittery and seeing things.

The riverside road was a main artery, busy with cars and taxis, but Eugene made the walk entertaining, pointing out sights and spots, telling us the stories of the city, erudite but fun. It was a mix of Roman history and gossip.

— *run through with a sword, he died on the spot but his boyfriend ran forward from the crowd and dipped the hem of his cloak in the blood and wore it for the rest of his life.*

— *but no one ever found the money or the horses.*

— *so they cut out his heart and fed it to a pig.*

We arrived at the riverside end of the Via della Conciliazione, and only then realised it was the long avenue that swept straight up to St Peter's Basilica.

The street was full of tourist parties, busy and littered with papers and wrappings. Bins overflowed with half-eaten ice creams, plastic water bottles, bits of pizza and Starbucks coffee cups. Detritus blew slowly around the feet of the people on the avenue but it was still beautiful. Nothing could hold the eye for long when every line led to the rise of St Peter's Basilica.

'Isn't it something?' said Lamberg, smiling as if he'd built all of this himself.

We were walking towards it, tractor-beamed by the geometry, when Fin caught my sleeve and tugged to hold me back from the others. He showed me a news alert on his phone: a girl had been found dead in woodland a mile from Bob Lee's house. Police were 'not looking for anyone' — that meant it was a suicide. Her identity was being withheld until the family were informed.

The news winded me. My father killed himself,

I've been on the ragged brink myself once or twice, I know how easy it would be to stand on the edge and just . . . tip. And I know all the wonderful things that happened because I didn't tip: Hamish and my girls, my friend Fin and my kind, mad bitchy friend Estelle. I saw all the wonders and ice creams and good sleeps and funny films Lisa Lee would never see flash before me, all the sex and adventures and strong tea she'd never get to have. It made me think of my girls in ten years' time, of Jess staggering out of a hotel at five in the morning with blood running down her legs, of Lizzie crying so hard on a night bus that her make-up ran and everyone moved away from her and the driver stopped and called the police to come and help her.

Fin held my hand and asked if I was OK. I said I was, though I wasn't really. He said he was fine too but that was a lie. He's had his bad days. Saving Lisa meant something special to him as well.

We didn't know Lisa. We shouldn't have been as sad as we were, but she was young and had struggled and I think we both saw ourselves in her.

Fin whispered that it might be best not to mention Lisa's suicide in front of Marcos and I agreed.

'We should tell Florian and Gregor,' I said and we stopped to send an email asking them to call. Mailer-daemon bounced it back. They'd deleted their account. Fin called the number they gave us but it was unobtainable.

Ahead of us Marcos walked between Bram and Eugene, listening to them talk. We followed them to the mouth of St Peter's Square.

Bram was arguing that the casket shouldn't be in an open sale. If Callis got it she'd claim it supported her faith and if it went to Hammersmith he'd rip it open

149

and claim there was a picture of Billy fucking Graham in there. Even an arch-capitalist like him thought that was a ludicrous way to answer complex theological questions.

Eugene listened carefully. 'I can see you're angry about this,' he said, reflecting back like a therapist. 'But it's out of your control and you have to accept that.'

It was late afternoon and the final few tourists were lining up under the colonnades to have their bags X-rayed before they got into the Basilica. Security was tight. Concrete roadblocks had been set up to stop car bombers, and watchful police officers cradled big guns, nodding us through while eyeing the far distance.

Eugene led us over to the obelisk in the centre of the square. A flock of teenagers left as we arrived, laughing and chatting, and it made me think of Lisa, how she could have been with them, hanging off to the side with the shy kids and the sad kids and the wildcard outsiders.

We sat on the steps and Eugene told us that the obelisk had been brought here from Egypt by Caligula. He had it erected on this spot, in what used to be Nero's Circus. St Peter, one of the twelve apostles, was executed in sight of that obelisk. And look, see where the crucifix is at the top? When St Peter was martyred here there was a brass globe in its place, a hollow globe, said to contain the ashes of Julius Caesar.

We all looked up, open-mouthed with wonder, like an obedient tour party.

Eugene continued: the obelisk was moved in the fourth century when the church was being built. It was taken down very carefully, laid on its side, and the brass globe that contained the ashes of Julius Caesar was replaced with a crucifix. When the obelisk was raised again the cross dominated the circus, could be seen from everywhere. Every angle.

But what to do with the brass globe? They opened it.

He smiled and glanced at Bram. 'There was nothing in there.'

Bram was a little defensive. 'Imagine if there was though.'

'Well, maybe that was the problem. They looked and the mystery was over. It was worthless. If they hadn't, Julius Caesar would still be in there.'

'If we open the casket we might find proof, Eugene. Spores from Judaea. Desert dust. Physical proof.'

Lamberg smiled at his choice of words. 'Faith is the substance of things hoped for, evidence of things not seen, Bram.'

'Is faith so fragile?'

'Faith is a willingness to sustain a belief *while* entertaining doubt.'

Bram nodded softly at that, at his old friend who he'd supposed dead and had missed all these years. Then he took off a gold watch he was wearing and gave it to Eugene. It was a Rolex, solid gold, he said. Eugene smiled and replied that it was a very sweet offer but he didn't really want to take it. He had no use for such things.

'Take it to remember me by. Or else you can come to Paris? We could go to this auction together?'

'No, Bram,' Eugene took the watch reluctantly and slipped it into a pocket. 'I can't come with you.'

'You don't want to see it one last time? Before

151

Callis declares Catholicism a crock of shit and Ortho-dox Christianity the only way?'

Eugene pulled up his trouser leg and showed his ankle. He was wearing an electronic tag; a thick black band with a small plastic box on the outside. It blinked red.

'I'd love to come, Bram, to spend more time with you, though, not for the casket. But it's a condition of my release that I don't leave Rome. There are worse places to be stuck.' Then he looked up at St Peter's. 'My wish, if it pleases God, is to die here.'

16

Bram told the taxi driver to stop outside the St Regis Hotel. Fin and I got out and Bram rolled down his window and said he'd take Eugene back to the college because it was late. Our rooms were reserved though, so if we checked in we could order whatever. He'd see us at seven tomorrow morning in reception, don't be late.

It wasn't until the car pulled out into traffic that I realised he'd left Marcos with us. We could have been anyone. Flags hung above the door, the lines clanging dolefully against metal poles as we all watched their car disappear into a busy roundabout on our left. Just then, through the busy traffic on the road, from the right came the blue Nissan Micra. It was small and dirty and being driven with eye-catching care, all the more noticeable in Roman traffic.

'Look!' I pointed at it as it slid in front of a bus. 'We're being followed.'

'Oh, don't think so,' said Fin. 'There's loads of that model of car.'

I might have conceded that I was wrong, that this was a common car, but Marcos laughed in my face, mocking me because he had been dumped and felt foolish.

'You're paranoid,' he said, picked up his bag, and walked off.

'They *were* following us,' I said to Fin. 'I've seen that car four or five times today.'

'OK,' said Fin, unwilling to argue.

I didn't know what else to say.

We went inside.

The hotel was intimidatingly grand. A huge chandelier hung over a loud yellow rug. Sculptural pieces were placed around the central hall and a row of three reception desks stood at the far end of the room, each of bottle-green marble. We managed to check in and were told that a card had been left to cover all expenses. This was a key to the spa. This was the internet connection. Room service was twenty-four-hour. Here was the massage menu.

The check-in clerk was very keen for us to spend money.

Upstairs I went with Marcos to make sure he was OK on his own. As far as I know children under sixteen should be supervised in a hotel. The room booked for him led into mine through a connecting door, which I thought impertinent. His own father hadn't booked them rooms together, nor was Fin chosen to mind his son. Just me. Because I had ovaries. Actually, I was offended but also found it a bit reassuring. I wouldn't have liked Marcos to be on his own, but still. Ovaries.

Each room had a massive bed and linen sheets as crisp as rice paper. We each had a sitting room and a small writing bureau overlooking the street, laid out with a beautifully designed stationery set stamped with the name of the hotel.

I waited for Marcos to drop his bag and told him we were going downstairs to eat.

'I only want some nuts and chocolate,' he said, looking at the minibar selection.

I said he was in Rome, and should eat a proper dinner first and have chocolates and nuts when he came back up, because I have ovaries. Then I made Fin come to the hotel restaurant with us so I could embarrass him into eating as well.

The restaurant was intimidatingly formal. We lingered at the door in our soft shoes and comfortable clothes and decided to opt for the bar instead. We all ordered pasta, which was exquisite.

Fin had trouble with the vegan pasta but managed two-thirds of a plate, which I found incredibly satisfying. Marcos ate his own and then finished Fin's and had some of mine. We all ordered lemon-and-basil-flavoured gelato which was delicious and surprising, two sensations that rarely go together.

We'd been there for almost an hour and a half, not knowing what was happening or whether Bram was even going to come back. My eyes were burning. I kept thinking about Lisa, thinking that we could have looked after her better, which was stupid because I didn't even know her. I wouldn't have even heard of her by the time she got to the woodland and sat down. I couldn't have done anything anyway.

I ordered a glass of wine but it just made me relaxed and sick and unsteady so I ordered another one. I turned my annoyance to the matter of Marcos. We were babysitting a child that we didn't know in a city that we didn't live in and the best-case scenario was that his stranger father came back and got him.

I tapped his phone. 'Call your mum, Marcos. Tell her she has to come and get you.'

He refused.

'Are you scared of her?'

'Of my mum?'

'Yeah.'

'Yes I'm scared of her.'

'Are you scared of Bram? He was giving you a pretty hard time back in the airport.'

He smiled. 'You haven't met my mum.'

Fin was full and I know that made him uncomfortable and anxious. He went for a walk around the hotel to call Trina Keany and check she was getting the audio files we were sending her. He was away for a long time. When he came back, he sat for a bit and then got up abruptly and went to the toilet. I watched him leave, hoping I hadn't pushed the pasta too much, that he wasn't going to make himself sick.

This is when Marcos's phone shrieked like a warning from a diving seagull. The screen said 'Giver of Life'.

He answered it nervously and turned away, his voice very high.

'Hi. Yeah. No. I'm in a hotel with some people . . .' He shrugged one shoulder and it stayed up there. 'Just . . . people. He's coming later. St Regis. I don't know. Rome, somewhere.'

'Let me speak to your mum, Marcos.'

His back rounded away from me, protecting the phone. 'Uh-hm?'

'Marcos, let me speak to your mother.'

I think I must have been a bit drunk because I grabbed his shoulder and prised the phone out of his hand in one swift motherly don't-put-that-in-your-mouth move.

'Hello,' I said smoothly, 'am I speaking to Marcos's mum?'

'. . . Who's this?'

'OK, Janine, you don't know me but I'm with your son.'

Marcos was frightened and struggled to get the

phone back but I ducked away and heard Janine snarl, 'Who in the name of fuck is this?'

Janine had the scariest voice I have ever heard. Her accent was thick Boston, I couldn't place it more closely than that but I could hear the oesophageal graze of every cigarette she'd ever smoked in her voice and she sounded as if she was drunk.

'Ah ha, yes, hello.' I felt very unsure suddenly. 'Yes, hello. So, um, I am travelling with your son and my name is Anna —'

But Marcos was shaking his head, eyes wide, mouthing NO NO DON'T SAY YOUR NAME as he ran his fingertips across his throat.

'Anna McDonald,' slurred Janine. 'I know who you are, honey. I know where you are. You think I'd let a fucking stranger look after my kid, you're fucking crazy.'

'Am I? Because at the moment he's with a very volatile man who may or may not be quite ill.'

That stumped her. 'Bram's ill?'

I wasn't going to lie. 'Well, maybe. He's shedding belongings and talking about being done.'

'Oh, OK.' She sounded as if she was smiling. 'Poor Bram. Such a nice man . . . ' She veered into trying not to cry. 'Did he say confession with Father Lamberg?'

Fin came back and sat down next to me. He grabbed my arm but I wrestled it away. Maybe I'd had too much wine. 'How do you know we saw Lamberg?'

It was confusing, with Fin trying to get my attention, Marcos gesturing to get his phone back and the noise in the bar, but I distinctly heard her suck her teeth and it sounded like a hiss. 'Jessica and Elizabeth.'

157

I sobered up quite suddenly.

'Yeah,' she drawled, 'twelve and ten. I know all about you, Anna. So, listen up: did Lamberg give him a small painting?'

'He asked for it. Lamberg said he never had it in the first place.'

There was silence. A little tipsy but attempting to seem nonchalant, I took a noisy sip of wine.

Janine growled, 'Bitch, stop drinking.'

'I could say the same to you.'

'Fuck you.'

'Yeah, well, fuck you too.'

Marcos was frantic at me saying that but Janine, mood-swinging Janine, laughed. 'I'd like to get drunk with you one day, bitch.'

'Why are you doing this to him? He's a good kid.'

'Yeah,' she sighed. 'He's a real good kid. Families . . . you know, loyalty.'

Fin was urgently patting my hand, then my arm, then my face.

'OK,' said Janine but it sounded like 'aye kaye'. 'Look up. See the guy at the bar with the blue suit on?'

I looked up. A man was sitting at the bar dressed in a blue suit, a white shirt and a pink tie. He had a small briefcase with him and was sipping a glass of whisky with ice.

'He's watching you.'

'There is probably a man in a blue suit in every bar in Europe —'

'His friend has a red sweater on.'

Then I saw that he wasn't alone. The man next to him did have a red sweater on.

'Wave to the nice man,' she said.

Unsure, I raised my hand and gave him a stiff side-to-side wave. The man in the blue suit waved back but my view of him was cut off by Fin sliding his phone into my line of vision. A headline. Body found that of local mother of two. Police. Tragedy. Lisa was still out there. And just like that, I wasn't sick or angry or even especially tipsy any more.

'These guys are the best. German ex-military. Top of the line. You don't need to worry about Marcos. They won't let you out of their sight. Put the fucking kid back on. Do it now.' Janine didn't shout because Janine didn't need to shout.

I was in a completely different mood now and said, 'Oh, righto! Nice to meet you, anyway.' And cringed as I handed the phone back to him.

Marcos grinned at me and curled over the receiver. 'Yu hu, hm, sure, yup. Yup.' He looked straight at me in a way I found chilling. 'Yeah. OK. No, he didn't. No. Never had it. They're gone. I don't know.' He hung up and said to me, '*Never* do that again.'

'Marcos, who is your mum?'

'She doesn't want anyone taking my phone away from me. It's the only way she can get hold of me. You don't know what you're getting into. You don't know her or her people.'

'OK,' I said. 'OK, but, Marcos, I think it would be safer if you went home.'

'You don't know my home.' He looked at me with a tired old man's eyes. But he was alive and so was Lisa Lee.

'Marcos, what's the painting of?'

'Don't ask questions.'

'Why did Bram give Eugene all that money for it in Bari?'

159

'Just don't. Don't.'

'Did Lamberg steal the painting from your mum?'

'Look, some dumb-fuck uncle gave it to Father Lamberg for the last rites or something.'

'Uncle Dumb-fuck gave him a painting to black-mail Bram? Why's Janine interested in it?'

'Looking for Lisa Lee, that's fine, no one cares, but Janine doesn't like you recording this. She's only allowing it because it means I'm not alone with Bram, but if you find something she doesn't want you to know . . . well.'

'Well?'

'*Well.*'

A story ran across his face, a frightening story, full of regret and resignation. I could see him as a grown man, in a dark bar late at night, lonely-drinking. I think Fin saw it too.

'Nuts and chocolate?' he said to Marcos. 'We can go to your room and watch a bit of TV if you like.'

Marcos gave him a small nod.

'Go and have a shower and get into your PJs, I'll come up in half an hour.'

Marcos left. He liked Fin, I could see that he did. He nodded, took his phone and his key card and walked away. The man in the blue suit slipped off his stool and was gone. Red-sweater man stayed though, watching us from the corner of his eye. I told Fin who they were and he said maybe Janine was a good mum after all and I said maybe she was and that she'd asked about the painting.

'Send me that screenshot you took from Lisa's film,' said Fin and I did.

He pinched the image open, closing in on the painting on the wall. I'd screenshot the frame just before the torchlight flashed off the cellophane, visible, grainy but discernible. He put it in an image-recognition app but the image wasn't clear enough. He tried another one and while it ran I asked if I had to come and watch TV with them. I was knackered.

Fin tutted at that. 'So am I.'

But he had offered and I hadn't.

'Thanks, Anna, always thinking of others,' he said, which is as close to a proper fight as he gets.

This app came through. It gave us five options and the one with the lowest percentage of matching identifiers was from a Monet called *Chez Tortino*, which had been stolen in Boston in 1990. There was a $10 million reward for its return.

'Well, that explains a bit,' said Fin. 'He's in deep shit.'

It was too much to take in. We went upstairs to our separate rooms and parted on the landing, saying we'd see each other downstairs in the morning.

Up in my room I found myself hypnotised by the biggest, whitest bed I've ever seen. The room had blue velvet sofas and a bathroom tiled in black and white with underfloor heating and more free toiletries than an airport chemist shop.

I took a shower and brushed my teeth and walked out of the bathroom swathed in giant white fluffy towels, sat down on the bed and looked out of the window. The street was dark. A soft pink light spilled over the cobbles from a restaurant round the corner.

I sat for a moment, taking in the events of the day. This must be how it was for the very rich, I thought, the whole world must feel as if it was two bus stops away.

I wanted to call the girls but had sort of waited until

161

I knew they'd be asleep. To assuage my guilt about that, I called Estelle instead. She wanted to know where we were and I told her. Sofia had packed up and was leaving for Milan in the morning.

'Shit,' I said.

'I know,' she said.

'I feel responsible.'

'None of it is because of you.' That was a lie. 'Fin's emotionally stunted. I've been telling you this for years.'

She said we needed a strategy for talking to the girls about Sophie Bukaran and I said I needed to work something out but my head was full.

'I'll think about it. I promise,' I said and meant it.

'If you don't, I'm just going to tell them the truth, Anna. I love you.'

'I love you t —'

She hung up on me and I was glad. Sincerity is exhausting.

I walked around the room, trying to think about Lisa, Bram, Eugene, Nero, anything but the commitment I'd just made.

It was a lovely room. The writing set on the desk was of creamy pale green paper with pink marbling along the edge, the name and address of the hotel was embossed in green at the top of every sheet with pink shadowing underneath the proud letters. I felt it, noticed the weight of the paper, the texture of it and the soft edging. I became mesmerised by it, thinking about Jess and Lizzie, how much they'd like this stationery. I lay down, thinking about them holding it and smiling, my fingertips stroking the paper as if it was their cheek, as if they were fretful and I was trying to get them to sleep after a worrying day.

Suddenly it was a quarter to seven the next morning. I sat up with a start, and the drool-covered pad fell onto the duvet. I ran into the bathroom for a shower and looked in the mirror. The green lettering had transferred to my cheek. I had to scrub it off with a hot flannel.

Downstairs I found Bram sitting in an armchair, wearing sunglasses and looking rough. He had taken Eugene home last night, and gone drinking. He reached up to scratch his cheek and I saw that his gold rings were gone. He had his satchel with him but it was lighter than before. He hadn't gone back for his bulky tape recorder.

'Bram, what's the significance of the painting in Lisa's film?'

He huffed a sad laugh. 'Not a painting. It's part of a painting.'

I couldn't see his eyes and when he stopped talking I didn't know what it meant. But suddenly he said, 'You see that Saran Wrap around it?'

I nodded.

'Keeps fingerprints good. Ties me to some things. Bad things with bad people who don't want to be connected to those things. But that was a long time ago. That was Boston.'

He stopped talking again but the pause went on for so long I thought he probably wasn't going to say any more.

'Why are you giving away your things?'

He smiled queasily.

'If you don't find the painting . . . is it bad?'

He tipped his head to the side, frowned, and looked away across reception. But his chin buckled and I saw that he couldn't speak.

163

So I told him about my conversation with Janine, about the men in the bar and the blue Nissan. He seemed surprised that she'd spoken to me.

'You know sometimes,' I said, 'when people have resigned themselves to dying they feel better for a short while but the relief doesn't last. It's no solution. I know I've felt quite down at times.'

He grinned at me. 'I'm not suicidal. I don't have those thoughts.'

'Well, Bram, maybe you should start.'

He snorted at that. I think he would have laughed out loud if he wasn't so hung-over. 'I'll go to the auction and find out who the seller is, that's how I'll find the painting. It's all going to be OK. I just know it is.'

He didn't know, still, that the chateau had been looted. It wasn't going to be OK. I sat there, with the means to crush his spirit, and wondered about sending him the link anonymously, but the consequences of doing that filled me with panic. And what did I know anyway? In short, I bottle it.

The hotel was coming alive. Guests in crisp morning clothes crossed the lobby to the breakfast room and the uniformed cohort of staff gathered behind reception, briefing each other and passing on gossip and pleasantries. The noise began to swell in the lobby.

Fin arrived, looking beaten and depressed. Sofia had phoned him. She was leaving and taking all his furniture. She was going to give an interview about him to a journalist. She wanted him to support her financially until she found her feet in Milan again.

'She's being spiteful. Fight her, Fin.'

'I will,' he said, but he said it softly, as if he didn't know what fighting was.

Marcos arrived at the same time as our car and we had to break the speed limit to get to the airport in time to keep our flight plan.

17

The 1990 Isabella Stewart Gardner Museum heist in Boston changed the international market in stolen art forever.

It was the highest value heist in art robbery history, or at least known art robbery history. Conceivably other robberies have taken place of art or artefacts that are worth a lot more money but were never reported or quickly resolved. What is bafflingly unique about the 1990 robbery, though, is that no one involved ever broke ranks and told, despite a $10 million reward.

Before it happened there had already been a series of art thefts in Boston, of Rembrandts, mostly. These were messy smash-and-grab affairs: windows were put in, security officers bashed on the head, paintings and sketches were cut out of frames and taken away in the night.

The robbery at the Gardner Museum was part of this pattern and not that surprising, but it was the scale of it, the calm assuredness with which it was done, and the value of what was taken that were astonishing.

It was assumed, not unreasonably, that whoever was stealing the artworks was solely moved by the resale value of Rembrandt's work and saw them as negotiation chips, either to hold for ransom or for bargaining with other criminals. They must be taking these works of transcendental beauty to trade them for the sorts of things low-born people like: guns or drugs or money. No criminal could have been captivated by Rembrandt's work.

But maybe they had.

Conceivably, someone without an art history degree or country club membership stood in front of Rembrandt's

166

self-portrait in the Isabella Gardner Museum, met van Rijn's eyes and felt a shock of recognition across the centuries.

Conceivably they went to a bookshop and found a book about him, pored over it, underlining passages and turning pages, reread it several times, and saw themselves in the great bathetic mess of van Rijn's life: his Catholic mother and Protestant father, his worship of his wife, his dead children and his money worries, and the compulsion to collect art and antiquities that brought Rembrandt to the brink of ruin.

Maybe they loved his art.

Love was never really considered as a motive because the museum was a monument to avarice, to Golden Age wealth. Stewart Gardner didn't even choose the objects herself. She had a buyer who chose all the works for her. Boston was an organised crime town. The Italian and the Irish Mafia operated there and everyone knew what they wanted. They were criminals. They were soulless. They wanted money and guns and drugs and sex.

Art meant nothing to them.

Expensive art couldn't move them or answer some deep-rooted need for connection and beauty in their heart.

Isabella Stewart Gardner had come from money and married more.

She had begun buying art when her only child died at the age of two, of pneumonia. When she was later widowed the loss was too much to bear and she began to plan a memorial: she bought a plot of land in the Fens on the outskirts of the city of Boston and built a mock-Venetian palazzo to house the collection she and her husband had amassed, so that the public could see the antiques, early editions of Dante and other rare manuscripts, carpets, crockery, paintings and sketches — a whole big bunch of

167

slightly random stuff.

The collection was ramshackle.

If it had a central theme, other than things bought by Isabella's money, the theme was expensive things made by dead people. The holy icons of capitalism.

Maybe to eyes that loved Rembrandt, to a heart that saw in his brushwork a plea for connection through time, finding him in such a collection would be an insult. A cheapening.

Maybe to such a heart each work by Rembrandt should be in its own museum, instead of crammed in next to other expensive baubles commemorating a sad rich lady's buying compulsion.

It was St Patrick's Day in Boston in 1990. This was a huge and wild event. The parade was watched by over half a million people. The city had already begun drinking, not just heavily, but patriotically.

Boston braced itself for the unexpected.

There were two security guards on at the Gardner Museum that night: Rick and Randy. Both were in their twenties. Randy had just graduated with a master's from a music school, he was marking time until he could find a better job. Rick was in charge. He was sitting at the security desk while Randy did the rounds.

They weren't alone, though.

There were motion sensors and alarms set up all over the museum. If someone broke in the alarm would wake up everyone within a mile of the museum. The motion sensors tracked the movement of anyone in the building.

Earlier in the evening Rick did a tour of the grounds. He went over to the Palace Road door and opened it. Then he shut it. Then he walked away. No one knows why he did this.

Afterwards eyewitnesses came forward to say that they

168

had seen two men sitting in a red hatchback outside the museum between half past midnight and one o'clock.

This is not a residential area.

It's the sort of area where sitting in a car, however innocent, is suspiciously loitering in a car.

The eyewitnesses reported that one of the men was a bit fat and one was a bit thin. Other than that they looked the same. Both had moustaches, both had dark hair, one wore glasses. Just sitting in a car.

At twenty-five past one in the morning Rick heard the buzzer sound on the side entrance. He looked on the video monitor and saw two police officers. They showed him their badges. They were responding to a report of a disturbance in the building. Could he let them in?

So Rick let them in.

They followed him to the desk. Was he alone in the building? No, he said, Randy was walking around, checking the rooms, making sure everything was OK. Could he call Randy on the walkie-talkie and ask him to come here please, sir? Sure. So Rick did that.

When he got there one of the men dressed as a police officer announced, 'Gentlemen, this is a robbery.'

The alarm on the wall was blinking at them and the robbers knew it was there. The guards and the second robber watched as the thin man with glasses walked over to the alarm and disabled it by using his nightstick to smash it off the wall. The alarm didn't sound, which was not reassuring. Then he came back over to the group and they led Rick and Randy downstairs to the basement.

No one fought, no one tried to run. They led them into separate rooms and tied them up, using thick silver duct tape looped under their jaws and chins and around the top of their heads so they couldn't shout. They duct-taped their faces around the nose, making sure they could breathe, and then they handcuffed them to radiators, asked if they were comfortable and then left them there for an hour and twenty minutes.

The police released photos of what was done to Rick and Randy that night. They are quite strange pictures. Rick's face is wrapped up in duct tape and he's handcuffed, hands behind his back. It doesn't seem to be a reconstruction because the tape is stuck to his long wavy hair and looks uncomfortably close to his eyes. If it isn't a reconstruction then, when the police arrived at eight thirty the next morning following a panicked call from the locked-out day shift, they must have refused to take the tape off Rick until the police photographer arrived. Rick loved his hair. It came down halfway to his elbows, looked like a perm but wasn't. Everyone has a peak look, one that they never quite move on from because it has so many happy associations for them. It becomes their forever style. Rick loved his poodle rocker hair so much that he never changed it. Decades later he was photographed in the street and still had the same hairdo.

Back to that night: the motion sensors in the museum tracked the robbers coming back from tying up Rick and Randy in the basement. This is what they did then:

They walked up one more flight of stairs to the Dutch Room on the first floor. They walked straight over to Rembrandt's only sea painting, Christ in the Storm on the Sea of Galilee and his A Lady and Gentleman in Black. They took the frames down from the wall, lay them on their backs, lifted the frames off and sliced the canvases out of the wooden stretcher frames.

They took down an etched self-portrait by Rembrandt, a young one in which Rembrandt is jaunty and happy, before he knew much of death and before his compulsive behaviour ruined his life. It was on paper, sandwiched *between the protective glass covering and a wooden board.*

But this was more complicated and speaks to their state of mind. There was an extra sheet of paper behind the etching, sitting between it and the board. When they laid the picture on its face and cut around the tape holding the frame to the back, they lifted the board, discarded it and stole the extra sheet of paper instead of the priceless etching.

Oblivious, they moved on. They picked up a Vermeer. They turned their attention to a Chinese drinking vessel, stuck to the table with a heavy base. They tried hard to get it off, battering it until it became detached.

One of the robbers went off, walking down a long corridor, through the Early Italian room, passing Piero della Francescas and gilt altarpieces, through the Raphael Room, to the Short Gallery.

This was a small room with wooden cabinets on the walls like shutters covered in priceless drawings. They went straight to the Degas drawings and took them down. Then they tried to get the finial of a Napoleonic flag out of its casing. The casing was fiddly though and, according to the motion sensors, one man was in here for quite some time while his comrade was slicing up priceless masterpieces in the Dutch Room. He gave up on the flag and just pulled the eagle off the top and took that. Then he went back to the Dutch Room, following the exact same route the motion sensor had traced Randy taking half an hour before they arrived at the door.

Either before they came up to the first floor, or after they'd been there, they turned the corner to the North Cloister, went through another two rooms crammed with valuable ornaments and artwork and went into the Blue Room. They took one small painting from here: Édouard Manet's Chez Tortoni.

Even for Manet, it's a small painting, just 26 x 30 cm. It

171

was hung on the wall underneath a far larger Manet. The bigger painting is a portrait of Manet's mother dressed in mourning clothes. Financially this is significant because it is not only a painting by Manet but one that addresses his personal biography, which adds value. Because the image is of his grieving mother it will be cited in most major biographies, referred to whenever his life story is told. And it's bigger.

By contrast Tortoni's was a cafe in Paris where aspiring writers and artists hung out. It wasn't a grieving mother. It was just somewhere he went sometimes.

In Chez Tortoni, a man in a top hat and black suit sits at a table with a large glass of white wine, a window behind him. He's writing something but looks up at the viewer with a slightly startled gaze, as if he has just noticed the painter or us, the viewer. The brushwork is soupy, and in the centre and foreground of the painting are his hands. One is flat and passive, holding paper flat while the other one, his right hand, holds a yellow pen.

The robbers spent an unheard-of eighty-one minutes robbing the museum of very specific items, almost like a shopping list. They stole thirteen items that night, collectively valued at $500 million. After the sacking of Rome, it was the highest value art robbery recorded in history.

There were many suspects. The Irish Mafia, the Italians, Whitey Bulger, a random gang of two, Poodle Rock Rick with the wavy hair, another guard who'd recently left and knew how lax the security measures were. It's not that interesting.

What is interesting is that not one of those items has ever been found. Not one. And no one involved has ever come forward.

Despite the FBI weighing in, despite a reward of $10 million, despite the supernova egos of individual art investigators, not one trace of the stolen artworks has ever been recovered. That's unusual. That's strange.

Whoever took them, whoever got them, whoever ordered them, they were frightening enough to have that kind of hold over everyone involved.

Isabella Stewart Gardner left instructions in her will that the exhibits in her museum were never to be moved or sold or added to, and if they were, then the entire collection should be sold at auction and the proceeds given to Harvard University. Because of this legal stricture, the curators left the empty frames on the wall with a small notice explaining the absence to visitors.

The works were either hidden or destroyed; the museum says it expects to get the items back because they are so famous. They have to say that. Admitting the loss is permanent vitiates the conditions of the Trust.

What investigators never say is this: someone chose those paintings carefully. They didn't pick the most marketable or the most expensive. They didn't even choose the best of their kind. Someone chose the ones they liked. The ones that spoke to them.

They didn't pick a set either, most of them didn't go together. Some of them did speak of a certain taste: the Vermeer was a fine companion to the Rembrandts. The Chinese vessel and the Napoleonic finial may have been taken for resale. Maybe the Manet was as well.

If they were going to sell those things they would need a specialist, a dealer, a smuggler in questionable items who wouldn't ask questions and knew buyers all over the world. Someone like Bram van Wyk.

The reward for information was a complication. $10 million was a fraction of the value of the stolen items, but still plenty to some. It created a small industry of amateur detectives looking for clues, listening to local gossip.

173

Any potential lead was thoroughly explored by the army of people who were now investigating the theft. Nothing was ever heard apart from baseless rumours and outright fabrications. This suggests that it was done by people with a lot of power, a lot of money and an intense interest in never being found.

It was always suspected that the robbery was done to the order of one of the richest criminal gangs working in Boston at that time. In the decades since the robbery, many of those families have left their criminal backgrounds behind. It was another generation, after all.

Fingerprints on a single, significant object have been used to link someone to a crime but, more importantly, when that person is found and interviewed, their movements and contacts have been used in investigations, and in court, to link them to networks of people, dangerous people, powerful people.

Any single loose thread could lead to every member of that family being arrested, their fortunes being seized and anyone unlucky enough to be that missing thread would be in danger of being quietly disappeared.

18

Paris was wild in the run-up to the Voyniche Casket auction. In the images online it looks as if it was full of crazy people but I was there and it wasn't like that.

A lot of people had come a long way to be there and, for many, it would be the most profound spiritual experience of their lives. It was humbling to witness their sincerity. It made me yearn for the comfort of faith, for conviction and community and fervour, instead of the melancholy conviction that always haunts me, that nothing really matters and death is the end. Bram said he felt it too. We were jealous and moved.

Our car from Le Bourget Airport dropped us four blocks from the auction house, on the Rue Royale, a wide avenue being used for the very Haussmannian purpose of controlling a riotous assembly. A chaotic mob had gathered around the mouth of the Rue du Faubourg Saint-Honoré. They were in festive mood though.

Metal barricades had been erected across the street entrance to keep everyone out and a large black police van behind it blocked their view. The crowd clustered at either side, trying to see past it.

The Villeneuve Auction House was in a shop-fronted property in a commercial street. But it was also straight across from the Élysée Palace, the official residence of the President of France. It couldn't have been a more secure or securable location.

As we walked down the Rue Royale people spilled

out into traffic and drivers made liberal use of their horns. I found myself scanning the faces for Lisa Lee and saw her sometimes: looking forward as she filmed herself, glancing shyly, smiling or catching sight of herself and cringing.

Marcos was reading out the placards. There were a lot of different agendas jostling with each other: prayers and demands, saints being invoked, cases being pleaded, all in different languages. Some were in Hebrew, some Chinese, some Cyrillic.

Most of the people there didn't have placards or agendas. Most of them just wanted to be near the casket and were rubbernecking the sights just as we were. Some were praying or singing in groups or silently standing alone to the side, eyes cast down. We passed one young woman on her own, underweight and overwhelmed, slumped against a wall, weeping, her thin hands clasped in front of her. Later I heard she died on her way home and people have started praying to her.

But everyone was excited to be here, so near to a possible proof. It felt as if we were on the brink of something huge happening. The Rapture or the Second Coming. The world watched and held its breath.

The French police were unmoved. They carried guns across their chests and bullied their way around the crowd, demanding passports and information, heavy-handedly shoving at people when they blocked traffic or got too close to the metal barricades.

'We shouldn't be going to see it,' whispered Bram. '*They* should be able to see it.'

He led us up to the mouth of the Rue du Faubourg Saint-Honoré and approached the cop in charge. He showed him a code on his phone to verify that he was a registered bidder in the auction: viewing of the Voyniche Casket was not open to everyone. The cop glanced at it, scanned it with his own phone, asked to see Bram's passport and photo ID from all of us. He checked our papers and walked away without speaking, disappearing behind the big black van.

He came back and uncoupled the barricade without looking at any of us or explaining that we could come through and gestured impatiently when we hesitated. We slipped through, passed down the side of the van and entered the empty street.

The shops were shut and shuttered. Cameras whirred on rooftops and lamp posts. Helicopters circled overhead. Further on, at a turn in the road, two burly cops held machine guns and tracked our approach.

We passed them and came upon a wooden platform in the middle of the road, built for the press to broadcast from. There was no one there now, just seats and mic stands. Concrete bollards blocked off all of the surrounding roads.

The air was crisp and bright and a cold breeze found its way around the gold sandstone buildings. The wide forecourt of the Élysée Palace lent the street in front of the auction house a wide-open aspect. The security officers there were very vigilant, briefed to shoot anyone acting odd and we were certainly that. I'd have shot us.

It was only then that I noticed how nervous Bram suddenly was. The pink had drained from his cheeks and his breathing was shallow. I hoped he wasn't planning to steal the casket or do anything dangerous but I knew he was planning something.

We stopped in front of a shop with three high

arched windows with pale grey blinds half drawn. Bram looked up into the camera above the doors and they swung open slowly.

We followed him in.

It was dark, took a moment for my eyes to adjust to the grey light.

Just inside the doors stood a man in a pale grey suit, narrow shouldered, with a small pencil moustache. He greeted Bram, bowing and welcoming him back.

'For you, Monsieur Bram van Wyk,' said the man, perfectly accenting Bram's name as he handed him a hardback catalogue of the items in the sale.

Bram took it and nodded, flipping it open to the centre spread photo of the casket. It was the image WBGrates had sent us, the one on the website.

Accustomed to the dark now, I could see a man and woman at the back of the room, he sitting at a yellow walnut desk, she standing next to him. She was slim and young, wearing a very tight pencil skirt and white blouse and holding a tray of champagne flutes.

She walked across the room, eliciting an appreciative collective sigh, even from me. Her honey-blonde hair hung loose about her shoulders, her lipstick scarlet. Her heels were so high that the sight of them made me arch my back and thank fuck it wasn't me wearing them.

She strode over to us expertly, the glasses of champagne held perfectly steady. When she reached us she tipped her head a little to the side, her hair tumbling softly over her shoulder. I didn't take one and neither did Fin but Bram did. Even Marcos took one, which I didn't agree with, but after one sip his whole face puckered and he put it back on the tray.

178

She tried me again, disappointed that I didn't want a drink, and then turned her attention to Fin. At the sight of him her shoulders dropped, her spine seemed to soften. They matched. She was as tall and slim as he, as effortlessly chic. If they had been dogs I would have attempted to breed them.

She offered him a champagne flute.

'Thank you very much, but no.'

I saw her eyes flicking between Fin and the rest of the company, trying to make sense of the connection. If my French had been better I'd have told her that we didn't really know what we were all doing together either.

The man from the desk came over. This was Philippe, a handsome man with a head of thick white hair and the air of someone who didn't really need a job.

'Bram, hi. Looking forward to seeing it again?'

'Philippe, yah . . .' They kissed each other's cheeks as if they were bored.

'A reunion for us.'

Philippe said we would all have to hand in our bags and phones before we went into the viewing. The man at the door held out a small black box.

'No.' Bram took his satchel off over his head. 'We're recording for a podcast so we'll be taking a voice recorder in.' He handed his tatty satchel to Philippe. 'But you can hold on to this for me.'

Philippe wasn't sure that was OK and had to make a call to check. We got permission but he looked the little recorder over first, making sure there was no camera on it.

Philippe gave it back to Fin and took Bram's bag with a thumb and forefinger pinch, keeping it away

179

from his body and handing it to the beautiful woman.

Bram watched and then looked her up and down, his eyes coming to rest on her breasts. I didn't like that. I slipped between them to shield her from his leery gaze.

But she was irritated by me, more than she was by Bram. She sidled around me to him, which left the three of us standing in an uncomfortably tight knot.

We put our phones in the box as Fin fitted the mic to the DAT machine.

Bram teased Philippe: 'So, who did you say is selling this casket?'

Philippe gave a dry dutiful laugh, halfway between a cough and an expression of disgust. 'Oh, Bram. You know how it is. Please —' and he raised an arm to a small door at the back of the empty room.

Bram strode across to it, neither slowing nor breaking stride and the door unlocked and opened to meet his outstretched hand.

We were in.

The viewing room was lined in black velvet and it felt like standing inside a jewellery box. Air conditioning kept the temperature cool, the lighting was soft and black plinths of varying heights were topped with glass covers, each down-lit with its own spotlight. A camera turned languidly towards us, moving around the group, taking us in.

'Why won't he tell you who the seller is?' I asked.

'That's standard. They don't want people contacting the seller independently and arranging a private sale. The auction house gets a high cut of the hammer price.'

There were other viewers in the room already, all expensively dressed and quaffed, standing well away from each other. A large woman with scarlet hair whispered to a man as they stared at a Benin bronze head.

Two men stared wordlessly at a small black box.

Another man walked slowly round the room, nodding, hands clasped behind his back as though he didn't trust himself.

Fin held the mic up to Bram and the scarlet-haired woman saw it and nudged her companion. Uncertain about what was going on with the recorder, they left.

On the nearest plinth a gold choker was perched on a glass stand, a glint of blood red in the middle. Bram smiled at it and moved over to stand in front of a blackened icon. It was small, the size of a cigarette packet, looked like nothing at all, but Bram's shoulders dropped in awe.

'Wow.'

'Can you describe what we're looking at?' asked Fin, holding up the mic.

'Sure,' said Bram. '*We're in the viewing room of the Villeneuve, one of the oldest auction houses in the world. The President is across the road, it's a rich place, in power, in history, in money. We're looking at the auction items in tomorrow's sale.*

'*Over there is a gorget from Ireland, Bronze Age, a gold choker with a ruby inset and enamelling. Would have belonged to a queen. Found near Dublin.*

'*Here, this small icon, is from the workshop of a master in Georgia, icon of the Theotokos, which means 'bearer of God' which is a better translation than 'mother of God', you know? More accurate to what is said in the New Testament. A Theotokos of the Hodegetria. This is where Mary, the Theotokos, is presenting the child Christ as a saviour to the audience. These are technical terms, you don't really need to worry about them. But here —*' he stepped

181

around a plinth to the dead centre of the room — *'is the Voyniche Casket. I last saw this on a boat in the Adriatic thirty years ago.'*

It was delightful to listen to Bram talk so knowledgeably about these things. He knew so much about it all. His eyes flared and his face softened as he leaned into the well-lit plinths. Familiar with the history and terminology, he had nothing to prove or sell, he just loved these things, and his pleasure and his awe were enchanting. Even Marcos smiled as his father talked, respectful of the joy he radiated. He liked Bram in that moment.

Suddenly the room felt warmer, not uncomfortably so, just right, in fact.

Fin was smiling and so was I as we gathered around the glass box.

The casket was smaller than I had expected but almost painful to look at. It was like staring into a neon sign. The white spotlight shimmered on the polished silver. The detail was amazing, the faces so well defined I could have picked out any of the characters in a line-up, and the careful inscription of Pilate's name on the top was legible, looked fresh and new. My eyes strained to make sense of the light-reflecting symbols.

A sudden voice from the ceiling asked us, please, ladies and gentlemen, move back from the display case.

We had all been craning slowly forward, obscuring the view of the security camera.

We stood back and Bram made sure the mic was close by.

He said very loudly, 'Pah!' He looked at Fin. 'This — this is fake. This casket is a fake.'

Surprised, Fin pushed the mic closer to him.

'Yes,' declared Bram, 'I can tell. There was a scratch, right on the gold seal. See? There are no marks there now, where the lid sits on the top.' He was bellowing in the showroom. 'Anyone who buys this is being made a fool of.'

People looked round at us. It was awkward. Embarrassed, Marcos shifted away.

'It's wrong, this casket. It's a copy.'

A small bald man standing behind another plinth snickered nervously. Marcos had come full circle of the room and back over near us.

'Fake!' said Bram to the camera in the ceiling. 'A fake.'

'You're lying,' said Marcos plainly.

'FUCK OFF AND STAND OVER THERE,' ordered Bram.

Marcos did as he was told, shuffling carefully backwards, eyes down.

'This is a fake,' repeated Bram to no one in particular. 'A copy of the Voyniche Casket. You have been tricked into listing it as an original. Let's go.'

We went over to the exit but it didn't open. Bram stepped back into the room and motioned to one of the cameras. The door unlocked with a whirr and we walked back out into the main room.

'I need to see Philippe,' called Bram to the room. 'I need to talk to him right now.'

The atmosphere was electric. The blonde came over with our box of phones. She liked me even less now. I said we had a train to catch to London in less than two hours, did she know where we'd be likely to catch a cab?

She was curt with us. We'd have to walk back the

way we came to beyond the cordon. Taxis were all very busy so good luck.

She'd heard from Bram and knew something unplanned was happening, something bad.

We stood outside, the machine-gun men vigilantly staring at us. The door locked softly behind us: click, crunch, whirr.

'Fin, we should move.'

'Yeah,' said Fin, and we started to walk back to the van. 'Is he saying it's a fake so he can get a better price? But isn't provenance important?'

'Hammersmith doesn't care about the provenance, he's not selling it on.'

We hurried out through the barricades and found a taxi immediately.

'*Gare du Nord, s'il vous plait.*'

He pulled out, found the road blocked by a group of religious tourists and sat on his horn until they moved.

I told Fin then what Marcos had confided in me back in Glasgow: Bram had a copy made of the casket. I thought he'd only told me because he wanted to fuck his dad up and expected to get away from all of us.

Fin was surprised at that but said Marcos was trying not to be like his father, not be duplicitous. He was trying to differentiate himself.

'Where would you even get something like that made?'

I didn't know. Fin looked it up. The most skilled silversmiths in the world were in Thessaloniki in Greece, he said. The secret skills had been handed down from generation to generation over two thousand years.

I nodded. 'That stupid hat with the gold braiding was from Greece.'

Fin brightened. 'They'd just been there. It was a giveaway. That's why Bram wanted to get rid of it.'

'And why Marcos wanted to keep it.'

He was going to sell the fake to Paul Hammersmith, a man who had already blown millions of dollars on shoddy fakes from fraudsters.

We sat back and looked out of the window at the throng, at the fake Messiahs and humble pilgrims. They tailed back all the way to Place de L'Opéra.

I was glad we were getting out of Paris, if only for the afternoon.

19

Alan Johansson's house was in Cavendish Mansions on the Clerkenwell Road. It was a nice area, trendy and full of coffee shops and small restaurants. I'd expected a slightly nicer building, as had Trina Keany, our podcast partner who lived in London and met us at the train.

'Oh,' said Trina when we got out of the cab.

'Hm,' said Fin.

It was a tall brick Victorian building on a very busy road with a defensive workhouse-y facade. The windows were small, the stairwell was open to the elements and painted council-grey up to shoulder height and then white. The entrance was sprayed with paint and a big turquoise sign on the wall identified it. 'Mansions' seemed a bit of a hollow boast.

'Social housing in London though,' said Trina, 'lucky people, still.'

We buzzed the intercom. Alan had forgotten we were coming but he let us in and told us not to take the lift because it kept breaking down and it stank. The lobby didn't smell too good either, a mix of urine and bleach. Alan was three flights up.

We found the door, knocked and waited. We could hear a loud telly. Footfalls inside as someone shuffled to the door. It opened a crack and he peered out with one eye like a nervous shut-in, saw it was us and opened the door a little wider.

Alan Johansson was a very big man. He filled the door frame upwards and outwards, a chubby giant swathed in a washed-out Darth Vader T-shirt with the legend 'I AM YOUR FATHER'. His hair was black and thick and his stubble so dark it looked like the mould in Lisa's film. He looked as if he hadn't slept.

Alan couldn't remember what we'd texted about ourselves but listened carefully as Fin told him that we had a podcast and that the arrangement wasn't for next week but today.

'Oh yeah, that. Forgot, sorry, bit of a night . . . Come in.' Using the side of his foot, he slid an ancient sleeping cat out of the way and opened the door.

'This is Maggie,' said Alan of the cat. 'Maggie's nineteen so she gets to sleep wherever she likes.'

Maggie was fat with greying fur pitted with bald patches that looked red and sore. She raised her head and half opened her eyes up as we slid sideways, one at a time, into the cramped hall.

Fin leaned down to pet her but Maggie didn't appreciate it. She craned her neck to escape the touch without bothering to get up and move.

The narrow hall was busy with coats and shoes and bags and smelled of toast and milk on the turn. A bassinet pram was crammed against the wall. It had been parked and moved from there many times: there were massive chips in the paintwork where it banged against the wall. A sound of forced laughter from a children's cartoon was coming from the front room.

The flat was small, every room needed sidling through, and it was dark, painted by someone with a taste for deep colours and the wrong brush. In the purple hall every stroke was visible, so thick that, at first glance, it looked like textured Artex.

'Come on,' said Alan and opened a door into a tangerine living room. The way in was partly barred by a sofa back, where a big woman sat facing an enormous TV on the wall. She looked over her shoulder and muttered, 'Yeah?'

'This is Harriet,' said Alan and introduced us as friends of those Belgian blokes, Florian and Gregor.

We sidestepped in a single line around the sofa and into the room proper.

Harriet was breastfeeding a very new baby with a head so big it made me flinch. She saw me and gave me a tired, sweet smile, 'Yeah, ol' big head, here,' she said and grinned.

I winced. 'Well done!' I said.

'Bow to stern,' she said and laughed.

Neither Fin nor Trina knew what that meant and I didn't want to explain. It was too graphic.

'He's given me a hell of a time, haven't you, Bubby? Haven't you, Bubby? Yes, Bubby, you have.'

Harriet wore pink brushed-cotton pyjamas with red love hearts on them and looked exhausted but very happy. Her skin was dry and flaky and her kinked hair rippled with crazy greys, looking like a cushion a child had been punching.

Alan pointed at the baby. 'Baby Justin,' he said, unable to look away from his son.

The baby was chubby, the fat folded over at his wrists. He looked incredibly content.

'Baby Justin . . .' echoed Harriet, mesmerised by the child.

She met Alan's eye and they both smiled, still in that golden moment when first-time parents believe that the miracle of their child, so evident to them, will be recognised by the rest of the world.

Unembarrassed, Harriet took him off the breast, slipped her giant nipple back in her PJ top and sat big-headed Justin on her knee, supporting his head with a finger and thumb on either side of his chin.

Justin looked astonished. She barely rubbed his back once when a burp surprised him and brought up a flying teaspoonful of milk that landed on the floor. Harriet and Alan both cooed until Maggie ambled out from under the sofa and tried to eat it and then they chased her out shouting at her *Dirty cat!* and *No!* and *Out, Maggie!* Baby Justin watched all of this, following the cat with his floppy neck, amazed at this brand-new world.

Fin asked to hold him and Harriet handed him over. He held him tenderly, flattening the big baby to his chest, nuzzling his face into his wispy hair and drew in a lungful of his smell. Then he gave him to Trina.

She held the baby close, kissed his head, told Harriet that she had nieces and nephews and loved babies, which was news to me. She just loved them.

'Go on,' said Harriet. 'Smell his hair.'

Trina took a lungful and held it. She's lovely, Trina, patient with Fin and me and all our nonsense. She's been very kind to us. Fin knows her better than me and has guided her through the pitfalls of mild celebrity since her podcast took off. They spend an awful lot of time together, editing.

She gave the baby back, her eyes lingering on the details of him, his arms, his chubby little legs, his molten expression that shifted from horrified to delighted in a moment. She was mirroring him unconsciously, grinning then frowning. Fin didn't give me the baby, I noticed. I took it as a comment on my

189

parenting skills.

'Come on into the kitchen,' said Alan and we all turned sideways and shuffled off. Harriet called after us, apologising for the mess.

The kitchen was tiny and messy. Drying baby clothes hung on the radiator, empty milk cartons and dirty cups and plates cluttered the sink. Black crumbs of toast, a pot of honey and an open carton of marg sat on a small table with three seats. Fin stood against the worktop and let us take the chairs.

'So,' said Alan, licking a finger and wiping up toast crumbs from the tabletop to put in his mouth, 'what is this about then? Why'd Flor and Greg give you my deets?'

Fin explained that we wanted to ask about his trip to the chateau. Lisa Lee had disappeared. Alan was shocked by that. He didn't watch the news. He didn't trust it. He got his news from YouTube.

Fin asked if he could record but Alan said he'd rather we didn't. He didn't know why, he just felt strange about it, which was honest, if annoying. But this is what he told us:

Right from the off, he didn't like Lisa or trust her.

He knew Florian and Gregor from before. They'd been over here on a shoot, down Southampton way, and a mate asked Alan if he'd use his drone to get them an overhead shot. Alan was happy to do it, it wasn't far and well, yeah, the shots turned out really good actually, and Fin and Greg paid him cash, good money for a morning, so that was pretty great. He was part of a community history project and that was how he got the drone in the first place, bit of fun, so it was nice to get paid for a hobby, you know? Then after that they asked him, maybe three times that year, gave him first refusal, because they liked his footage so much. If he could do it, he did. Happy to. Nice blokes, Florian and Gregor. But this time was different.

First of all it was in France, which Alan didn't mind, it's not that far and they were paying handsome but he didn't know if he needed permission. They said not to worry about that, though they weren't really supposed to be there anyway, which did sort of worry Alan. They were younger than him. He'd be the one to get in most trouble if they all got caught, he felt.

Then there was the Scottish girl, Lisa, she was there too when he got there. He didn't know her, she was their mate, but they'd had a bit of an argument on the way down. It was a funny atmos, you know? Not like before when it was just them and him. He didn't know if one of them was going out with her or what, but it wasn't nice.

Anyway, Alan never went in the house because he was worried about what they'd said, yeah? He'd done the job though and gave them the footage on a USB and was packing up to go home when Lisa came out of the house at the side and she was crying. She didn't like it in there. Gave her the creeps. And he sat with her and she was crying and he saw her arms.

Cutting herself. Quite bad. Long-term. He felt for her.

Alan was pretty low at that time, but that trip wasn't nice, and it wasn't just his mood. She didn't want to drive back with Florian and Gregor. She said they'd been picking on her in the house, but Alan didn't know if that was true, they didn't seem the types, but she was a bit all-over-the-place and he didn't want to leave her with them, in case, you know? She was upset. He said she could get the ferry with him as he was driving. She said she'd go with him to Dover and he could drop her at a train station and she could make her way back to Glasgow.

They left after Florian and Gregor. She never said much but she'd found a letter in the place, with the owners' Paris address on it and she was going to contact them, she did say that. Didn't want to talk to Alan, they got stuck in Calais for hours because a ferry broke down, but she was chatty with other people. Met a man on the ferry, chatted away to him quite happily, so she wasn't shy or anything. But she was quiet when she was alone with Alan.

Maybe she needed to talk to someone who hadn't been there because she talked to that other man for a long time.

It happened as he dropped her at Orpington Station. When he got her luggage out the back the shoulder bag, the one she had in the house, it was well heavy, like it had a big bottle of water in it, like three-litre-bottle-of-Coke-style heavy.

She was looking at the station, at where to get her ticket, and he looked in. It was a big silver thing. Something from the house. She'd nicked it.

'I mean, that — that is so not right. I could get done for that, you know? I'm already in bloody France as a bit of a favour. I's really angry. I'm only bringing her home because I feel sorry for her and she's went and done that. No.'

Did he say anything to her?

No, he said, what was the point? He made her give him the Paris address of the people that owned the chateau though, and he wrote them a note, posted it on the way home, explaining that he hadn't gone in there at any point. He didn't take anything. He did it

192

to cover his back. Why should he get into trouble?

He'd come home a bit low and didn't think they'd see each other again because it had all gone wrong, and he was a bit sad about it because Florian and Gregor were nice. But then, when he got home — Alan changed over the course of the telling. He was bent over, shoulders rounded, chin down, but at this part of the story he straightened up and looked to the living room behind my head and began to glow — when he got home Harriet was waiting for him and she told him then that she was preggers and they were going to have a baby. They'd been trying for such a long time and it just kept not happening. Then he came home and she said she was expecting. Fin reached over, took Alan's hand in both of his and squeezed it. Alan was as surprised as I was by that. I think he was a bit uncomfortable and peeled his hand away.

But Trina grinned and asked if Alan spoke to the man on the ferry.

'Nah.' He sighed here, glanced back out at Harriet and Justin to remind himself that they were real.

Then she asked him to describe the man.

'He was about fifty, you know, older? Foreign. Dressed nice, smart suit, loafers. Said he was going to Scotland on holiday and she was telling him about where she lived. I thought Lisa fancied him. Then the horn sounded and we had to go back to the van.'

He gave us the family's address in Paris.

I asked, 'Have you ever seen that man again, Alan?'

'No.' He looked towards the kitchen door. 'Anyway, I've been busy with other things, you know?'

And he smiled, remembering that it wasn't those times any more, that it was now, and he was happy in his small warm flat that smelled of toast and milk and honey.

I told him, 'If you see that man again, if he comes here, lock the doors and call the police.'

20

It was dark when we got back to Paris. As we stepped out of the Gare du Nord both our phones pinged. Bram had sent us a text: he had booked us rooms in a fancy hotel on the Place Vendôme, three blocks from the auction house, he and Marcos were in the master suite, and he had booked a table at Saint George VI. We were to meet them both in the lobby in an hour.

We decided not to go. We were scared of him.

Every word from Bram's mouth was a lie, it had been him on the ferry, the satchel was a giveaway, but we couldn't figure out why he was pretending not to know Lisa Lee, why he had come to get us, why he would involve witnesses to all of this or confide that he was Paul Hammersmith's agent. He might not know that Marcos had told us about the copy of the casket but he must have known that his son was unreliable, angry with him and trying to mess up his plans. The chaos made him more frightening.

I didn't even know if we should come back to Paris but Trina and Fin both felt it would be a missed opportunity for a great story. We decided to say that we had missed the last train back. We would turn up in the morning to go to the auction with him. Our main reservation was leaving Marcos alone with him.

So we stood outside the station, in the eddy of commuters and beggars and cops and pickpockets in the forecourt and tried to book a hotel for the night but Paris was full. Even Airbnb was full. The closest rooms we could find were forty kilometres away and that wasn't even close to a train station. We'd have to go to the hotel, to Bram and Marcos. We had no option.

We should be seen with him by as many people as possible, said Fin. It made it less likely that he'd kill us.

We walked to the hotel, turning it over, guessing meanings that made no sense, trying to see it from Bram's point of view. He'd met Lisa on the ferry and she had the casket with her. He wanted the casket to swap for the painting. Did he know that she had it with her? Probably not. How did he know she'd be on the ferry? Why had he followed her if he didn't know where the chateau was? Did he go to North Berwick? Did he kill her? Why would he take the risk of being recognised by going back?

We started from the beginning and tried another hypothesis: Bram wanted the casket to exchange for the painting. He thought Eugene was dead. Did he do a deal with Lisa on the ferry? Did he have a copy made to exchange for the painting but then the real casket turned up?

Honestly, it was like cutting through a sweater to look for something and ending up with a handful of loose wool.

On the other hand, said Fin, Bram was not a fit man and murder was probably a prohibitive amount of cardio for him.

Maybe he didn't kill her. If she was WBGrates and DMd us two days after she disappeared, she was probably still alive. She must have contacted the family in Paris and we had their contact details from Alan.

We stopped in a cafe, I called the number and got put through to a voicemail account. I left a message saying we were Fin and Anna, friends of Lisa's, and we were in Paris. We'd like to speak to someone, if that was at all possible but we'd understand if not. I left my mobile number but I didn't expect a reply. If Lisa were alive and interested in our whereabouts we'd be easy enough for her to find: the Paris pilgrims were posting every sighting of every player on social media and we were there with Bram. She could probably tell us what we'd had for breakfast.

We ordered wine and sat and talked for the first time in a long time. It was nice. Fin was sorry for getting in the car but not sorry that we were here, doing this again, and I wasn't sorry either. I smoked a little and sat quietly.

'Is that Sofia out of the picture then?'

'Yeah. She's going back to Milan. Back to her family.'

'I'm sorry for asking her to come. I can see why you didn't want her there, she wasn't very nice to you.'

'I wasn't very nice to her.'

'That's the low self-esteem talking.'

He smirked. 'You don't know me, Anna, not very well.'

I was quite indignant about that. 'I think I'm a fairly astute judge of character, to be honest.'

'Everyone does. You think I'm a dickless wonder because you can't be friends with me unless I'm a dickless wonder, but I'm not, not really. I love you. You're safe with me. I got in the car because I was afraid of leaving you on your own, not because I'm afraid of confronting Sofia. There's stuff going on that you don't know about —'

My phone rang and I was so annoyed and distracted by Fin that I answered it without thinking. It was Jess.

'Oh, hello, darling!' I said and cringed.

She was excited and happy, over at her friend's house for a sleepover with some popular girls. Lizzie was home with Daddy and Estelle. They were going to the cinema. I heard the girls laughing in the background, shouting over each other the way girls do. I thought the conversation would be OK, light and meaningless, but then Jess moved away to a quiet place to speak and my heart tightened in my chest. I slumped over the table and covered my eyes with my hands.

She spoke as if she had rehearsed it: 'Mum? You know that thing Sofia said —'

I said, oh, listen, no, there's a lot you don't understand, you're too young. Sofia's very angry with Fin. They barely know each other and, well, *that's* a real shame but, I mean, come on. She was annoying. You're too young to really understand that, don't worry about it.

I was wilfully misunderstanding, talking over her.

'OK, Jess?' I wanted to force her to agree, wangle a fraudulent yes out of her mouth. I was so ashamed of myself that I pressed my fingers into my eyes until they burned.

'OK?' I said again. 'OK, Jess?'

'OK,' she said dutifully and then got off the phone as quickly as she could.

I dropped my hand. I was cold. I wished myself gone. Not dead, honestly, just not there. I didn't want this for her. I wasn't really angry at Sofia because Jess already knew, I just didn't want it to be so soon. I thought we had longer together, a longer season of innocence.

I looked at Fin. 'Let's go.'

198

We walked to the Place Vendôme in silence. The dark city glittered and growled, cafes thrummed with drinkers and diners, and taxis and cars sped by us, cyclists dodged us, but all I could think about was the girls and what I had done to them, what the fact of my existence and all the luggage I dragged behind me meant for them.

When we got to the Place Vendôme I wasn't even moved by the grandeur of the setting.

It was a wide and elegant oval of high-end shops and hotels, a space so wealthy that it felt dead. Sleek black cars idled nearby, the uniformed drivers waiting patiently.

Our hotel was across the square from the Ritz and further down, identifiable only by a discreet green awning. Doormen welcomed us and someone bolted over as we walked in and wrestled our plastic shopping bags of hastily bought toiletries away, insisting that he carry them the twenty feet to the desk.

It was a white marbled lobby trimmed with rich brass piping and smelled of jasmine and coconut and fresh starched linen. I could have lain face down on the floor and slept.

We gave Bram's name to the woman at reception.

'Ah,' she smiled at Fin, 'yes, Monsieur van Wyk.' In a way that made me think she didn't know him but was being paid to pretend she did.

As she got on with the gubbins of checking us in, taking our ID away to photocopy, she explained that breakfast was served in our rooms, just call down and they would make anything we wanted.

A bellhop took our keys and invited us to follow him to the elevator, if we would be so kind.

Every member of staff was better dressed and more

refined than us. Fin and I were angry and out of our depth, confused by the story we were in and dressed in travel-worn clothes.

In the lift the bellhop admired Fin's brogues and told him there was an artisan cobbler a street away, he would be happy to effect an introduction? Fin said thank you but we weren't going to be here long. The man looked me over for something to compliment. After a momentary struggle, he said we were very welcome. Then we all stared awkwardly at the back of the lift door. I have never felt more inadequate.

We stepped out on the landing and the man swiped the key card to the door, stepping back and bowing to me.

We walked in. He showed us the features of the room: the bar is here, the bed is here, this is a wardrobe. Then he stood by the door, staring at me until I remembered that I should tip him. I fumbled my purse out of my battered second-hand McQueen handbag and gave him not enough.

He took Fin away.

I turned out the lights and sat on the bed. I was there for a while until my phone pinged a text: it was from the owner of the chateau telling us to come to this address tomorrow at nine.

I stood up with surprise and, at just that moment, an envelope slid under the door, breaking the beam of light from the corridor.

I sprinted over and opened the door, more on impulse than anything else and found the bellhop. He smiled. A letter, madame, hand-delivered to the front desk.

Who by?

He shrugged. A courier, he said. They gave my

name but not my room number. No, he didn't know what they looked like, he hadn't seen them.

I retreated to my room and opened the letter.

It was a handwritten note in childish writing.

This isn't safe. Go home, Anna.
WBGrates

The bar of the A crossed back over from the tail. It made it look like a star. I read the envelope. Just my room number, written by another hand in fat, neat letters.

I called down to the front desk. Who delivered this? The bellhop brought it up, madame. But who delivered it to the hotel? A courier. Young? Old? Oh, she was quite young, red hair, slim. The receptionist had offered to call me but the person only wanted to leave the message. Was she alone? Oh, yes, she said, couriers are always alone.

I took a picture of the words 'home, Anna', sent it to Bob Lees. Was this Lisa's handwriting? Then I felt even worse about myself. I shouldn't be presenting a grieving father with the possibility of hope. His wife had died, his daughter was missing, he'd been told a body was found and then was told it wasn't her. I sent him another text, saying it was from a letter she'd sent a while ago and I wanted to be sure it was from her and not someone posing as her.

My phone buzzed a text from Bob Lees. The handwriting was Lisa's. He sent me a comparison from a note she'd left her sister.

Amy these are my boots and they don't even fit you.
Stop it.

201

The bar of the capital A crossed the letter, turning it into a star.

I called Fin.

'Lisa Lee just dropped a note at reception for me.' I explained what had happened. 'So she's alive and she's in Paris and her hair is red.'

'If she dropped it in herself they might have CCTV of her.'

We met down in reception.

The woman who had checked us in was still behind the desk. She welcomed us warmly by name but cooled off when we asked if they had CCTV in the lobby.

They did, she said, but no, she wouldn't let us see it. The hotel guests relied upon their discretion and other residents might be visible in the background. I argued that the woman we were interested in wasn't a guest, she was someone who had come to drop a letter off for me. A threatening letter. We didn't need a shot of the lobby, just of her face to see if she was who we thought she was. Couldn't they find the image, take a photo just of her face and show it to us?

Please?

She smiled and blinked and we knew she wouldn't do it. She needed to call her manager and let him decide but unfortunately he was not on the premises at this moment but if we were prepared to wait for an answer he would communicate to us his position as soon as he could.

It was luxy hotel for fuck off.

But Lisa wasn't dead so Bram hadn't followed her home and killed her.

We were even more baffled than before.

202

21

We tidied ourselves up as much as we could and took the lift down to the marbled entrance at nine-thirty. There, sitting on a big silver velvet armchair, were Bram and Marcos, dressed in matching new linen suits, blue shirts, Bram's with a green silk cravat tied loosely at his neck. He was stroking his new blue suede loafers. A green cigarette idled, unlit, in his hand. Marcos stood up when he saw us, smiled and greeted us as though we hadn't seen each other for a year.

He was cheerful this evening, lighter, as if he had resigned himself to something or handed in an essay, and Bram was relaxed too.

He asked us how London went and our answer was cagey; Alan said he got Lisa home on the ferry. It was a long journey. Then we both watched to see if Bram would react. Yes, he said, faster to fly. But the ferry journey must be nice, on a good day.

Fin asked him if he'd ever taken the ferry to England before but he just said nah.

Marcos told us about all the crazies he'd see in Paris this afternoon, praying and singing and crying.

'Don't be rude about people's faith,' said Bram with unexpected sincerity. 'It's a beautiful thing. They want to know they're loved. That's all any of us want.'

Then he threw his arm around Marcos's head, turning him to the street and walking him out.

Fin and I followed them out to the rain-washed Place Vendôme.

'Doesn't Marcos look handsome this evening? We went shopping today.'

'Don't patronise me,' said Marcos, but he smiled a little and stroked the pocket on his lovely jacket.

Bram didn't seem to mind his hostility now. They fell into matching stride as we walked down through the arcaded Rue de Castiglione.

It was evening in central Paris but eerily quiet on this street. There were no people, few cars, no taxis. Everything was so tasteful it was making me feel queasy.

Down at the Tuileries Gardens a still, grey sky was topped with a white glow coming from the left bank. Paris was busy somewhere else but not in this ossified district. It felt as if the great thrumming mess of Parisian humanity was near, just over the river or across a park or through a wall, beyond our line of vision. But here all was still and frighteningly calm.

We weaved as we walked, pairing and uncoupling, making our way through the silent streets, Fin and I buoyed by the possibility of Lisa being alive and nearby, Bram on good form and Marcos infected by his dad's mood.

I heard Bram telling Marcos that all would be well and, even when his mum called him back to Marbella, which could happen at any moment by the way, but even when she did, Bram *would* see him again. There wasn't just going to be this one time. And he was going to be rich after this auction, so rich that he'd buy Marcos an apartment around here if he wanted. But Marcos smiled and said he was a kid and kids weren't allowed to own apartments. Okay, said Bram, I'll buy you a school. I'll buy two schools. And you can burn them down if you want. Every kid hates school.

'My daughters love school.'

'Oh,' he said, 'you have kids?'

It was the first time he'd expressed any interest in anything about me. I pretended to be very touched and fake-sobbed and Bram laughed at that and put his arm through mine.

'No, I *like* crazy bitches. Well, I hated school. They beat us with sticks and kept us hungry.'

'I thought you were rich and spoiled,' said Marcos, smirking because he'd finally caught him in a lie.

'Yes.' Bram was only slightly thrown off his stride by that. 'Well, that's what the Juvie warders said, as they beat us. I was glad to get back to my parents' stud farm.'

'You didn't say they had a stud farm.'

'Oh. What did I say?'

Marcos shrugged. 'An estate or something?'

'Then that's what it was!' he declared and linked arms with his smirking son, 'You don't want to know the truth, kid, it's better I make it up.'

I have to say this: this Bram was quite a different creature from earlier Bram. He walked taller, he was kinder, quicker to laugh at himself. I didn't know what had happened.

'So did you get some good news?'

He shrugged. 'Oh, maybe I came to an accommodation with some people, maybe,' he said and treated himself to a quiet little smile.

'About a certain painting?'

'Possibly.'

'So you won't have to say goodbye to Marcos?'

He grinned, looking back at Fin and Marcos who had dropped quite far behind. 'Maybe not. I want to keep being his father for a little longer. I think I can work it all out after all.'

We'd reached what seemed to be the edge of the dead zone. We could see people at the end of the road.

'Where are we going?' called Fin.

'In here,' said Bram.

It looked like a shop or the lobby of another hotel. The glass walls were smoked but when we stepped inside the floor was white, the room made dazzlingly bright by mirrored walls. A grey-suited man behind a mirrored desk greeted us, bowed when Bram gave him his name and invited us to go through a door. There didn't seem to be signs anywhere. In the next room, beautiful, panelled in cherry wood, another man took us to a brass lift and shut the cage door on us. It rose gracefully to a red foyer with oxblood leather walls and a huge pistachio-green door.

Through the door, we stepped into an exquisite ballroom decorated in Louis XIV style. Foxed mirrored walls made this room seem vast and busy. A giant oval painting was set into the panelling, a pastel scene of a gentleman in white silk jacket and britches gaily pushing a pink-cheeked woman on a swing garlanded with roses. Tables were covered in immaculate white cloths, stiff with starch, set with silver and fine bone china. The floor mosaic was of fleur-de-lys lozenges. Huge curtains of pale-green watered silk framed windows that overlooked the park and enormous chandeliers rained soft orange light over the room.

The style was opulent and baroque. When we walked in I assumed it a vulgar, heavy-handed recreation, but after tasting the food I think the décor was genuine and antique. If it had survived the Nazi occupation it must have collaborated. I could imagine this very room full of Nazi officers. I still can't think of anything more Parisian than startling beauty coupled with moral opportunism.

It was a room that commanded lowered voices and quiet steps. Everyone was in conservative French uniform, well-fitted suits, mute colours with occasional flashes of peach or red. We shambled in like a circus act who had won a voucher.

The maître d' sat us down, masking his superiority very well. When I went to put my quite worn McQueen handbag on the floor a man appeared out of nowhere and slid a small velvet stool underneath it. The restaurant was so mannered that it was a little bit bizarre, like one of those dreams where you're onstage but don't know your lines.

We ordered and were served aperitifs and Bram proposed a toast: to the Voyniche Casket, to the real one, which was not in the sale on the Rue du Faubourg Saint-Honoré. He had a way of fixing everything and then we could all go home. It was very nice to meet you, Fin and Anna.

Marcos was pleased. Fin was relieved. Bram was smug. I didn't want to go home. Home was the very last place I wanted to go and I didn't want this to be the end of the story.

But maybe it was. Maybe we'd find Lisa alive and well, Bram would go off and become a good dad, Marcos could be happy, Fin would make a great podcast. Maybe everyone would be happy except me.

Well, there's another fifty pages so obviously that isn't what happened but, at this moment, in this restaurant, before the note was delivered to the table, that was the end. Life is a series of moments.

OK, said Bram, now we'll have a meal celebrating

this week, Holy Week. He called the waiter over and ordered for everyone except Fin, the vegan, because he didn't understand that. The waiter offered an off-menu vegan-compromise.

When he left Fin whispered to Marcos, 'It's going to be fancy pasta. It's always just fancy pasta.'

It was not just fancy pasta. Nothing was just anything in that restaurant.

I usually have no memory for food. I can remember that I liked eating somewhere and I could probably remember whether it was a bag of chips or a lobster, but I have no memory for flavours. Something could register as pleasurable or very pleasurable, but that's about it. That meal, though, comes back in similes and snapshot images: bread rolls that were still warm inside with a crust so fine that it broke like an egg.

A butter pat served with greaseproof paper on it with the name of the restaurant printed on it in red. The butter tasted of rain and had an aftertaste of very mild, fresh cheese.

A single circular raviolo in a pool of white chanterelle sauce that gave out a tiny warm burp of truffle-scented fog when I cut into it. The smell dampened the inside of my nose and stayed with me for half an hour.

A chocolate pot the size of a thumb that made the saliva glands in my mouth ejaculate. I was instantly ashamed that it happened in front of other people and felt exposed and anxious for quite a while afterwards. I'd much rather have been alone when that happened.

Of the wine that was served with each of the five courses, I remember only snippets. A white so smooth that the taste hardly registered until I swallowed and then my mouth was jealous of my stomach. A robust red that seemed to enhance the flavours of everything on my plate without detracting from it. We drank rather a lot, I'm afraid, and even Marcos had several half-glasses but only because we didn't want him to miss out on any aspect of this once-in-a-lifetime meal.

We ate, often in astonished silence, sometimes asking each other if they had tried this bit yet. We talked about the restaurant, the decor, the other clientele. We talked about the day, and Lamberg, wishing him with us, about our hotel and the history of the local area. The geometry of the table made the restaurant a place for light conversations: the tables were too wide for confiding, too broad for any fast-moving exchange of views. This was a place for lying and performing the role of diners for the staff and for other tables.

By the time the coffee came the mood in the room was suddenly looser. Diners were smiling sleepily, speaking louder than a murmur, touching each other across acre-wide tables.

That was when the grey-suited man from downstairs walked across the room towards us with a very serious expression on his face, his eyes trained on our table. He was carrying a tiny silver tray and stopped next to Bram, gave a little bob of the head. 'For you, Monsieur van Wyk.'

Bram was not pleased. 'I didn't ask for the bill.'

'Sir, no, sir, your bill has been paid. This is a message from the gentleman who paid it.'

Bram smiled smugly. 'A certain billionaire's office.'

He lifted the note casually, opened it and shuddered at the first word. I though he was going to be sick. He sat up and finished reading, arched back, eyes transfixed by the note.

'Fuck.' He looked up at us. He didn't seem to know what to say. He looked at the paper. He looked at the grey-suited man as if he had insulted him.

'The gentleman requested a response, sir.'

'Yes. Tell him yes.'

The waiter bowed, thanked him and walked away.

'Ludovic Voyniche. He's here for the auction. He wants us to join him on the *Terra Nova* at Le Havre for a nightcap. He has sent a car to take us to a heli-pad.'

We didn't know what to say.

'Is that safe?' asked Fin.

'I don't know,' said Bram. 'Let's all go.'

I thought that was a bad idea but Bram insisted we were all going and we should tape all of this and podcast it.

Fin said, 'We're going into an environment totally controlled by him. How do we know he wasn't responsible for Des O'Brian's murder in Bari? We should leave Marcos in the hotel.'

'Listen,' said Bram: Voyniche had invited us through a third party which meant he wasn't going to kill us. And if he knew we were in the restaurant he'd certainly know if Marcos was alone in a hotel.

He looked at the retreating grey-suited man, 'He's telling us it's safe by leaving a paper trail. And there's a driver waiting for us outside, he knows, and a helicopter with a pilot. And the person who took the booking for the helicopter. You can't get the whole of Paris to sign an NDA.'

Then Marcos said, 'We're going in a helicopter?'

'No,' I said. 'No, let Marcos stay. I'll stay with him.'

'Anna, you don't understand who Marcos's mother is,' said Bram quietly. 'If Marcos comes with us we might even come back.'

22

The helipad was a half-hour drive across the city in a limousine, doubling back to the Opéra and then skirting the Seine. I would have thought the driver was ripping us off if we'd been in a taxi but Bram insisted that this was the route. He always took this road when he was going to a helicopter. The way he said it made me think he'd never been in a helicopter.

When we got there the pilot came out of the office to shake all of our hands and lead us out to the helipad. Ominously, he was wearing a smart uniform and aviator sunglasses. At night. His monosyllabism and formal manner convinced me that he was stoned. I kept thinking about Diana and Dodi.

But I got in. Fin got in. We all got in and did up our seat belts so that we would be securely attached to the giant lump of metal as it hurtled through the air towards the sea.

Often in TV and films characters tell each other things while they're in a helicopter, pass on some essential morsel of exposition or a twist in their relationship. In reality, you can't hear anything and have to wear ear protectors. There's a mic in the earphones but it's voice-activated and there's a delay before it clicks on so even if you were saying something pertinent like '*I killed your mother*' all anyone would hear is '*— your mother*'.

We took off in a flurry of noise and terror, rising up into the night sky. The Eiffel Tower appeared on our right, gold and glowing on the flat skyline and we banked abruptly, tipping sideways as we turned to the coast. I felt a sudden need to hold on to something, realised that my hands were straying to the door handle and I clamped them between my knees. It took forty minutes to get to Le Havre but it felt like forty days.

If you've never ridden on a helicopter I would say don't. Just don't do it. It isn't safe and it's terrifying and, yes, it gets you somewhere quicker but it's hard to enjoy a destination if you're shaking the whole time. As I say, it really wasn't for me but it sobered me up so quickly that by the time we landed I could feel a hangover dawning over my right ear.

Fin busied himself during the flight fiddling with the mic. He told me later that he was terrified too and pretended to himself that he was in a bus on a bad road to keep himself calm.

I watched out of the window as we followed the white lights of the motorway, anticipating the lights of Le Havre, expecting to see great ships lined up. I glimpsed it, I think, but we took a left and landed on an industrial estate with fields on either side. We were all wide awake now, sitting up tall, frightened. The pilot landed and spoke to us on the headphones: the residents' committee on the *Terra Nova* had passed an ordinance that helicopters were not permitted to land on the ship after nine o'clock at night. A limousine was waiting to take us the rest of the way.

This was on the tarmac with the lights on and the doors open. There was a minibar inside with little lights all over it and a bottle of cheap champagne in a bucket of ice. Bram found that hilarious. Voyniche was a man who didn't like to pay more than he needed to, he said, he was a cheap man.

The drive took seven minutes along the quiet industrial concrete docks of Le Havre, past long warehouses and cranes folded in on themselves like sleeping herons, down long concrete quays and round a corner to the dockside.

The *Terra Nova* was a fine ship, high and white, with five decks of balconies all the same size and shape, each lit with a small white lamp on a small white table with a single chair on either side looking out at the view. It was strangely uniform, more so than a normal cruise ship. There were no towels hung over rails to dry or snorkels dumped outside, no glasses left on tables. It was almost regimental, as if the rich and elderly had formed an army and taken to the sea.

As we approached the ship it seemed to rise up out of the sea, getting taller until it felt crushingly vast, like driving at the base of a mile-high cliff.

The car passed it, circled round and slowed to a stop at the security clearance area for the *Terra Nova*.

It was a tented room manned by four large, suspicious men with taser guns prominently displayed on their matching uniforms. Behind them, twenty feet above the dock, a motorised walkway jutted tantalisingly out of the ship.

They looked very smart in tight black tops and trousers, very muscled, puffed up, with big round shoulders and thick necks. They were wired when we arrived but relaxed when they saw us getting out of the car with a kid and what was clearly his father. We were frisked, made to empty our pockets onto a table, our bags checked over by a metal detector wand.

The long walkway lowered slowly to the dock, the security guards caught and tethered it, and a small door opened in the side of the ship, inviting us in.

213

Walking out over the water on that narrow gangplank, I remember the sound of the sea licking the dockside, the unsteadiness I felt after the helicopter ride and the soft give of the walkway under my step.

Inside we were met by two men big enough to be security but dressed in white polo shirts with a red 'TN' crested logo embroidered on the breast. They led us down a long service corridor of white metal walls lined with pipes and then out through a small door.

We were in a wood-panelled lobby with a deep grey carpet and several corridors running off it.

The lighting in here was twilight-dim and we could hear nothing but an engine purring beneath us. Discreet black signs in tasteful fonts sat low down on the wall, pointing the way to the 'Drawing Room', 'Sun Lounge', 'Gym IV' and 'Library'.

Bram was having a lot of feeling about the ship. I think he was very jealous. He kept looking around and shaking his head, fingered the wood panelling, sneered at the signage and the carpets as if he was a hotel inspector come to suggest improvements. He tutted and ran his finger along a handrail and indignantly showed us his clean finger.

We were led into a library by a crew member who whispered a request for us to wait here please and disappeared through a soft-closing door. Above us blinding spotlights shone down on deep reading chairs, making the rest of the room harder to see.

My eyes adjusted slowly to the contrasting dark.

We were standing in a circle of curved bookcases, huddled in a tight, nervous clump as if we were expecting to be hunted for sport.

Bram was nervous, I could tell. He felt at a disad-

214

vantage and took out his cigarettes.

'I'm very sorry, sir,' said a voice and a bodyguard stepped out of the dark, 'but smoking is not permitted in here.'

Bram looked him in the eye. 'No smoking?'

'I'm very sorry. There is a smoking lounge but it isn't permitted in the library.'

'Good,' said Bram. 'That's a good rule. I like that. Personally I have never smoked.'

He lit his cigarette and smiled. The steward smiled uncomfortably as Bram exhaled over his head, daring him to insist.

The man didn't know what to do. Finally, maintaining his smile, he slipped back into the dark and returned with an ashtray. It was smaller than the well of Bram's hand, made of glass and had the ship's crest stamped in the middle. It was handed over graciously and Bram actually thanked him which made me realise how nervous he was.

He was gracious and polite when he forgot himself.

I could see now that the room was two floors high, walls of shelves loaded with a lot of unloved leather-bound books. A spiral staircase ran up to a mezzanine level, the whole room topped with a fake stained-glass ceiling lit dimly from behind. None of the winged reading chairs were marked or sagging from being sat upon, no arms ringed by a wet glass of something lovely, sipped while lost in a story. Everything in the room was brand new and the old-but-newness of it highlighted the virtual-reality sense of the place. If McDonald's had libraries this is what they would look like. It was a cathedral to reading that would brook no joy, tolerate no legs slung over the arms of a chair, no absent-minded nose-picking or slumping while reading. It felt soulless and sad.

We waited. I felt the subtle shift and switch of the sea beneath, as if we were all standing on the back of some great breathing beast.

'Hello.'

Bram jumped. Ludovic Voyniche had materialised among us without apparently approaching. Marcos laughed and Voyniche chuckled, mimed a creeping walk to show us how he had snuck up to us through the dark places.

He enjoyed our surprise.

'Oh!' he said, throwing his little hands up to mimic our surprise, *'Odös bérgyilkos!* Grandpa assassin! Haha.'

Voyniche was just under five feet tall, in his early seventies but spry and twinkly-eyed. He was bald, his face clean-shaven over sunken cheeks, and he wore bifocals with brown plastic frames, a patterned sweater and slacks.

Bram was right, he looked almost universal.

'And so,' he said, 'Bram van Wyk, so long since we met. I'm even smaller now.' He shoved his hands into his pockets and stood tittering, his thin lips twitching kisses.

Bram smiled down, pleased to find this neat, playful little man when he'd expected an antagonist.

'Bari,' said Bram.

'We were so young.'

Disarmed, Bram grinned back. 'We were.'

'Mmm-hm,' agreed Voyniche, rocking on his heels, smiling off into the distance. 'A lot has happened.'

His gaze swept the library shelves as if he wanted to say look at me and all I have: a small apartment on this mid-sized cruise ship full of other paranoid, tax-dodging millionaires.

Voyniche turned to look at Fin and raised his hands. 'And this is your boy?'

'No,' said Bram, taking a big stride over to Marcos and wrapping an arm around his head, wrestling him still to kiss his crown. '*This* is my boy. The handsome one.'

Marcos struggled free. 'Fuck off,' he said fondly.

Voyniche gave Marcos a punch on the chin, a tiny bit harder than it needed to be. 'Don't talk to your father so. Show him respect.'

Bram liked that. He may have even blushed a little. I don't think many people had ever stood up for him.

Voyniche saw it too, and his eyes brimmed. He laughed, baffled, dabbing the tears away. 'Crying. I cry all the time. I actually wept when I saw your face today, Bram. Tears come uninvited when you're old.'

'You saw me today?'

'On camera.'

'Camera?' asked Bram.

'The camera in the auction room. I heard you say it's fake.'

He stopped smiling abruptly, dropped his voice and leaned in to Bram. 'Why did you say that?'

Bram cleared his throat. 'Well, it's — you know . . . '

'No.' Voyniche's mouth contracted. 'I don't know. What is it?'

Silence sat heavy in the room as Voyniche waited for an answer.

Bram took a drag on his cigarette and the paper fizzed audibly.

'Put that out,' ordered Voyniche quietly. 'You are in my house.'

Bram exhaled through his nostrils but stubbed the

cigarette out in his ashtray, keeping his eyes on Voyniche. A bodyguard stepped out of the dark and took it away.

'Thank you,' Voyniche said to Bram, tipping towards him.

'You're welcome,' said Bram, uncertainly.

'OK. Serious. Why did you say the casket is a fake? It has my name. If it is a fake maybe I am a fake. Maybe I am a man who sells fakes. You see?'

'Oh no,' insisted Bram, 'I don't mean that you sell fakes, not at all, that's not what I meant.'

Voyniche leaned in and his voice fell to a whisper: 'Then what do you mean, Mr van Wyk?'

Bram didn't answer.

'*What the fuck do you mean?*'

I was suddenly aware that we were surrounded. Men had materialised from the shadows, not smiley men wearing polo shirts. These men were wearing black and had pistol-shaped lumps under their arms, standing as if they expected us to run. By the time I noticed the first one we were surrounded. Fin stepped nearer to me. I pinched Marcos's shirt and pulled him closer to me.

Voyniche ignored them. 'Explain.'

Bram did a brave thing: he took out his cigarettes and lit a pink one. Then he blew the smoke over Voyniche's head in a thick stream. 'I wondered why you didn't kill me too.'

Voyniche was surprised by that. 'Kill you?'

'In Bari. Why you let me go.'

Voyniche watched the burning cigarette. Bram took an exaggerated drag and held it in.

Voyniche looked at his feet. His body began to shake, just a tiny tremor, at first it looked as if the air conditioning was ruffling the shirt on his back. The tremble grew, his head nodding, his stomach twitching in and out. He looked up at Bram and a sound came from his mouth, a thin wheezing laugh.

'All these years, Bram, I thought it was you. This is why I was so pleased to see you on camera. Because if you killed that man in Bari, you wouldn't be at the Villeneuve viewing room today. If you killed to get that box and lost it somehow, you wouldn't turn up to buy it, too many eyes on it, someone could make a connection, you'd send someone else.'

Bram dropped his shoulders and nodded, gave a faint smile and I noticed the armed men disappear into shadows again. But we knew they were there now.

'So,' said Voyniche cheerfully, 'speaking of agents: who are you bidding for? Hammersmith?'

Bram was panicked. 'No. *No.* Just for myself.'

Voyniche waved him away, 'Oh, come on, Bram, you don't have that sort of money. They'll be looking for Hammersmith. If he doesn't arrive they'll be watching for whoever could be his agent. Are you his agent?'

'No!'

'If they guess it's you they'll block you from getting it. Callis is serious. Hansen has a keen eye for a profit margin. But it could be good for you not to get the casket.' He said this without rancour. 'Because if Bari wasn't you and it wasn't me then it was Eugene Lamberg. He's a fanatic, he's not moved by money, he'll kill whoever gets it.'

None of us wanted to believe that.

'No,' said Bram, 'not Eugene. Bari is full of Mafia. It could have been anyone.'

'Sure,' nodded Voyniche. 'What do you know about

Lamberg? He's charming? He's a handsome man, yes? You know about this Balaton girl, the one who found the casket in the ground? Lamberg told the Secret Police she was selling antiques. He was an informant. They killed the girl. He thought he would get it but they took the casket from the mother's house.'

'No,' said Bram. 'No.'

Voyniche smiled. 'I know. Incredible to us now but so obvious at the time. How does a priest, a good-looking foreign priest with good teeth and a Viennese accent, move around Communist Hungary giving Masses and praying with people? Of course Lamberg was an informant. Everyone was an informant then, it was how we survived. Even I gave them information. They sold me the casket, let me trade for trinkets, didn't kill me and in return I told them who was selling. But I ask you this: if Bari wasn't Lamberg, why isn't he here for the auction?'

'He can't legally leave Rome,' I said. 'He'd get arrested again.'

Voyniche looked at me and narrowed his eyes. 'He's just been released from prison?'

'Yes,' I said. 'And it's a condition of his release that he stays in Rome. He's wearing an electronic tag on his ankle.' I glanced at my ankle and he looked at it.

'He showed you his ankle with this electronic band?'

'Yes,' I said.

Voyniche frowned. 'That's BS, Lamberg was released from Caen. He was in prison in France. He killed the woman in France.'

Bram dropped his cigarette.

'But he's so nice . . .' said Marcos.

Bram picked up his cigarette. He was shaking, 'No, no. No way.'

'Yes. It's Eugene,' said Voyniche. 'You're resisting but you know it is.'

'But Bari could have been Mafia, or what about that man with you, that man on the boat that day? What about him?' implored Bram. 'What about him? He could have done it.'

Voyniche didn't like that at all. He clasped his hands behind his back and began to rock back and forth, nodding, twitching his lips at Bram as if warming up for a kiss.

'The man on the boat with me? You remember him?'

Bram struggled to recall. 'Tall? He was handsome, a grey sweater? He was a funny guy, he let me talk at him and nodded and made faces at me —'

'*Faces?*'

'Expressions, faces, as if he understood but then it turned out he didn't speak English. He was playing a joke on me. He was joking but not mean, kind of nice. A nice man.'

Voyniche nodded seriously and rocked. 'Yes,' he said slowly, 'he was my cousin. He died in the Balkan War. He died. In the War. Died young. And he was a nice man.'

He kept rocking, slowly, meeting the pitch of the ship, comforting himself.

Bram did an unexpected thing: he lurched over to Ludovic Voyniche and hugged him, just once, very tight, and then let go, stepping back as though he was afraid of the liberty he had taken.

At first Voyniche didn't react at all.

He glared into the middle distance so hard that his eyes watered. Then, without looking at Bram, he slowly raised a hand and grabbed him and dragging

221

him close, kissed both his cheeks as tears spilled down his cheeks.

Bram stood straight and looked at him. Then he hugged him again. I heard him whisper, 'I'm sorry.'

They let go of each other, slapping each other's arms as though they were pushing each other away, knocking the memories back into their containers.

Then Voyniche gathered a breath and spoke to all of us.

'I'm sad about this too. I like Lamberg, always have. I've known him for forty years, from way back. Old days. Budapest. Bad times. Very bad. We did things to survive that no one should do. Terrible things.' Guilt flitted in his eyes and he looked up at Bram, suddenly angry. 'Give me a cigarette.'

Bram took out his packet and flipped it open, lifted the gold leaf papers and ran his fingertip along the cigarettes to a yellow one. He held it up. Voyniche shook his head. He looked at the purple one. Bram held out the yellow one. 'Sometimes you have to make yourself pick yellow. For better times.'

Voyniche took it and Bram gave him a light. Voyniche inhaled, tipping his head back like a drowning man breaking the surface. A steward slipped out of the dark margins, holding out an ashtray and gave it to Voyniche.

'So, you knew all of that about Eugene but you always suspected me?'

Voyniche shrugged. 'I liked him better. I preferred it was you.'

Bram liked the honesty of that, 'How did you know him from Budapest? I thought you were from Durrës.'

'No, during the war I was in Durrës, sometimes. Good business, war. My cousin Geza and I . . . Lamberg contacted me, asked if I could find the casket, he didn't know I had it, I didn't know what it was. Lamberg did, of course, he can read Latin, knows who Pilate is . . . It was in my safe for ten years and he was trying to contact me. Couldn't find me. I almost melted it down. It's just a box and my safe was filling up, you know? But Lamberg found me in the end and told me if I could find it anywhere he'd buy it for so much. I said, oh, let me ask around . . .'

'What did you know about him?'

Voyniche opened his hands. 'Who the fuck knows, he's a fanatic. A priest. I knew that. Religious. But we were surrounded by fanatics in Hungary, then in the Balkans, even on this ship, not always religious. Some people worship money. Fervour helps them hide, the true crazy ones. That woman he killed in France, it was in a chateau. Does this mean anything to you?'

Bram exhaled a thin stream of smoke. 'The chateau the casket was in? He had it all this time?'

'Probably.'

'What did he want it for?'

Voyniche shrugged. 'For 'religious reasons'? I understand falling in love with an object but it always wears off. Does the box do anything?'

'No.'

Voyniche shrugged. 'Well, I don't know then. But he was arrested and taken away and the secret room was left. Maybe he meant to go back after prison and get it. I don't trust religious people.'

Bram leaned in to him. 'You can trust me,' he said.

They laughed at the unlikelihood of that, hearty and honest. It was sweet to see that. They nodded to each other, respectful.

'I'm sorry about your cousin. Sorry for your loss.'

223

Voyniche nodded. 'You're the first person who's remembered him for, maybe, twenty years.' He touched his chest, cleared his throat and when he spoke again his mask was back up. 'So! You're doing good business. This fake thing, it's OK. I won't — you know. Good for you. Good, good.' And he patted him on the shoulder to turn him to the door. 'I do trust you, Bram.'

They pointed at each other and chortled at his joke.

'So.' Voyniche brought his heels together, cutting the laughter short, rocking forward one last time. 'Lamberg. You see now what he'll do for the casket. If you get it Lamberg will try to kill you.'

'I'm not worried.' But we could all see that he was.

'Hm, but they won't let you get it because you're Hammersmith's man.'

'I'm not with Hammersmith!'

Voyniche ignored the lie. 'But if you do get it for Hammersmith then Lamberg will kill you.'

Bram stubbed his cigarette out in Voyniche's ashtray. 'Well, he'll have to get in line if I don't get that painting.'

'The Monet?'

'Hm.'

'So, OK.' Voyniche looked up at the ceiling. 'You want this casket?'

'Yeah.'

Voyniche craned towards him. 'You sure?'

Bram nodded. 'Sure I'm sure.'

'OK.' He turned to address the rest of us. 'Thank you for coming, now leave. And Bram: I warned you, so I wish you good luck. I hope you live past tomorrow but I'm not convinced.'

Voyniche was not prepared to lie about how much danger Bram was in and it hurt him: Bram's brow crumpled and for a terrible moment I thought he might cry.

'Bram,' murmured Voyniche, 'we're where we are.'

Bram nodded heavily.

'It is what it is.'

'Yah . . .' Bram took out his cigarettes, an attempted act of defiance, tried to light another cigarette, his hands shaking too much for the flame to meet the tip. He tried again, let the flame go out and relit it. He couldn't do it. He dropped the lighter to his side and threw the green-and-gold cigarette to the floor, then looked up at the fake stained-glass window.

He spoke in a sigh. 'This life . . .'

'I know.' Voyniche nodded once, looked at us and raised his smile and said, 'And now you leave.'

Our escorts were behind us, herding us out of the door, hurriedly chasing us down to the service tunnel, out of the door in the side of the ship and down the gangplank to the waiting car.

We all got in and it drove off. The window separating us from the driver was down.

Marcos was worried. 'What did you mean by 'get in line'?'

Bram waved a hand in front of his face, forget it, he's just a crazy old man. But his voice was low and his eyes were frightened.

I didn't really know what had happened in that library on the *Terra Nova* but Bram was softer on the journey back to Paris. He was tender.

We were in the car to the hotel, lost in our thoughts, when I saw his hand creep across the back seat to Marco. He took his son's hand and squeezed hard.

Marcos looked at his father, eyes wide and worried, and he squeezed back.

23

Fin had set up the recording equipment and hidden it in his jacket even before we stepped into the street in the sixth arrondissement, one block from the Luxembourg Gardens.

It was litter-free and bright. The apartment blocks on either side had immaculate stonework and clean windows. The only other person walking in the street was a woman in a grey tabard with three yipping chihuahuas on a trident leash. She tugged them resentfully from tree to tree as if she was trying to get somewhere. I said hello as we passed her and smiled, perhaps a little patronisingly. She shot back a look that was half warmth, half disgust.

We found the door we were looking for. It was imposingly large, framed in a stone arch with an intricate iron grille on the transom window.

I rang the call button for the apartment.

We were expected.

A lock buzzed and the giant door opened as lightly as a soft-touch kitchen cupboard. Fin pushed and I followed into a white marble entrance hall that radiated cold.

Behind us a side door snapped open. A man stepped out. He was wearing a nice suit and a tie-less white shirt buttoned stiffly up to the top.

Fin told him who we were there to visit. He looked sceptical and kept his eyes on us as he picked up a wall phone and called to check. He agreed with everything being said to him, smiled unctuously and bowed to the wall as he hung up, less of a gesture than a memory.

Please to follow him for to go up, he said in English that was not so much broken as reluctant.

Round the corner a brass birdcage lift was tucked into the turn of a spiral staircase. He used his weight to draw open the collapsible gate door. It didn't really look big enough to hold both of us, but we got in, cowed into compliance by the unfamiliar situation. He slammed the door on us. We were pressed tight together. Fin's hand was dangerously close to my groin.

'Well —' Fin met my eye from an inch away '— this is unpleasantly intimate.'

The man told us to press the button for the seventh floor and then stood watching as the lift gave a jolt and took off, moving so slowly that I held his eye for a full twenty seconds before the first floor separated us.

The cage shuddered gently as we rose through the centre of a beautiful stairwell of white walls, green runner carpet and a handrail of bright summery brass.

We weren't sure the lift was going to make it but, finally, at the seventh floor, it bounced to a stop. Fin pulled the grille open and we got out onto a landing. There was only one door, a small, flat wooden panel. No bell.

We stood in front of it, unsure what to do. I knocked lightly and it was opened by a neat man with a grenadier moustache.

Fin asked him if he was the Count.

His face twitched bitterly but he invited us in.

We shambled into a circular hallway that was two storeys high. Soft morning light sifted in from windows high above. We were in the cupola tower at the

227

edge of the apartment building.

The man shut the front door tight, set an alarm, told us not to touch anything, then he left.

Through open doorways we could see other rooms, large with high ceilings, expensive art and tasteful furniture. There was none of the usual clutter of life, no half-empty cups or books left lying around. No one had come in, kicked a shoe off and then run to the loo in the other one or put a bag on a chair for a minute. It looked as sterile as a movie set.

A low murmur of conversation came from a room beyond a room. Steps. The man came back, his eyes doing an inventory of the objects in the hall, making sure that we hadn't touched or stolen anything. He walked across to closed double doors and invited us to enter a bright lounge with a large glass dining table.

Dominating the room was a huge chandelier, an arrangement of radiating glass shards, like a still image of an explosion. And underneath it, at the table, an unlikely pair sat side by side.

Comte Gaspard de Lornasse was in his late sixties but his health seemed to be in a galloping decline. He was bug-eyed with wispy grey hair, not an attractive man, his dewlap folded in the middle and trembled when he swallowed. But we weren't looking at him. We were transfixed by the other person sitting at the table with him, a girl with a scarlet bob and green lipstick.

It was Lisa Lee.

This was too formal a room for fucking-helling: this was a room for unspoken tensions and brittle moods.

Lisa looked fresher than she had in the film and was dressed like a native Parisian in a simple grey linen dress.

228

She gave us a nervous wave, her hot hand leaving a smoky imprint on the glass tabletop.

'Perhaps you and your party would like to sit down?' asked Comte Gaspard de Lornasse, sweeping a hand at the row of seats across the table as if he was inviting us to an interview.

We sat down.

A wall of windows behind Gaspard looked out into the central well of the block, white tiled and pitted with the small back windows of other apartments. Two walls were caramel-coloured leather, a third held a maze of brass shelves but they were largely empty. At the far end of the room stood a glossy black grand piano, the open lid reflecting the day back at us, and two large sofas faced each other across a large coffee table.

Far away, somewhere across the city, a horn sounded.

I'm rambling on about the furnishings and impressions, I know I am, but this was what it felt like to be in that room. I was distracting myself because Gaspard de Lornasse had the most melancholy eyes I've ever seen. His sadness was of a depth and profundity that could not fail to affect everyone around him. Lisa could stand it though. She was perfectly comfortable, neither thrilled nor saddened, as if she was inured to an older man's misery and preferred Gaspard to Bob because he, at least, was a stranger.

Fin thanked them for seeing us and we all shook hands. Gaspard pressed my fingertips limply as if he didn't know how to shake hands.

'Lisa,' I said, as if I'd caught her smoking behind a hedge, 'your dad is worried sick.'

'Oh.' She sighed and cringed at that, just as she had

in the film, bringing her shoulder up and shutting one eye a little, but she didn't try to excuse herself. 'I'm sorry. Dad's always upset.'

Fin tried to make her understand that Bob was more than a bit upset. 'The police're searching the North Sea with helicopters looking for your body.'

She looked away. 'Oh.'

'Amy's worried.'

'Is she?' That piqued her interest but only for a moment. 'I can't go back. You don't understand, it's not safe.'

'Because of Lamberg?'

She looked at me and saw that we understood a bit of what had happened.

'Did you meet him on the ferry?'

She nodded and looked at the Comte. 'I didn't know who he was. I thought he was just a nice man.'

'Did he follow you from the chateau?'

'No, I don't know. We looked up the dates, didn't we, Gaspard? I think he'd just got out of prison then and was going there. I think he arrived and we were there. He must have gone in after and found the casket missing. Then he followed me and Alan in the van. We were hanging about Calais for a bit. He could have caught up with us. That's as close as we can guess.'

'What happened in North Berwick?'

Lisa looked at Gaspard for permission. He nodded.

'I was expecting a pizza. I heard the doorbell, saw headlights through the window and thought it was them but when I opened the door he was sitting in a car . . . Gaspard had warned me by then. I'd told him about the ferry, told him everything, and he says if I seen that man again, Des O'Brian or Eugene or whatever he's calling himself, I've to run. He's very

230

dangerous. He's told me what happened to his wife. So I just ran out the back, I've jumped a train to Edinburgh Airport, came back here.'

'You flew? How could the police not have noticed that?'

'Used my mum's passport. He's never cancelled it, my dad. Never got round to it.'

It was interesting that Lisa spoke the way she did: hardly moving her mouth and using working-class colloquialisms that marked her out as quite ordinary. But to someone who didn't come from Scotland, who couldn't read those signs, she was unplaceable in the social order, couldn't be reduced to a type. She would be judged on her own merits. And, seen objectively, Lisa was gorgeous and chic and clever and brave.

'My dad's got a lot of problems,' she said shyly.

I said I could see that. She needed to call him though and tell him she was alive.

'I'm gonnae. Soon as the auction's done, I'm gonnae. The casket'll be away then and it won't be our problem any more.'

She grinned suddenly and said it was nice to meet us, she'd been following us both for a long time.

'Are you WBGrates?'

She nodded. 'I shouldn't have brought you into this, not with a lie, I did take it but I was ashamed of doing that. I took it to give to Gaspard but then everything got complicated. I didn't want people to think I was pilfering. It was more than that. I'm dead sorry, but their house, it really affected me. I know the feel of a house like that. I knew somebody had died in there.'

Lisa and her friend the Comte looked at each other, and then, as if the reflection of their grief was too much, they broke off and stared at the table. Gently,

231

Gaspard's hand moved across the glass until his little finger met hers and withdrew again. I wondered if they were sleeping together and found myself grimacing.

'There was that much stuff left. Personal things. I told Gaspard he needed to get the place emptied because when the films got posted people would come and strip it. I mean, I knew from my dad — every jumper, every scrap of paper, what it all meant and how much it would hurt to lose all that.'

Gaspard seemed to wilt over the table and Lisa rapped lightly on the glass, waking him up. He sat up, blinking hard.

'I came to see him with the casket. Worst thing I could have brought. He couldn't clear the house, couldn't stand it, so I did, to make up for what I'd put him through, bringing that thing here, to his new house. I put everything in storage and he paid me.

'So the house was already empty when the location was leaked?'

She nodded. 'I brought the casket to him because it looked so valuable, I didn't dare leave it. But that upset you, didn't it? Set you back?'

'. . . This is why we left,' he said.

'I felt so bad. I couldn't have brought anything that hurt him more.' She looked at him regretfully. 'His wife was killed because of that thing, you know? She'd found the secret room and told me about the casket. She wanted to give it to the Catholic Church. He made her write a letter and he killed her. They were friends, I think, is that right?'

Gaspard took a deep breath and rolled his head up to face us. He trembled as he spoke.

'He lived with us, hiding from police, but we didn't

232

know. My wife, my Liliane, she was younger than I. Very devout. It was a comfort to her in her illness. She had cancer, uncomfortable treatments but completely curable. She took Mass every day. She had great faith. But then she drowned in her bath, found by the children, drowned.'

'It was the next day, in the morgue, the bruises on her chest had become darker. A man's hand on her chest and neck. No accident. They found O'Brian in Innsbruck, speaking perfect German, using the name Lamberg. He had a letter from her saying she wanted to die, because she was so ill. He didn't know she told me about the casket or that she kept a journal . . .'

Lisa took over the telling now because Gaspard has slowed down, his energy was flagging, whether it was the effort of remembering the terrible events or just talking, I wasn't sure.

'She'd written about finding the casket and how amazing it was, how exciting. They never saw the journal until I emptied the house, sure you didn't, Gaspard?'

He shook his head and his wattle went in the other direction, 'We left with Liliane's body. We did not go back. We asked everyone to leave, Father O'Brian, all of our staff. We locked up our chateau, thinking we would all be going back. We had not one idea of what had happened to my wife . . .' His voice trailed off and Lisa left a pause, watching his face for any indication that he had more to add. She took over.

'I said just sell the casket, give your children the money, you'll never hear anything about it again, but now it's everywhere. It's all we hear about.'

'You couldn't know, Lisa,' said Gaspard. 'You couldn't know.'

She looked at us earnestly.

'He was wanted for other stuff, you know? Lamberg? They'd been looking for him for something he did in Beirut ages ago and into the priest he was pretending to be, Des O'Brian. Couldn't charge him though, not enough evidence, even though he was in prison. He just waltzed out of there. Am I getting arrested if I go home?'

I didn't think so. She hadn't done anything except leave, not really, not unless Gaspard was going to charge her with breaking and entering, which seemed unlikely. But she should phone her father, I said, even if she didn't want to go home.

Lisa's hand had moved across the glass to Gaspard's, not squeezing or expressing any emotion, just skin on skin, passing warmth, as if he needed the contact. Gaspard's eyes were on the tabletop. It was sad that she could show this compassion to Gaspard and not her own father, but who knows what goes on in a house. There may have been too many claims on her.

'And the yellow painting in the room with the casket,' asked Fin, 'where did that go?'

Lisa didn't know what we were talking about. I had to show her the screenshot from her film.

'Oh. Never saw that when I went back. Someone must have gone in and taken it before then.'

24

The Paris sky was a brilliant, blinding blue, the spring air smelled sharp and fresh. We could hear the mob as we gathered in the hotel lobby, the whistles and singing and calls muffled through megaphones. It was the sound of an angry circus and car horns, a clamour that rebounded off the face of the buildings and circled the hotel, filling the empty street outside.

We were waiting for Marcos to come down.

Bram had the pallor of sliced sandwich meat left on a radiator for a week. Fin said he looked ill.

'I am,' said Bram. 'I think my heart is paying me back for all those cocaine nights, but I still have to go.'

I told him, look, Fin and I knew he had a copy made. Did he need both? Couldn't he just give Eugene the fake and get his painting back?

'But if I don't get the casket at auction,' he said, 'Eugene will suspect the one I give him is the fake. Even a good fake won't work on him. He knows it so well. He handled it for years.'

'You're giving Eugene the real one then? What about Paul Hammersmith and all the Christians in the world, waiting with baited breath for it to be opened? These people in Paris, don't you care about them?'

He gave me a cold look. 'Anna, from what you have seen of me, do I seem like a man who would risk his own life to give Paul Hammersmith the real one? Why would I do that? Because I see how much they want to be loved by their father and it makes me love them? Because deep in my thieving, rotten, drug-baron heart, their yearning moves me?'

I didn't know what to say to that. 'If you get the painting back, what then?'

He stood tall, arching his back to take a deep breath. 'If I get it I can give it to Janine. If I give it to Janine, she gives it to her family, the ones who want me killed. They call the contract off. I get to live.'

'And Paul Hammersmith gets the fake casket.'

Bram shrugged. 'Takes no talent to fool a fool. Howzit, Marcos.'

Marcos arrived and Bram fussed over him, did his shirt up and made him tuck it in, flatten his hair and turn his phone off. Marcos was in an unusually good mood though, more engaged and awake than I had seen him before. He only told his dad to fuck off once and it was said affectionately. Bram didn't seem to mind it either.

We stepped out of the hotel and into a wall of noise.

There was no mistaking where the sound was coming from.

The crowds had been swelling since the day before and the mood was febrile as we approached the barricade again.

Even more cops with guns were manning the entrance to the road. Bram showed his barcode to the chief and he scanned it, checked it, and walked away behind the van.

He didn't come back.

Bram got panicked, demanded that the officer nearest him go and get the chief, but the man kept his eyes forward until a young man tripped and shoved at Bram, making him grab the barricade to steady himself. The officer reached over and pulled Bram's thumb back to make him let go. It felt as though a riot was about to kick off.

We were not getting in.

But, slick as an eel, the chief reappeared round the side of the van and swiftly uncoupled the barricade enough to let us all slip through. The crowd didn't try to push it open. I got the impression that they didn't actually want to be any closer, they just wanted to be nearby.

When we stepped round the van we could see all the way down the narrow street, denuded of even parked cars. It was eerily quiet after the uproar we'd come from.

As we walked along the road the first person we came to was a security officer with a GoPro in his hands, recording our every step. It's an itchy sensation, being monitored as a potential threat to life. I found myself walking stiffly, trying to communicate innocence by bobbing less and keeping my hands out of my pockets.

Bram was sweating furiously now, his head down, walking like a man about to meet his fate. Marcos said something to him, some muttered comment about the crazies in the crowd, but Bram didn't react. I don't think he could hear.

The media platform was full of colour and kit. Presenters were addressing cameras, having their make-up applied, next to banks of long-lens still cameras, any one of which would have been a perfect cover for a gun. The police lined the shopfronts, watching up and down the street. Figures moved on distant rooftops.

As we passed the press platform, a blonde reporter in a red suit shouted down to him, 'Bram van Wyk, is it a fake?' but he ignored her and barrelled on, his pallor that of a man about to win the world or have a heart attack, or maybe both. We trailed in his wake to the darkened doors of the Villeneuve Auction House.

The blinds were fully drawn. The doors were blacked out, but as soon as Bram arrived in front of them they swung open.

We stepped inside.

The doors shut behind us and we all took a moment to breathe.

The reception desk had been removed, replaced with an airport-style baggage X-ray machine with a conveyer belt and metal-detection arch. Two very muscled men in suits and ties made us strip off our coats and belts and watches and run our bags through the machine.

Our phones and laptops were requested by a security official. We would not be permitted to tape this. Each person's electronics were stored in a separate small white box which was taken away by a man who then returned and gave each of us a small metal luggage tag stamped with a barcode.

Bram had to hand over his ever-present satchel.

We were invited to gather in front of the door of the viewing room which then opened with a noisy click. We stepped in and the door shut and locked behind us.

The walls were bare concrete now, the velvet curtains had been taken down. At the far end of the room a lift door opened with a light-hearted ping.

Bram waved a thank you up to a camera and we all got in. The door slid shut, the lift juddered and we ascended.

We found ourselves in a large room of duck-egg-blue walls trimmed with gold *boiserie*, a dark parquet floor and floor-length windows onto the street, all shuttered tight.

Along the far wall young people were sitting on a rostrum, looking out over a long table. They were all dressed conservatively, like much older people, and busily tapping on phones or laptops, fitting earpieces, ready to take phone bids. They were rehearsing, solemn and intent, thinking their way through the moments ahead as they arranged their pens and paper or checked internet connections.

In the centre of the room, organised into a square, were ten rows of chairs and among them milled a thin gathering, finding seats, greeting acquaintances, moving slowly as they nodded hellos. Everyone held catalogues.

M. Philippe came over to Bram. He shook his hand warmly, sympathetic to his nerves, and offered him a drink of something, perhaps? Bram said no, thank you, Philippe, no, so uncharacteristically gracious that it was alarming, almost last-word-y.

'Monsieur van Wyk will sit at the front and you, his entourage, will take places towards the rear of the grouping, *d'accord*?'

No one else answered so I said, yes, of course, fine, thank you.

He motioned us to the very back, then led Bram to an aisle seat in the third row, quite far away from us. We could just see the top of his head. The seats at the front of the room were full but all of the serious money was in Bram's row. The clothes in that row were packet-fresh, the wearers quite old, often attended by younger sidekicks dressed in a poor imitation of them, cheaper blazers, smaller statement necklaces. The sidekicks looked around the room, reporting back to their bosses in tight-lipped whispers.

I spotted faces familiar from the news headlines.

Sitting at the opposite end of the same row as Bram was Tom Hansen, the Norwegian billionaire. He had a head of thick black hair, gelled back like an eighties banker. He was mid-thirties, angular, sitting with his elbows out as if hoping to jab someone in the ribs. Anger radiated from his weatherbeaten face as he looked around the room, accusing and combative, dismissively batting away attempts at conversation from his aide.

Elena Callis sat in the middle of the row. This protector of the Eastern Orthodox Church looked like a comedy WASP in a long beige cashmere cardigan over a beige blouse and beige leather trousers. Her hair was unmoving, a carefully honeyed dye job that set off her statement jewellery of fat gold necklace, bracelets and rings. As the tide of bodies waxed and waned between us I saw her ringed hands resting on the catalogue, her index finger tapping a slow beat. It was a calming technique. She was in turmoil.

She was aware of Bram, her chin twitching towards him, as if she was desperate for a delicious, full-face ogle but was too controlled to allow herself.

Everyone, I felt, was wondering who was bidding for Paul Hammersmith.

The audience settled down, cued by the lights dimming very slowly and gradually, and then we heard the purr of a large white projector screen lowering across the far window.

The crowd sat upright. A man in front of us cleared his throat. A light behind us buzzed awake and the name and logo of the auction house were projected onto the screen.

A tense quiet fell over the room.

240

We heard the clip-clop of steps before we saw the auctioneer.

She was a tall woman in a grey wool dress worn under a houndstooth jacket. She stalked up to the podium. Her cropped white hair was dramatic, her jewellery restrained. A ragged ripple of applause broke out around the room as she stepped up to the rostrum. She looked up to acknowledge us with a disdainful nod.

She drew a deep breath and in a clear, clipped voice welcomed everyone, seated attendees, phone bidders and those joining on video links — here she glanced up to one of the security cameras. She explained that the footage would be held solely by the auction house and no recording would be held for longer than a week, she hoped this was acceptable.

All of this seemed to be filler, a chance for the gamblers present to gather themselves, mark their moves and settle down, because she finished with a final gliding gaze around and then lifted a small wooden gavel.

The audience opened their catalogues to the first page, a congregation turning to the first hymn, and it began.

The projected image changed to a close-up of the blackened icon, so massive on the big screen that I hardly noticed the two men carrying the small item onto the stage. One set up an easel the other placed the icon on it. Then they stood on either side of it, cupping themselves and watching the audience for stage invasions.

She read out the catalogue description of the icon, the artist was Chyorny, and announced the reserve price of fifty thousand euros. Then she paused, looked up, nodded and began. The bids rose by five thousand.

Elena Callis's aide bid on her behalf, calmly raising her numbered paddle a fraction each time as Elena looked diffidently away.

The auctioneer's eyes flashed around the room like a cat hunting a fly. She saw micromovements no one else did, spotted leaps in the bid price that seemed to come from nowhere. Callis's aide had reached seventy-five thousand when the auctioneer stood still, watching. The room held its breath. She raised her gavel and brought it down, the loud 'clack' clattering around the room.

Several people turned to congratulate Elena Callis as she muttered to her aide and allowed herself a jerky smirk. The aide wrote something in the catalogue on her knee.

The auctioneer kept a neutral face as the men lifted the icon carefully and carry it offstage.

Two other men took their place, one carrying a black velvet plinth, the other a gold amulet cradled in his gloved hands. They set the gold piece on the plinth on the stage and stepped back.

The auctioneer looked accusingly at her audience as if hoping to catch them out in some breach of protocol. An obedient quiet fell over them and they turned the page of their catalogue. The projected giant image changed to the object on the stage.

I had seen it up close in the viewing room. The gold was red and soft and looked like putty, moulded around irregular rubies and enamelling.

The room stilled. The auctioneer drew a breath, raised her chin and the bidding began again.

Forty thousand. Forty-two. Forty-four. Forty-eight. Sixty-five. Seventy. Eighty. Eighty-five. Ninety-five. One hundred and five.

I shut my eyes to listen, wishing we could have recorded that soft soundscape of people moving in concert, holding their breath in unison, a distant electronic muttering on telephones and the tick-tock chant of the velvet-voiced auctioneer. But I was aware that this was history being sold, time and faith commodified and palmed off to the highest bidder to dispose of as they wished. Elena Callis could take that icon away and blow it up if she wanted. There was nothing to stop her. She had paid for it.

It was absurd.

I think a lot of the room was aware that the people outside had a real connection to many of these objects, that they were held behind barriers with guns pointed at them.

I think the wrongness of that added to the excitement in the room.

The amulet sale was longer, a call and response between two bidders in the same row. Left bid one hundred and forty, right a hundred and fifty, left a hundred and sixty-five. Right came back with one hundred and seventy-five and left waited. Left bid two hundred thousand euros. Right. Right. Right? Right? Right bid again, two ten, and then left two twenty, then right two thirty. Left seemed to demur but suddenly, at the very last moment, came back with three hundred. Right seemed to panic. The auctioneer was enjoying it. She held right's eye and smiled, raised her gavel and . . . right bid three twenty, left three thirty, then right three fifty. Right. Going to right. Left shook their head. Gavel down.

They had bid too much, seemed to be the consensus in the room. The winning bidder looked a little startled.

Several other objects were set on the stage and sold, most for fifty or sixty thousand. Tom Hansen bid for and won a small gold medieval reliquary containing a saint's finger bone that had once belonged to Charlemagne. He got it for the bargain price of forty-eight thousand. The floor disapproved of Hansen's bidding style though — he was waving his own paddle high in the air like a schoolboy desperate to be excused. Several tutted at him as the reliquary was taken down from the stage. I distinctly heard him tell someone to fuck off.

Suddenly the room was bathed in white light as the image of the Voyniche Casket was projected onto the screen. A trill of excitement ran through the crowd.

The auctioneer explained that, because of certain circumstances, this item was not present in the building for the sale and she flashed us all a knowing smirk. The audience responded with a collective nasal snort that sounded, honestly, kind of evil. I thought of Lisa, of the praying people outside, and of Father Des O'Brian in Bari, blood spiralling from his slit throat as he tumbled into the dark.

I looked for Bram's head. He was shifting nervously in his seat. The person next to him glanced over and a man in the front row turned as he scratched his nose, stealing a look. Tom Hansen half stood to look around the room, giving a half-smile as his eye settled on Bram and Elena Callis. His eyebrows bobbed and he sat back down. Someone tutted at him.

The auctioneer raised her chin at the room, daring anyone to misbehave. Everyone froze. The bidding began at fifty million and rose quickly, five hundred thousand each time. Fifty-one, fifty-one point five. Fifty-two, fifty two point five, then, abruptly and inexplicably, sixty.

The price was rising fast. Elena and Tom were bidding against each other, driving the price up in a neat syncopated rhythm, back and forth, back and forth. Bram watched as the price rose to one hundred and five million. The audience craned forward slowly, backs losing contact with chairs. Tom broke step, hesitating for a beat before bidding a hundred and ten.

Suddenly a phone agent made a play. Tom Hansen smiled over at the rostrum as if an expected visitor had come to the party. Two hundred million. Two one. Two two. Two two point five. Bram still hadn't bid.

I saw his jaw clenched tight and light from the projected image catching beads of sweat on his forehead. He looked grey, his breathing shallow and fast.

The projector's fan buzzed high, cut through by the clear, clipped sound of money.

The back and forth between Elena, Tom and the phone went on until they reached two hundred and sixty million. Then bids began to stutter, Elena was trying to break the rhythm, coming in fast, staking leaps in the bid price. Finally the phone bidder dropped out at two hundred and sixty-five million euros.

Just Elena and Tom.

I looked at Bram. He wasn't even following the bids. He seemed to be staring at the lap of the person next to him, his colour a ghostly grey, sweat oiling down the back of his neck. It looked as if he was about to have a stroke and I was afraid to stand up and go to him in case I made a bid.

Both Tom and Elena vacillated at two hundred and seventy-three million euros. It was over. Tom had it. Bram hadn't even bid once as the auctioneer wrapped her hand around the gavel, scanning the room, giving it one final check as a small smile twitched on her lips.

Bram threw his left hand up so high the auctioneer wasn't entirely sure it was a bid but realised it was. Then Elena came back in and Bram started bidding quickly, left hand flailing, raising it to two seventy-five, Hansen bid two seventy-six, Bram two eighty, conquering by confusion, doing what he always did.

Tom Hansen was infuriated, missed a bid to Elena and stood up to shake a fist at Bram for his vulgar, chaotic style. He dropped out. This left Bram and Elena Callis bidding against each other.

The bidding slowed to a calm trot. They were working the auctioneer, making her wait when she wanted them excited, dragging their heels to show that they were in charge. She remained impassive but the room was annoyed at them for toying with her. An audible huff sparked a titter.

Bram raised his left arm and bid two hundred and ninety million euros.

Elena looked at her hands. Bram was staring at the back of the head in front of him, jaw grinding, left arm tucked tight across his body. His right arm wasn't working. That's why he was throwing his left up to bid. He was having a stroke.

The auctioneer allowed herself a small smile as she raised her gavel, her gaze doing a victory lap of the room as she gave his rivals one last chance.

It felt like spite. Tom Hansen came back and upped the price by a leap to three. The phone agent came back and offered three ten. Tom bid three hundred and fourteen. Bram was losing it. He bid three fourteen point five but it was too conservative a raise and it made him look weak, as if he was hitting the limit of his resources.

Hansen raised it half a million to three fifteen.

Bram wavered. He wavered until her gavel was up to her shoulder. And then he came in strong, upping the price to three twenty.

Three twenty-five on the phone. Elena, certain now that the phone bidder was Hammersmith, twitched her chin to Tom as Bram bent forward, cradling his right arm in his left, barely listening to what was being said.

Three twenty-five on the phone, she repeated. She looked at Bram, she raised the gavel in her hand, she drew a breath and then Bram threw his left up. Three hundred and thirty million to Bram.

The phone agent listened. He muttered something. He listened again. He folded.

Tom Hansen crossed his legs. Elena Callis slapped her catalogue shut, but neither had lost to the phone agent. They were content to capitulate as long as Hammersmith didn't get it.

The gavel came down.

A round of awed applause broke out. People leapt to their feet and turned to see Bram, bent double over his chair.

Fin had seen what was going on too. We both stood, ready to rush over and call an ambulance, but Bram got up, rising unsteadily above a sea of heads and turned to give us a little wave and a weak smile. He grinned over at Marcos as if they'd been separated for a year.

He was not dead. And he had won.

The audience slapped their catalogues shut in a collective full stop, looking around, remembering who else had been here for this. The auctioneer thanked everyone for attending and the phone agents for their kind attention but the audience were already out of there, standing up and gathering their belongings. The lights came up.

It had taken twenty-five minutes.

Bram was holding his right arm, his fingers clawed tight, panting, as he stumbled over to us, ignoring the outstretched hands.

He was shaking. 'I won,' he whispered, 'I won.'

Fin congratulated him and reached for his clawed right hand.

'I won,' he said again, eyes unfocused, face damp. He was panting.

'You need to see a doctor right now.'

Bram nodded, yah yah, he said, yah, and then his right hand bloomed open. He looked at it, held the hand up, and the colour came back to his cheeks. 'Oh my God. I won.'

'Monsieur van Wyk?' It was the phone agent Bram had been bidding against. He was holding his hand out. 'Monsieur van Wyk, congratulations for your success.'

Bram took a deep breath, rolled his head back and took the hand, pumping it. 'I won.'

'Mr Voyniche asked me to extend his felicitations.'

Bram froze. 'You were bidding for him?'

'His felicitations, Monsieur van Wyk,' he said and then he stepped back and was lost in the crowd.

Bram grinned at us. 'That old fucker. He did that so they wouldn't know I was here for Hammersmith.' Then he looked up to a camera in the corner of the room and blew him a kiss.

Philippe materialised from the crowd to take Bram away to sign the papers. Bram wanted Marcos to come with him, wanted to show off to him, I think. Fin whispered in Marcos's ear: *if his hand does that again call an ambulance.*

They were turning away and Bram called back to us: they would meet us at the hotel, in the bar in two hours, we'd have good champagne this time.

25

We didn't go straight back to the hotel. I regret that now, but the pilgrims and the gawkers were leaving and we wanted to record interviews with them while we could.

Then we went for a walk and something to eat. I was worried about Fin, watchful of him. I felt I'd forced his relationship with Sofia and ruined it. I could only tell myself so often that he got into my car. At least I could make sure he didn't get ill again.

We found a vegan falafel place, bought him a wrap and sat outside so I could smoke. I made him eat the whole thing. I didn't care, honestly, that I shouldn't nag him about his eating. Neither Hamish nor Estelle would forgive me if I came home with him and he'd lost weight.

He ate it though and it was big. Not American big but big for France. He didn't want it, I could tell, but not for eating disorder reasons. He just got full quite quickly and didn't really want any more but ate it to make me feel better. I watched him eat and wondered how much longer I could look after him. I did, honestly, think he was dickless. He was right about that.

By the time we walked back to the hotel the crowd were almost all gone, around us just the normal rumbling growl of the faithless city. I missed them.

The hotel lobby was empty but the man behind reception watched us walk in with the slack mouth and worried eyes of someone with very bad news. For a moment I thought Bram had died of a stroke or skipped on the bill.

'Monsieur Cohen, Madame McDonald, I wonder if you might go to Monsieur van Wyk's suite?' he said.

'Is he ill?'

He wrung his hands. 'Not quite exactly. But. Well.'

He looked so concerned that Fin and I took off up the stairs. Outside the suite we heard muffled noises and a scream coming from inside. Fin banged on the door.

The room fell silent.

'BASTARD.' It was Marcos's voice. He screamed as loud as he could, a fierce throttled cry that rose to a frantic pitch.

Fin banged again and the door opened.

We walked in to a mess.

Bram banged into me, smashing his shoulder off the wall of the bathroom. His shirt was ripped off his back and red raw scratch marks marred his skin. He slammed the bathroom door and locked it. The sound of a tap gushing.

'Marcos?'

We stepped into the room.

A coffee table lay splayed on the floor, the legs splintered on one side as if someone had fallen on it. Red splatter stained the white linen on the bed. It was ketchup from a tray of room service food that had been thrown and fallen down the side.

Marcos was on the floor behind the sofa chair, crying and frightened, his face red and swelling under knuckle marks on his cheek.

'Come here,' I said to him. 'Come out and come here.'

He got up unsteadily and reached for my hand. I

took it.

Now, Marcos was not a small child, he wasn't even a sympathetic child. He kept telling me to fuck off but I've never felt more of a mother than I did then. If Bram had come for him again at that moment he'd have been looking for his jaw on the back wall. I hugged Marcos. He held me tight just to keep himself up.

I led him out to the landing, a public space, and walked him carefully out over to the stairs, Fin just behind us.

Bram came out of the bathroom and we backed away but he didn't come for us. He almost didn't see us. He slammed the door behind himself so hard that it shook the building.

We stood still, listening, waiting.

The door flew open. Fin grabbed Marcos's arm and ran him upstairs but I stayed and I watched Bram leave with his bag. He didn't look back at me.

I went upstairs and found them outside my room. I let them in. Marcos was shaking, he was so angry. I wet a flannel and held it to his face.

He said a series of things about his father, just normal angry things kids say, I don't want to go into too much detail, but it took a while of listening and nodding and saying calming things, take a breath, it's OK to feel sad, until the red left his cheeks and the tears dried.

Bram had beaten him pretty badly.

This is when Marcos told us how they saw Eugene in the road at the airport and everything had gone wrong.

After the auction they were taken into a back office to sign some papers. It was a formality but his dad wanted him to see it because it was historic, Bram said. One day in the future, when Bram wasn't here any more, Marcos would be able to go to America and see the casket in a museum and he'd remember being here with his father.

Bram signed the deed of sale, two sets of them, and a lot of men were around handling the paperwork, shaking hands with Bram, talking about the bidding. The auctioneer came in and she was shaking hands with everyone.

Then they were taken to another part of the building, a cellar, and Bram paid with a bank transfer. Everyone cheered when the money went through. Then Bram asked for the casket.

They didn't want to give it to him.

Philippe tried to persuade him to let them keep it until he could arrange for a security team. That was the first thing that made Marcos suspicious. Bram said no, give it to him now, and everyone went quiet.

They went away and then they came back with a trolley and a wooden crate on it. The casket was inside.

Bram made them prise the lid open, pull the nails out and lift off the lid so he could take it out and hold it.

He let Marcos hold it. It was heavy.

Bram put it back in the crate and they wanted to nail the lid shut again but he made them leave it loose. They didn't like that and Marcos knew something was up. He knew because the atmosphere was so weird. No one wanted them to leave, they didn't think it was safe, but Bram picked up the crate and got in the lift.

They couldn't stop him.

When they got outside Bram was really excited. He had the crate under his arm as he walked down the

253

street to a car.

This wasn't a limo. It was an SUV, really high up and black. Look, Bram said, knocking on the window, bulletproof glass. The auction house had laid it on to get them through the crowds.

He made Marcos get in the front seat next to the driver. That seemed wrong too. Bram got in the back, sitting right behind Marcos so he couldn't see him, and he told the driver to take them to Le Bourget, the airport we landed in when we came here from Rome.

I remembered that morning as if it was a month ago: an art deco building, glass bricks glinting in that morning sun, and Bram's hangover lifting like the dew, the excitement we'd all felt at seeing the casket in the viewing room.

They arrived at the airport. The SUV stopped and they got out. The lid had been taken off and put back on upside down. Marcos knew then that Bram had switched the caskets because the lid was on differently from how it had been when they got into the car.

He didn't say anything though. Not at that point. Four men wearing sunglasses came over to the car, American men, and they tried to take the crate but Bram insisted that he'd carry it so they just walked next to him. They were taken into a room by a side entrance.

It was small, leather chairs, a bunch more men in there. All American. One of them stood up and came over and shook Bram's hand and introduced himself: Paul Hammersmith. He looked American, you know, cheap shirt, bad shoes, big teeth.

They shook hands and Bram talked too long. He asked everyone if they'd been watching the auction, did they see what happened. But the men weren't interested. They wanted to look inside the crate.

So Bram got the casket out and let them hold it. It looked the same as the one in the auction house. It looked just the same but Marcos knew the crate lid had been moved, he knew Bram had been in there. They passed it to Marcos and it felt heavier this time. He just knew it was heavier than the one he had held in the auction house. And the lid had been moved.

All these men were smiling and taking turns to hold the casket and they were all saying hallelujah and how great it was and glory be. A lady came and looked at the casket with a glass thing on her eye. It had a light on it and she checked the seal and compared it to the catalogue picture and she gave Paul Hammersmith a nod. It was the casket. But Marcos knew the crate lid had moved when Bram was in the back of the car. He was the only person who knew. He thought of all that stuff Bram had said about respecting people's faith and all that and he knew it was wrong to cheat and lie your whole life.

He was tearful now, conflicted by what he had done because he wasn't moved by that, he didn't have an urge to do the right thing, he was just angry with his father and wanted to belittle him. He couldn't admit it to himself though.

Marcos announced to the room that Bram'd had a copy made in Thessaloniki and the lid had been moved in the car and the one they were holding was a bullshit fake. They'd been ripped off.

Everyone went quiet.

People started whispering. Hammersmith smiled at Bram, all big teeth, and thanked him but the security men came storming over and took Bram's bag and emptied it onto the floor. There was nothing in it but cigarettes and newspapers and crap.

Two men went out and searched the SUV. Marcos watched through the windows as they pulled up the floor mats and moved all the seats and checked every inch inside and out. They didn't find anything.

Then they came back and strip-searched Bram in front of everyone. They made him bend over and cough and everything, in front of the woman, and Bram kept shouting that he couldn't hide something that size on his body, what the fuck were they thinking? Who could fit that up a backside?

But then suddenly everyone went off to talk to each other in a huddle and then they left through a back door. They took the casket and the crate with them.

They were left alone.

Bram didn't say anything for a while. Then he got dressed. He gathered his things and put them back in the bag and when he had finished he reached over and picked Marcos up by the hair, lifted him fully off the ground and took him outside.

Eugene was there, standing on the far side of the road, watching. He waved. Bram went to him and said, 'Where is it?' and 'Are you ready to swap it?' and Eugene said yes. Meet him tonight.

'Where?' asked Fin. 'Where are they meeting?'

'Des O'Brian's last address. That's what he said. Des O'Brian's last address at midnight tonight.'

He told us the rest of what happened, how Bram got him home and they'd been fighting for an hour when we came in, he told us the things they said to each other. It was bad.

'Bram killed that girl, didn't he?'

'No, Marcos,' said Fin, 'Lisa's alive. She ran away from home, from Eugene, but she's very much alive.'

That made it worse for him, because he needed Bram to be a shit. Fin said Marcos should go home, to his mother, just get out of all of this, and he agreed.

We went down to the smashed-up suite and found the hotel staff in the room, standing around, surveilling the mess. It looked worse the second time we saw it.

I apologised profusely but the cleaning staff said it was no problem, they'd seen a lot worse. It would be cleaned up in under an hour and we were very welcome to stay tonight, should we so wish. Everything was being paid for by an American corporation so money wasn't an issue.

Marcos snuck across the room and found his phone and we crept back upstairs to call his mum. Janine didn't pick up.

I said look, she's had people following us this whole time, she probably already knows what's happened. She'll send someone to take you home.

We waited, we looked out of the window for cars or men but we saw no one. Marcos put the TV on to the only channel in English: CNN.

It was a special report, live from Paris where the Voyniche Casket had been sold this afternoon.

Paul Hammersmith's private Learjet had blown up over the Atlantic. Suspected bomb on board. Fifteen people killed. Police issued a statement saying it was complicated because there were so many religious groups in Paris at the time. Terrorism couldn't be ruled out. A spokesperson for Hammersmith's church gave a tearful interview about what a wonderful man Paul Hammersmith was.

A sobbing American woman holding rosary beads was interviewed on the Rue Royale: it's Good Friday,

257

she said, today is Good Friday and he died.

And a missing Scottish woman had turned up, safe and well in Paris. Lisa Lee — I turned it off.

It felt like the end of days, as if signs and wonders were being fired out by the universe, yet to be deciphered. Everyone remembers where they were that day, when we heard about Hammersmith dying, how scared we all were about the casket and the times.

I panicked as much as everyone else and called Jess.

'Look, Jess, that thing Sofia said about me — you can ask anything.'

'OK . . . sure?'

'Sure.'

'Well, I've been looking this up. Your name used to be Sophie Bukaran?'

'That's the name I was born with. My dad's name.'

'So . . . I'm part Kazakhstani?'

This was not what I was expecting but of course this was what she cared about. She was twelve. She was working out who she was.

'I think you just say Kazakh but yes. My father was from Shymkent but my mum's family were from Tashkent, originally. That's how they met in London —'

'That's why I have black hair? I'm Middle Eastern?'

'Well, I think Kazakhstan and Uzbekistan are in Central Asia, technically.'

'So, I'm half *Asian*?' She squeaked with delight.

'Yeah, you're Asian. Is that all you've been reading about?'

'Yeah.'

I braced myself. 'Anything else you need to ask — ?'

'No, I don't want to know about that other stuff. Are you in Paris?'

I said I was and it was exciting, which was an under-statement.

'Mum, can we visit Kazakhstan together one day?'

'One day, maybe. Maybe.'

But at that point I didn't know if we would make it out of the hotel. We'd been waiting for an hour and now we knew Janine wasn't coming.

I called down and asked for a car to take us to the Lornasse Chateau, two hundred kilometres away.

'Certainly, Madame, and to return?'

I said yes. But, honestly, I didn't know.

26

We were on the edge of the dark woodland, the birch trees luminous in the moonlight. The ground was spongy and soft, uncertain, like standing on a towel at the beach. We all felt it. I looked down, pressed my toe into the ground and watched water seep into the hole. So we picked our steps carefully, watching water rise over the edge of our shoes and fill them, each ingress a fresh shock of cold.

Ahead of us was the Lornasse Chateau. It had disintegrated since Lisa filmed here. Slates had slipped like jelly from a plate and lay in shattered piles. Window shutters listed and a thick crack ran up the outer wall, wider at the top than where it began.

Someone was already inside: a set of footprints led across the ground, in-filled with water, their outline clear. Whoever made them had found the same break in the tumbledown wall we had. They had stepped over fallen bricks and taken our same soggy path through the wood. Most of the trees were down now, on the ground, or hanging drunkenly on their neighbours.

And there, at the end of the clear path, was Des O'Brian's last address. Inside the filthy glass on the front door, the orange tip of a cigarette flared.

Someone was watching us.

I looked down at the footprints again. I had noticed Bram's loafered feet often enough to guess that the footsteps were about the right size to be his. But they could be Lamberg's. I had no idea whether his feet were big, or small, or hoofs.

We really didn't have a plan. We were in the middle of nowhere and didn't know how to call the police, whether they would come, whether Bram would want them to come. They could arrest us for trespassing or child trafficking or being accomplices to a suspect in the Hammersmith murders. We were winging it.

'Let's go in,' whispered Marcos.

I said OK, but not this way, 'Someone's watching.'

We had asked him to stay in the car but, as he pointed out, at least on foot he could try to run away. If he was in the car he'd be easy to find. The driver might not be too eager to fight off a kidnapper.

We skirted along the edge of the yard, hearing nothing but the purr of a motorway a hill away and wind whistling through the valley, until we found another fallen dividing wall, this one to a kitchen garden. We climbed in over it and found a gate that led to the back of the outhouses. We stopped at the edge of the gravel driveway.

Ahead of us was fifty feet of open ground to the chateau.

I blinked and, for the briefest moment, pictured Alan Johansson standing by the steps on a warm autumn day, worried about being in France and sad at the mood of the group he was here with, not knowing that Harriet was waiting in her tangerine living room, breathless with joy, holding a pregnancy test, ready to change his life. I opened my eyes to the night and the rotting building.

Fin ventured a step out onto the driveway, his footstep gravel-grinding a loud crackle in the quiet night. We saw how impossible it would be to sneak across, unheard and unseen. We really didn't know what to

261

do. We were wary of giving up the cover of the out-buildings and watched the front door, waiting to see if the cigarette would glow again.

We just waited.

Suddenly Marcos bolted, spraying loose gravel, slipping and sliding, scrambling on all fours sometimes, until he reached the side wall.

Panicked, Fin and I ran after him.

We had made a lot of noise, or so it seemed to us, but no one shouted or came for us. We stood still with our backs to the outer wall and panted, not with the exertion so much as with excitement at having broken the silence.

Then we heard it: a wooden groan and then another coming from inside the house. Someone was moving about in there.

Fin nodded us to follow him.

We skirted the building, holding the wall, creeping low and staying quiet. I didn't think we should go in. Bram could be in there with a hammer in his head, a floor could collapse beneath us, it didn't seem safe, but someone was in there, moving around, picking their steps.

We came to an entrance at the side of the chapel down some steps, a modern fire door with a green plastic 'Exit' sign above it. The door looked shut but I could see where dead leaves had tumbled into the gap.

I stepped down, pushed with my shoulder and the door juddered into a concrete corridor with a flooded floor.

It smelled of rot and leaves and meat. I waded in, found the water less than an inch deep and shuffled inside. I turned on my phone torch. Ten feet away steep stone steps led up to a small door.

These were the basement steps under the staircase that Lisa Lee had filmed, but the floodwater was shallower than when she was here. I didn't know if that was good or bad.

At the top of the stairs I turned the door handle and pushed gently. As if it had been waiting for me to set it free, the frame cracked and splintered, plaster fell in big dank chunks and the door dropped, hanging from the top hinge. I turned back to whisper something but the final hinge snapped. I felt the draught as it fell on the back of my neck and heard it crash out into the hall.

We retreated down into the flooded corridor, guilty and afraid, and turned back to look at the doorway. A sudden fresh burp of grey dust exploded inwards. Something else had collapsed in the hall.

'We should get out of here,' said Fin.

I agreed but Marcos slid past us, hurried up the steps and we had no option but to go after him.

It was the ceiling above the stairs that had fallen in, the one Lisa was showered by. Alarmingly solid chunks of plaster lay on the floor and a knee-high plaster smog sat in the hall, gritty on the eyes, bitter in the lungs.

The chateau had emptied since Lisa's visit. Nothing remained. The rug was gone, the table was gone, even the holy-water font from the front door and the child's raincoat on the banister, it had been picked clean, first by Lisa's removal firm then by scavengers.

We stood still, listening for noises from upstairs. Careful footsteps, sounding as if they were two floors up and far along to the left. It had to be Bram.

Marcos felt his way carefully along the floor, hanging on to the wall until he reached the staircase. Two steps up he stopped, frowned, shaking his head as his heel sank into wood. He was scared enough to turn back and come down.

We felt our way into the dining room, looking for another set of stairs.

Through a butler's pantry of open and empty cupboards, we found ourselves in the kitchen with its distinctive green walls. Silhouetted shadows on the walls were all that remained of the copper pans. The cooker had been taken; the table, the baby chair and unravelling rug were all gone.

Fin nudged me to look at the floor. A set of fresh footsteps ran through the dust, hanging close to the wall and exiting through a back door. We followed them, retracing their route until we reached a servants' staircase.

The ceiling had fallen in here too and the plaster dust was half an inch deep. Fresh footsteps were sunk deep into it, taking them one at a time, being cautious, both feet leaving their imprint on every step.

We took the stairs one person at a time. I followed Marcos up and even the wooden handrail felt like dough under my hand. We trailed the steps all the way up two flights to the top of the house and a familiar corridor.

We knew exactly where they were going. Lisa had shown us this already but now it was filled with the heavy smell of decay, covered in black mould.

The steps we were following had been afraid too. They'd walked sideways, keeping their back to the wall. At one point their feet had sunk deep into a floorboard and they moved to the other side, walking carefully, a hand smearing oily black mould across the wall.

They led through a small doorway and, beyond it, we saw the narrow steps leading down into the reading room of dead pigeons.

Marcos was at the front of our column, followed by me and then Fin. I saw him freeze in the doorway, breath in a sharp gasp.

'Go,' I said.

But Marcos still didn't move.

'Marcos,' I whispered, 'keep going.'

He filled the doorway, blocking the light.

'Marcos?' A soft voice was calling in the dark.

But Marcos didn't move.

'Bram?'

'GET OUT!' It was Bram's voice, he was in the reading room and he was shouting.

I tried to get past Marcos but he backed up quickly, knocking me against the wall.

'DON'T MOVE.'

That was not Bram.

That was Lamberg. 'Don't you move, boy.'

Lamberg didn't know who was here because we were walking single file. He might have seen or heard me moving behind Marcos but he might not have seen Fin. I stepped over to the middle of the corridor and gestured behind my back to Fin, waving him into a side room, telling him to hide.

'COME IN HERE. BOTH OF YOU.'

'I don't think it's safe for us all to be in here,' I called. 'The floor won't hold.'

'Safe enough,' said Eugene.

'The floor won't hold four people, Lamberg,' said Bram. 'Let Marcos go.'

'We'll see. Come in here.'

Marcos held the door frame as he stepped down the shallow steps, clearing my view into the room. Books lay scattered all over the floor.

'Come on, Anna McDonald, come in here with your friends.'

I stepped down the three stairs into the rotting room. Bram was on my right, standing by the door to the secret room. He had his satchel with him, it hung heavy, and in his hand he held the small yellow painting wrapped in cellophane. Marcos was behind my shoulder, on my left, and Lamberg was standing by the dirty windows, beyond the pigeon carcasses.

It took a moment for his face to resolve in my eye. He was smiling but his eyes were sad. He lifted his right hand to me, a fraction of a movement, just enough to make me look down. He was holding something, something dull and grey. I thought it was a cigar tube but then I looked and blinked and saw it was a piece of pipe. He had taped over either end. It was a pipe bomb.

'Eugene . . . ' I said, wanting to warn him about this Eugene, this other man, a vicious man that none of us believed in. But he was that man.

'You brought a child to this,' said Eugene reproachfully. 'That's on your conscience.'

I saw then that his other hand was hanging by his side, holding an old-fashioned brick mobile phone, and his thumb was curled, hovering over the call button.

He nodded Marcos closer to Bram.

'No,' barked Bram, 'Marcos, get out. Run.'

The phone was holding everyone's attention except for Lamberg's. He was looking at me. 'You. Stand

266

next to the boy.'

'Hey, listen,' blustered Bram, '*listen*, come on, no. This is crazy, man, I have it! I have it here for you, like we said. An exchange. I give it to you, I don't give a shit about his thing, man. Take it.'

'FINDLAY COHEN.' Whether Lamberg had seen him or guessed he was there, I never knew.

No one moved.

'Fin stayed in the car.' No one believed me.

'MR COHEN, come in here or I will blow your girlfriend up.'

After a moment Fin filled the doorway and spoke. 'Um, Anna and I are not actually together.'

Lamberg tipped his head, confused.

'I don't think he really cares, Fin.'

Lamberg motioned at Fin to come down into the room and stand next to me. He stepped down, holding the wall to steady his steps and coming over to stand with us. He peered at Eugene.

'Is that a bomb?'

But the question was redundant. Of course it was a bomb.

Fin and I looked at each other.

What a shit way to die, in this grubby place, squinting hard with grit in our eyes, with two conmen and someone else's child.

'Trina's pregnant,' said Fin.

'Trina?'

'We're having a baby.'

'Fucking hell,' I said, because I didn't know what else to say.

'Fucking hell indeed,' said Fin, because neither did he.

No one else in the room cared about this. Bram

267

was talking to Eugene but looking over my shoulder to Marcos.

'Let me give you the casket, Eugene.'

'I finally gave you what you wanted,' said Eugene, eyeing the yellow painting. 'I'm sorry this is how it has to happen.'

'You want the casket?' Bram patted his satchel. 'I'll give it to you, Eugene. Hammersmith didn't need to die. I had a beautiful copy made for him just so that I could get this for you. You should have trusted me. I'll give it to you and we'll leave. We can leave them here.' He took a step forward. 'We can just go. They don't matter. Let them go, Eugene. I'll give you anything you want. Anything. I have it here, this is a crazy misunderstanding, come on, let them go.'

Lamberg looked disappointed. 'Bram, you know I can't.'

Far away, in another part of the chateau, something groaned and shook the floor. Something further away answered with a sharp report. Silence fell in the room.

Lamberg was breathing hard, his eyes narrow, a sheen of perspiration on his face. He was working his way up to doing something.

No one said anything until I blurted, 'Where did you get that bomb?'

He looked at me and half smiled, glad, I think, that someone had said something.

Bram lifted the satchel up. 'Eugene, come on, you want to see it one last time?'

Lamberg nodded.

Bram unzipped the satchel, reached in and took it out.

The Voyniche Casket was beautiful. The silver looked unnaturally bright in the filthy room, almost magical. It caught the shifting light through the dirty windows, winking back at the moon.

Bram shook it at Lamberg. 'You want this, yes? It's yours, my friend. Let them go.'

Lamberg smiled sadly at Bram. 'I don't actually want the casket.'

'But you've killed for it. You've killed for it many times.'

'I don't want it. It shouldn't exist. I should have destroyed it when I could. But I was weak. I kept it.' He glanced at the door to his secret room, reliving, I imagine, the time he spent with this thing, loving this thing, knowing that he and he alone knew where it was, that it existed and what it was.

'Why didn't you?' asked Marcos.

Lamberg looked at the boy, wet-eyed. 'Pilate met Him. *He knew Him.* How could I destroy it when I don't know what's inside? How could I do that?'

Marcos didn't understand. 'Why didn't you just open it and prove to everyone that Christianity was true then? If you really believe there's proof of Jesus in there?'

'Yeah,' said Bram, nervous at Lamberg talking to his son. 'Maybe you don't believe it. Maybe you don't believe at all.'

Lamberg knew why Bram was provoking him, drawing his attention away.

He smiled at Bram. 'I don't believe, Bram, I have faith. Faith is different from knowing. Faith is a God-given grace. People make this mistake all the time: doubt is not the enemy of faith. It's part of faith. The real enemy of faith is proof. Proof kills faith. People used to worship the sun but now we understand it. The sun is no less magnificent, no less powerful, but no one worships it anymore because we have proof of how it works and what it does. If this casket contains proof of a single tenet of Christianity it will ruin the faith of a lot of people, it will condemn people to hell . . .' He looked at the casket. 'What a temptation, to hold that in your hand. I should have destroyed it.'

Bram looked at it. 'Your logic is good but we're still here and you're still holding a fucking bomb. It's just a thing, Eugene, it's not a life —'

'It is much more than a life! A life is fleeting.' Lamberg was angry and I stood very still. An angry man with a bomb will do that to most people, but not to Bram.

'It's nothing, it's just a *thing*, a man-made piece-of-shit thing. Take the fucking thing. Blow it up. This faith of yours is worthless. You're lying to yourself anyway, you won't destroy it this time either. You'll never destroy it. You can't.'

We heard another sound, from the roof this time, a low tectonic sound through our feet, half sigh, half groan. Then a crash. The far side of the chateau was caving in.

'I won't have to.' Lamberg looked up and smiled. 'This place is unsafe. It'll collapse at any time. No one'll come back in. The things are gone. No one will come back. No one will ever find us.' He nodded over to our corner. 'Or them.'

'Then fuck your God,' spat Bram and he lifted the casket over his shoulder and threw it past Lamberg into the far corner. 'Take it. I'm giving it to you.'

Lamberg's eyes slid to the silver box. It had landed on its side; the gilded lady raised her slender arm and smiled gently.

Bram's voice broke. 'Let Marcos go, please? I'll give

270

you everything I have.'

'I already have everything,' said Lamberg quietly. 'I repent. The moment my thumb comes down I will be repenting this. But even if I am damned I'll save far more souls than the people I could possibly kill. And I may lose my soul to do this one thing I know is right. Would you sacrifice the thing you loved the most, Bram?'

Bram van Wyk snorted a laugh but his face contorted and suddenly he was crying, his chin tight, hands hanging by his side. He looked over at Marcos, his big face a wet mess, looking at the thing that meant more to him than anything else. He was looking straight at it and knew that he would be the reason it was destroyed. 'I'm sorry . . . '

Marcos was crying too. 'I'm sorry. I shouldn't have told them it was the fake.'

'It's not you, treasure,' said Bram, 'it's me. It's always me.'

But I wasn't paying attention to them, I was watching Lamberg.

He'd straightened his back. His eyes were vacant. He lifted his chin and I knew then that he was poised, saying his final prayer, drawing a deep breath as his eyes rolled back in ecstasy.

But there was something wriggling on his chest. It was tiny and it was frantic. It was red.

Bram was still talking. 'I'm wrong, everything I do is —'

A high manic tinkle sounded: glass breaking. Lamberg looked at the broken window as the room flashed unbearably bright.

A sudden smell of fire and blood. I was blinded, my irises branded with white.

I grabbed for Marcos, found what felt like a bit of shirt as Fin grabbed my arm and we all three clung to each other.

Movement in the room, steps, big bodies moving in here.

When my vision came back the sights I saw made me miss the blindness.

Bram was on his side facing us, his stomach a filthy mess of bloody ribbon, a hurried puddle forming by his head. Lamberg was praying, I thought, on his knees, his face freckled with his own black blood. He fell sideways, twisting, dropping his hands and showing us the hole in his chest.

The brick mobile phone lay on the floor in front of me. I kicked it to the wall.

Fin shouted and I reached out to grab his arm, thinking him shot, but he was shouting Marcos's name.

Fin was not shot. We heard ourselves breathing again, fast and ragged as shadows moved in, stealthy and careful, checking Bram's pulse, checking Lamberg. A hand reached out and picked up the casket and the painting, slipping them into a black bag.

A hand. '*Kommen Sie.*' And Marcos was gone.

A wall cracked loud, something crashed in another part of the building.

'*Kommen Sie.*'

This was later, I think.

Big gloved hands and men in ski masks reached out to us.

Fin pushed me into their hands. I pushed him. We got into a bit of a slap fight, or as much of a slap fight as terrified people can manage.

'Let me fucking help you, you mental bitch.'

I gave in. He handed me over to the gloved hands. '*Beide. Ihr beide.* Both, *kommen.*'

We were out of the building, I don't know how that happened, I don't know how long it took. But we were outside, in the wind and the night, standing on the edge of the jumbled wood and I lost control and shouted for Marcos, I needed to know he was OK.

'*Alles ist gut.*' A face through a ski mask.' *Alles ist gut,*' it said again.

We were taken round to the front yard and a very big silver car, so high off the ground that I had to look up to see him.

Marcos was sitting alone in a back seat, the door open, white tracks of tears scarring his dusty face. He was playing on an iPad. He wouldn't look at me.

'Mom says cops are coming,' he said quietly. 'She says get out of here right now if you want to see your kids again.'

The door slid shut and the car pulled away.

Fin and I stood, watching until the red brake lights were eaten by the dark.

27

You may already know about this. It was widely reported and broadcast as it happened and Netflix made a documentary about it called *An Anonymous Donation to Harvard*.

With the permission and cooperation of the Hungarian government the casket was transported to Oxford University under military-security conditions. An international team of experts from twelve universities around the world worked together to decipher the inscriptions and decorations, exploring the meaning and potential meanings in the interplay of symbols and writing and imagery on the outside of the Voyniche Casket.

After several months, again with the Hungarian government's permission, and this time with the blessing of the Vatican, it was unsealed, cut open with a fine laser inside a vacuum chamber designed to retain any dust or microbes or particles of sand that were inside. Once analysed these might prove that the contents of the casket had been in Judaea in the early first century CE, around the 0030s, preferably around Passover. They were looking for anything that could definitively place the casket near the approximate date of the crucifixion of Christ.

Livestreamed, broadcast live, and filmed from every angle, the lid was lifted off by a robotic hand with felt pads on the tips of each prong to apply a carefully measured amount of pressure. The lid was laid aside and the camera in the chamber focused on the contents.

Writing, astonishingly easy to read, though the letters are quite faint in the sharp non-UV lights. A brief message, written on a small scrap of greenish paper, very high quality, with pink marbling along the edge, and just four words:

Anything you want, kid.

It was only when they lifted the paper out that they found it. Tucked underneath, in mint condition, a mini bag of Haribo Tangfastics.

Acknowledgements

A great many thanks are due to those in the field of historical artifact smuggling who are so generous with their time and knowledge. I couldn't have written this book without their astonished indignation at the state of the world they work in.

Also many, many thanks to my mucker Jade Chandler. Also to Bill Massey for amazing editorial suggestions when this book was just a bucket of unrelated ideas. To Jon Wood, Liz Foley and Katie Ellis-Brown for their support, and for disguising their bafflement when I talked about the idea for this book. But particular thanks to Dredheza Maloku for trawling through the typesetting edits for this book which were many and utterly, utterly tedious.

We do hope that you have enjoyed reading this large print book.

Did you know that all of our titles are available for purchase?

We publish a wide range of high quality large print books including:
Romances, Mysteries, Classics
General Fiction
Non Fiction and Westerns

Special interest titles available in large print are:
The Little Oxford Dictionary
Music Book, Song Book
Hymn Book, Service Book

Also available from us courtesy of Oxford University Press:
Young Readers' Dictionary
(large print edition)
Young Readers' Thesaurus
(large print edition)

For further information or a free brochure, please contact us at:
Ulverscroft Large Print Books Ltd.,
The Green, Bradgate Road, Anstey,
Leicester, LE7 7FU, England.
Tel: (00 44) 0116 236 4325
Fax: (00 44) 0116 234 0205

Other titles published by Ulverscroft:

THE LESS DEAD

Denise Mina

When Margo goes in search of her birth mother for the first time, she meets her aunt, Nikki, instead. Margo learns that her mother, Susan, was a sex worker murdered soon after Margo's adoption. To this day, Susan's killer has never been found.

Nikki asks Margo for help. She has received threatening and haunting letters from the murderer, for decades. She is determined to find him — but she can't do it alone . . .